BEFORE I LEFT:

THE TAV OF JACK HENRY

by

Matt Simpson MD, Major (Ret'd)

© 2024, Matt Simpson

Library and Archives Canada Cataloguing in Publication
Simpson, Matt, author
Before I Left: The TAV of Jack Henry / Matt Simpson

Issued in print and electronic formats.

ISBN: 978-1-998501-23-6 (paperback)
ISBN: 978-1-998501-24-3 (ebook)

Cover Design: Paul Hewitt
Interior Design: Muhammad Tahir

Double Dagger Books
Toronto, Ontario, Canada

www.doubledagger.ca

Part One:
To the Manner Born

Chapter One
A Gucci Go

It is not an easy thing to talk about going to war and seeing people messed up like that. Everybody wants to hear about it though. As soon as they find out what I did, the first thing they want to know about is how many gunshot wounds I treated, or how many chest tubes I put in, and most of the time I don't want to talk about it. Most of the time I wish they didn't ask.

If you've ever been to war, you know what I mean. You have these memories that haven't been processed, and that's part of it, but it is more about how the words never quite capture the expanse of the thing inside your head. How do you talk about the way you were before, the way you are now, and the way it changed you if you only have a few flippant moments at a dinner party, or over coffee in the park.

To tell the truth, I never thought I'd go to war. None of us did. We grew up at a time when war-fighting was a thing of the past. A generation had passed since the big one. It had been peaceful for so long it felt like it would be that way forever.

As boys though, we dreamed of adventure. We joined the Canadian Army Reserves as soon as possible and came of age on the dirt roads of the Petawawa training area. Our instructors wore blue berets and regaled us with stories of Golan and Cyprus. Our Bombardier Iltises had 'UN' painted on the side in bold white letters. School became a quiet place for contemplation, and dreaming of our next convoy down the road. Our classroom walls were hung with pictures of our parents' prime ministers. Lester B. Pearson smiling with his Nobel Peace Prize. In the totality of the profession of arms there was nothing more quintessentially Canadian than peacekeeping.

But when was the last time you heard that word?

Things have changed now, since 9/11, but back then the whole world saw us as peacekeepers, and we revelled in it. We knew peacekeeping was only one function of our fighting force but we let it define us. We were proud of our heritage and it felt good to be peacekeepers. When we weren't sandbagging the Red River to keep the flood waters at bay, or clearing roads to deliver blankets to snowed-in widows after ice storms, we were digging trenches in the Petawawa sand and play-fighting battles our grandfathers had won generations before. We practiced fieldcraft and battlecraft and became proficient in the deadly arts, but our equipment was from a bygone era (the same helmets and web gear you see in old Vietnam war movies), and we were learning tactics from the trench wars of Europe. All that 'war-fighting' expertise felt—antiquated. The idea of shooting to kill an armed enemy was a whimsical notion from the distant past. Those were acts committed by our grandfathers so that we would never have to. We never thought we'd be a generation to go to war.

———

It was a time of innocence and peace, we only dreamed of wars gone by. On the fiftieth anniversary of D-Day, the Army set up an elaborate outdoor museum at Major's Hill Park in Ottawa, and all the WWII veterans came to see it. They were living history, walking around those displays with medals that no one even knows about dangling off their blue jackets. They would stop when they saw us boys in uniform, blow their noses with handkerchiefs, and sometimes, if we were lucky, they would tell war stories.

Most times they'd start with something quaint like finding a Luger pistol in the mud or pushing a piano over cobblestones in a French market square to dance with the Woman's Auxiliary Corps. They called those ladies 'wac's' and smiled sly, old-man smiles with untold stories shining in their eyes. But sometimes, if we took time to sit and listen, we heard real war stories. Something they hadn't told for fifty years. Stories they never told their wives or grandkids. Intense, harrowing stories about Panzer tanks clickety-clunking over a ridge, or the shock of cannons raining shells, or the German Army war-machine looming all around or close behind. Memories of dismemberment, trauma, and the death of friends. You couldn't imagine what they'd gone through, but you couldn't look away, or stop listening if you did. They needed to tell those stories before they died. And we were there to listen. Young soldiers in awe of heroes. But they never let you call them heroes. They said, "the heroes never came home."

We were tasked to guard displays that summer. My team and I were stoked about it. We spent our days walking in the sun and our nights were mostly free. As the man in charge, I arranged a skeleton crew for wandering security and allowed the rest some leeway to hit the town. We slept under canvass right there next to the Byward Market. If you don't know Ottawa, that's where all the clubs and parties are. I couldn't keep the boys away if I tried.

We were towering in the confidence of being twenty-one and paid to serve our country and filled with the passion of youth that sometimes makes you do dumb things. We lived on the edge that summer.

We were armed, too. It was rare and exciting to be armed in public. Our 9mm Browning pistols were heavy on our hips but the lingering sense of invincibility made them feel much lighter. At the end of each night, when the bars let out, and the ladies in their party dresses wandered through. We felt like kings.

Each morning we woke in the dew, stretched, and pushed our sleeping bags down those nylon and aluminum cots, dressed, and strapped our weapons back on.

Private Weiss was waking up in the cot across from me. He was one of those troops that everyone loved, always telling jokes and goofing off, and making us laugh. He was quick-witted, and capable. I gave him maybe too much slack. I should have been watching him more closely.

He had his pistol out. I listened as he pulled the slide back to engage the slide lock. That's what you do to clear your weapon. Nothing out of the ordinary. I was sleepy, sitting up, and rubbing my eyes.

Those Browning pistols are old, even then they'd already been in service for nearly a hundred years. They are rugged and reliable, but their mechanism is—antiquated. Clearing them requires you to put a magazine in the housing to release the trigger. Unless your fingers are freakishly long and you can reach up the housing and depress the sear lever.

Private Weiss didn't have freakishly long fingers.

He slid a loaded magazine into the housing and clicked the slide lock. I heard the slide move forward, chambering a round.

The sound is different when a round is chambered. The slide chunks heavier and moves a fraction slower when it picks up a round.

I heard it clearly.

"No, Weiss," I yelled. But it was too late.

He had done two things wrong: he should have clicked the slide lock before sliding in the magazine… And, he should have been pointing the weapon at the proving barrel between his knees. Instead, the weapon was raised and his arm was extended like a gang-banger. The bullet exploded out of the barrel, pierced the tent, and raced across the park and street, smashing a massive pane of glass about two hundred feet away.

The Canadian National Art Gallery seemed to explode.

Through the filthy plastic window of that canvas tent, it looked like the entire building was disintegrating. Glass crashed over the grass, hall, and asphalt. People were running and ducking for cover.

We froze.

I glanced across the field and back at Weiss.

"Oh shit," he said.

Our ears were still ringing.

"Oh shit is right," I said.

"What did I do, Jack?"

"You fucked up, Weiss."

He looked stunned, "What—What do I do?"

"You put the weapon down."

He did. I stood and took it from his hands. He sat on his cot and lowered his head to his hands as I cleared his weapon properly, and placed it on the table.

"Stay here. Rolly, stay with him. Call 911. The rest of us will check the damage."

I threw on my uniform, grabbed the first aid kit by the door, and ran across the field to the road. Jagged pieces of shattered glass were everywhere, inside and outside the gallery. One, embedded in the asphalt, wobbled in the wind for a moment, then broke, and crashed to the ground.

I looked around. It was early and a handful of people were milling about.

No one seemed to be injured. Thankfully.

Weiss got lucky.

When I got back to the tent the troops looked stunned and the police were on their way.

"Weiss, you sit," I said. "They'll want to speak to you. Rolly, take a small party to the gallery and help clean up. The rest of us still have a job to do. Our mission hasn't changed, boys. Let's get back to work."

That was not a good day.

It was supposed to be a 'gucci go'. We were supposed to have a pleasant, uneventful summer of guard duty, walking in the sun and listening to war stories. Instead, I was talking to police and filling out forms.

The shit-storm that followed kept me up for weeks but eventually things were smoothed over. Someone up our chain of command was an Ottawa cop who knew the team that showed that morning. I had all my 'Is' dotted and 'ts' crossed so it all went well enough. The incident made the back page of the Ottawa Citizen, but no names or reputations were ruined.

The shittiest part of the whole thing was having to write Weiss's charge report.

Charging a friend for an honest mistake is not fun. Weiss knew better. He was qualified on the Browning, well-trained, and knew how to handle it. It shouldn't have happened, but he was probably hungover, or maybe still drunk. Who knows. Doesn't matter. He knew the consequences and rules are rules. I had no choice but to write him up. And felt good doing it. That's what the system demands. And the system matters. And it works. A negligent discharge is an offence against the code of service discipline. Always has been, and always will be, an automatic charge.

He knew the fine was coming.

I felt terrible about that part, but it was his finger on that trigger. He messed up. It wasn't my fault that he needed money for school.

The orders-parade, a few weeks later, saw him predictably sentenced to a fine that he couldn't afford. We took solace in the fact no one was injured and he avoided jail time. I spoke about his character at the trial, but he didn't speak to me for years. He left the Army soon after that. The last I heard he was running a business in Montreal, selling fine art of all things. That was life in the Army Reserves.

Queue the sad trombones.

I went back to my undergrad that fall calling myself 'pre-med' even though that wasn't a thing. I had this notion that my degree in Biochemistry would lead me into medical school. A pipe dream I'd had for as long as I could remember. Becoming a physician was a thought, probably put there watching too many *M*A*S*H* episodes with my mom. I was sure it would manifest itself somehow.

School had always been easy for me, so I never applied myself. I was coasting, getting 'Bs'. My life energy spent on that part-time Army job. The Army felt more immediate. More like real life. School never felt like real life to me.

We took things seriously in the Army Reserves and we did serious things. There was joy in doing hard physical things. Working under pressure, subordinating ourselves to a code of honour, accomplishing impressive feats. Together.

That was real. It's hard to imagine what a platoon can do before you see it done, but you can't un-see it once you have. Sometimes I miss those glory days.

But playing silly-bugger in the Petawawa sand was never going to get me where I needed to go. And the fun was beginning to wane. Writing charge reports on friends was only the beginning.

***

The "Somalia Affair" was in the news that summer, and looking back, it probably pushed me to the edge. Things got much worse for soldiers after that. If you don't know the history, a couple assholes from the Airborne Regiment in Petawawa murdered a kid overseas. His name was Shidane Arone. I'll never forget that boy's name. Poor kid was scrounging for food, and they killed him. The whole thing was inconceivable.

We had been trained by the Airborne. They were more militant than most. By necessity. But they had difficult jobs to do. Most of them were fundamentally good, honourable guys. Most of them were skilled and fearless and left you with a sense they'd give you the shirt off their backs if you needed it. But they did run us into the ground. I can't say I enjoyed that. But we were better for it.

We were as shocked as the rest of the world that something terrible like that had happened overseas. There were murderers in their midst, and that was horrifying. We were glad when, in the end, those few got what they deserved, but things changed for all of us pretty quickly afterward. Everyone saw "airborne soldier" and thought "murderer". And then "airborne soldier" became "any soldier" and the whole Army was wrapped up in it for a while.

Guilt by association. It was a dark time to be a soldier. You couldn't escape the hate.

Walking through the Byward Market on my way home from the armouries one night, some boys, hanging out a car window, yelled, "BABY KILLER," as they passed. I knew it was nothing to do with me but it pissed me off, so I yelled back, "Go fuck yourselves!" And the car stopped, and four beefy boys piled out.

They presented me with a choice. I was indignant enough to stand my ground and try to school them on the error of their ways, but when one of them pulled a baseball bat from the back, I turned on my heels and ran.

The alley to my right connected to an adjoining street. I crashed through there as they chased, laughing and hollering, "You better run BABY KILLER," they yelled, and got close enough to throw beer cans. One of them grazed my shoulder and hit the corner as I passed. It splattering Molson Canadian over my face, but I kept running. I splashed through muddy streets filled with November rain and by the time I made it down the stoop to my shitty apartment three blocks away, I had lost them, but I was filthy with mud from the splashing. I collapsed in the entryway drenched in frustration and tried to reconcile all the anger.

I was just trying to walk home.

I recall sitting there taking a moment to catch my breath and contemplating my predicament like it was yesterday. In the end I couldn't blame them. We all group people into tribes. It helps us make sense of the world. Heuristics. Patterning. It's natural. But stereotypes leak around the edges and people get hurt. Those few airborne assholes had tainted everyone in uniform, and it didn't seem fair. But it was what it was.

My chest was heaving as I wiped my face with the olive drab, canvas sleeve of my coat, but it only smeared mud across my cheeks and into my eyes.

Filthy and dejected I stared at myself through the dark mirror in the hall.

That was the moment I decided.

Alone on that cracked vinyl floor in the cramped hallway of my sad, mouldy, one-bedroom walk-down on Clarence, I decided I was going to med school, if it was the last thing I ever did.

The next day, I put on my best suit, walked across town to the Medical School and sat across a desk from a sweet, middle-aged admissions officer who showed me my future. I was told my grades weren't cutting it, but I was given a solution: Stay the course, buckle down, focus on getting perfect grades.

So that is exactly what I did.

I applied myself to that end for the next three years.

Chapter Two

Medical School

Getting into med school was hard. Some might say I won the cosmic lottery by being born male in Canada in the seventies and all that, but I don't feel like I grew up with any silver spoon. My childhood wasn't easy. My mom joined the Air Force after finishing nursing school to make ends meet. She didn't have much choice after my dad left. The military helped her scrape together a life for us. She would say things like "whatever doesn't kill you makes you stronger," and "honour is the gift you give yourself," practically every day. Never making a ton of money, but always keeping us safe. Kraft Dinner and 'cheese on bread' were staples, and we always had enough 'half-moons' and 'freezies' in the cupboard for all the neighbourhood kids.

The base was a safe and decent place to grow up. My life was pretty charmed because of it, but getting into medical school was not easy. I taped quotes to my bathroom mirror like "The harder I work, the luckier I get," and "How bad do you want it," and got to work.

Lesson number one: A 'B+' and an 'A+' are two entirely different animals. The A+ requires a great deal of sacrifice and suffering. Balance ten stoichiometric equations, then balance ten more, then ten more for good measure: "No, I can't go to that party this weekend I have an organic chemistry midterm coming up."

I put in time, embraced the grind, and kept at it. I was always somewhat meticulous and orderly, and figured that would help, but there was never any guarantee. I learned by doing and began to love the suffering. When the grades rolled in, I saw it was good, and knew it was going to happen. I mean, you never really know. But I knew.

When it didn't happen on my first attempt, my mother and sister encouraged me to keep trying. My Army buddies thought I was crazy. They made it clear that a Reserve Army Sergeant, a fatherless son of the seventies, a base brat living in a languid basement apartment, had no business being that ambitious. They humoured me though. "Good luck with that, Jack," they'd say, razzing me relentlessly for missing our glory days with my nose in textbooks. But they were quietly rooting for me. They sat in the back heckling at my thesis defence, and teased me for stuttering, and screwing up answers, but they bought beers at the mess after, so it was all good.

I had been wait-listed twice but finally had the marks. Three academic years of perfect grades. Exactly what I'd been told. I was going to give it one last shot, and if it didn't work out, I'd settle down, get a job teaching at the community college, marry a pretty girl, have some babies, play beer league hockey, and settle back into that part-time Army gig.

But that was when I got in.

Remember when Forrest Gump got that letter that said he'd invested in "some fruit company" and the camera pans to the 'Apple logo' at the top and he says, "Guess I don't have to worry about money anymore." That is basically what it feels like to get an acceptance letter from a Canadian medical school. After years of hard work and sacrifice all my hopes and dreams right there in black and white. That was a great day.

And when you achieve a monumental success like that it's easy to believe the hype. As if it was somehow the force of your own will that made it happen. I fell prey to that notion for a time, but deep inside I always knew the truth: the Army played a major role in my success.

Not only did military service shape who I was as a young man: disciplined, regimented, and careful, all good things that set me on my path, but sentiment was shifting again by then. The Somalia Affair was beginning to be a distant memory. Soldiering had weathered it's 'dark period'.

When 9/11 happened everything changed. When those psychopaths flew hijacked planes into the Twin Towers, the world was reeling, but wearing a uniform was suddenly a noble and heroic thing again.

You probably don't recognize those ebbs and flows of sentiment. But if you've ever served you know exactly what I mean. That sort of thing impacts us in large and small ways. Hard to quantify. But I'm pretty sure it got me into med school.

Despite my trepidation and disillusionment about being a soldier at the time, it was suddenly an advantage once again. There was no more muddy beer cans in the street, no more "baby killer". I walked into that last med school interview wearing my uniform with pride, and when they thanked me for my service and shook my hand, I knew I was in. They probably had my acceptance letter in the mail before I even got outside.

It felt like providence had intervened.

In my heart of hearts, looking back, the prevailing winds, and those Twin Towers going down, played some strange part in my trajectory. And somewhere, somehow, there was a debt to be repaid. One greater than the contract I signed. Going to war for my country was probably a foregone conclusion.

So there I was, a base brat, going to med school.

Crazy how the world works.

———

Medical school is like drinking from a firehose. Four years of reading, regurgitating facts for tests, and repeating, then hoping to remember details when the time comes. And for the most part, you do. My classmates were smart, witty, and fun. I don't know why I was expecting a bunch of book worms, but that's not who I found. They were all quite impressive; outgoing, accomplished, driven, and well-rounded. And there was a familiarity to the manner in which we supported one another. All of us on the same 'academic mission', molding ourselves into that elusive end state we'd been dreaming of since childhood. Physician.

But I was a soldier first.

Which was different. An oddity many didn't know what to make of. I found out early most student-doctors shy away from the notion of military service.

"Why would you do that?" Allen said. He was one of those fit, wiry triathlon types shuffling along beside me toward the anatomy lab. The med building behind the hospital was brand new. All orange brick and glass with those polished marble floors with the stone speckles. We were waiting in a lineup for lab coats, making small talk.

I had mentioned signing papers that morning, joining the regular force. He seemed utterly confused.

"What were you thinking?"

"What? Why? Does that make you nervous?"

"No, man, I just don't get it. For one, the pay. Doesn't the Army pay doctors crap money?" I never liked Allen.

"Less than civilians, maybe, on the surface. It might seem that way. If you don't factor in the pension and benefits, and lack of business expenses." I had been looking at the Army pay scales that morning and almost shit my pants. That kind of money was astronomical to a kid from my side of the tracks.

"Okay, but what about 'hierarchy'. Didn't you just sign up to become someone's bitch? They're going to tell you how to practice medicine."

"No they won't. Maybe where and when, but not how. And what about hierarchies makes you nervous?" I could see how it might not sit well with him. Obeying orders does seem like subordinating free will. But it's not like that. If he ever served he would know. "You don't relinquish your personal autonomy. It's more like conforming to a standard. Within a structure. Like this line-up," I said, gesturing around.

We had been standing in that line for twenty minutes.

"No. Right. But really. Not the same thing," he said, "Don't they tell you where to go?"

"I'll be posted somewhere, yes. But I can see some advantages to that." I tried, smiling but he was done with me and our conversation. He started chatting up the girl in front of us, and I went back to thinking on my own again.

A chain of command can be positively edifying, but it's easier, for student-doctors in particular, who have the world by the horns, to see only down side. Most prefer to ignore that Canada even has an Army. My very existence was disturbing to some. But I figured that had more to do with the moral ambiguity of the violence of war than any real or perceived sense of who I was. Or at least that's what I hoped.

That was one of the only times I ever chatted with Allen. It was a big class and we rarely crossed paths. I'm pretty sure he ended up becoming an orthopaedic surgeon in Vancouver. I waited in that line, reading a pamphlet on curriculum and contemplating my decision.

The external gratification that comes from all the 'attaboys' you get in the Army was something I liked, and couldn't articulate at the time. It feels somehow base to admit that. But the fact is, in the Army, we sew our rank and accomplishments on our tunics. There's something satisfying about that. Most of us don't admit to ourselves how good that feels, but it makes a difference. Fundamentally, I think we all love that sort of thing.

Some of us even long for it.

Most physicians say they would never want to be posted but they end up moving someplace random anyway. It's about a sense of control for them. My mindset was always about the mystery adding a sense of grandeur. Your posting the start of your next grand adventure.

So, while my classmate rationalized not even thinking about the military, I remustered to the Regular Force with barely a moment of hesitation. It meant no more weekends in Petawawa, no more polishing for parades, and I was paid full-time to go to school.

Those were all good things.

The feeling I somehow owed the Army something, never even crossed my mind. Leaving behind good friends was the hardest part, but they saw it in my eyes that I was going where I had to go. And so, it was an easy thing to join the Army.

And by virtue of my new profession, they made me an Officer.

Chapter Three

Grace

The Army issued me a black leather doctor's bag as soon as I signed up. It is one of those sturdy flat-bottomed classics with the rounded sides and brass clasps. I love it. It makes me feel like a *real* doctor. To this day I take it on house-calls and lug it around the med school when I'm teaching lectures, and never say a word about it. Like it's normal for a guy like me to be carrying a bag like that. Like old Arrowsmith on his way to clinic back in 1905.

My wife, Grace, rolls her eyes.

A lot of things are different since I've been back from Afghanistan, but that is the same. She still rolls her eyes and she still makes me smile.

By far the best thing about medical school was meeting Grace. "My best day, her weakest moment". She sat across from me at our first group session and stole my heart.

We were assigned a case the night before, ingested everything available on the topic, then met in our team room to discuss. The room was small and plain, tucked down the hall like an afterthought. The stale scent of the lecture hall's coffee cart lingered from down the hall. A table dominated the room, its surface nicked and scarred from countess discussions. Chairs that didn't invite comfort, their padding worn thin from years of use. We would huddle around bowed over our laptops arguing over symptoms and treatments, the arena for our battles of wits.

Our first case was Wilson's disease. Or maybe Trisomy 21? Or Cerebral Palsy? It doesn't matter, all I remember is Grace.

I would go to the room early to finish my review and eat lunch. A habit from the military. Always early. In time to mark your map. The group would usually arrived just in time. I can remember like yesterday the breath I drew when Grace walked in on that first day. She was captivating. And I froze. It was the first time we had been close enough to speak, and I couldn't. Nothing came out. Not only was she stunning, but she gave me the gears, minute one.

I had an apple on the desk in front of me.

"You going to eat that?" she asked.

"Um... Not if... You are," spilled out. And like a fool I held it out.

"Well, that was easy." She snatched it from my hand, took a quick bite, and chewed with her mouth open. "I read somewhere women who eat two apples a day report better sexual functioning," she said as she wiped the juice from her chin with the back of her hand.

When I regained my composure I said, "Well that sounds like—bushels—of fun," and smiled at her.

She smiled back. "*Apple*—solutely!" she giggled.

Her auburn hair and dark eyes glistened under the lights and I thought, WOW!

"Ummm, I *apple*—aud that effort," I tried.

"That's because it was hard—core," she said, instantly, sitting down across from me, "but you should have—picked—something better." Her giggle stopped my heart.

I don't know if she had those quips lined up in the breach but how quickly she said them was striking. The speed of her mind amazed me. Taking another bite, she smiled directly into my eyes and I was done. That was it. The end of my childhood in a moment.

We went through the motions for three hours picking tidbits from one another and answering questions with the group. Her wit and intelligence were overwhelming. A classmate told us to "get a room" right there in group on that first day. I wasn't sure how she felt until much later, but I suggested dinner, and we went to a steakhouse that very night. In hindsight "Appleby's" might have a been a better choice, but I had completely stopped thinking about anything but Grace.

Before I left for Afghanistan our grand adventure was just beginning.

Before I left for Afghanistan.

Sometimes I lie awake at night trying to remember *before I left for Afghanistan*, as a meditation, to make the dreams stop.

Sometimes I reach far back into childhood searching for my earliest memory, which for me is in the school yard with my sister. We're running up an icy hill in snow, then down on a navy Crazy Carpet which throws us in the air and whips in the wind and slashes across her face, cutting the corner of her lip.

When I get up, she's bleeding and lying, too still, in the snow. I'm shaken and far too little to help, or know what to do.

I remember my sister bleeding on the snow. I'm standing over her watching blood congeal on her cheek. An older kid crunches over, nudges her, and she stirs, and I try to keep up as she screams and runs home.

But that couldn't be my earliest memory.

If I start there and go forward, I find more places and people and moments but they're all the same; always blood, always sadness, and they fade away.

Until Grace.

Grace doesn't fade away. She feels a part of me. The happy moments before Afghanistan are filled with Grace.

She is the most complete person I've ever known. Her wholeness grew on me by the day, the month, and year, as though I had loved her all the days before but hadn't met her yet.

Love is like that I suppose. If you love someone you know how that feels. How I feel now when she enters a room, or touches my hand, or rolls her eyes at my frumpy doctor bag.

Before we graduated, I had convinced her to marry me. In the following years we built a life with hard work, sleepless nights, and respect for one another that runs deep.

She has always been the possibility of a dream come true that makes life worth living. Without Grace waiting, I don't know if I would have made it home.

Chapter Four

Fantasian Hordes

For a few years Grace and I *lived* at the hospital. It's called residency for a reason. You probably have an idea from television and movies what that's like. I thought I did too, but I never could have imagined the soul-stirring reality.

We couples-matched to the Community and Family Medicine program in Toronto. There was no guarantee we'd end up in the same place but we were confident. Every program wanted her. She had perfect grades, stellar assessments, and a winning smile, and the fact the Army was funding me didn't hurt.

We powered through those years of service, learning, and study, moving swiftly between rotations, feeling blessed and useful. We could tell stories from those days that would fill pages, and break your heart; the first time you deliver life-altering news to a family in crisis, or sit with someone in their darkest moments bearing witness to terrible disease and tragedy. That's hard, and stays with you, more-so the first few times you do it, but that's not what this story is about.

Residency was trying, but happy, and it passed in a blur. We were moving forward manifesting the life we wanted and our dreams were coming true. We smiled a lot. Laughed a lot. Cried sometimes. But it all lead directly to our goal. And when you're *becoming* like that, it's easy to find meaning in the suffering.

And then we were family doctors.

Easy peazy.

Most things were like that with Grace. She had a way of making life grand. And just like that the Army posted its newest 'general duties medical officer' to Kingston. Which was fortuitous again because Grace was admitted to the Woman's Health and Obstetrics program at Queen's University which was her dream.

Our stars aligned. We bought a drafty house downtown near the university with old floors and heavy radiators and I went to work at the base hospital. Grace joined a family practice, filled her roster quickly, and started delivering babies at the Kingston General Hospital. I moonlighted on the weekends in the emergency departments at all the peripheral hospitals; short happy shifts that kept my skills sharp and filled our coffers.

We were practicing medicine.

Our hard work had paid off, and our delayed gratification was done. We finally started spending. We let loose and got *all* the shiny toys. Grace looked great in her black Porsche Cayenne. I installed a home theatre in the basement with all the finest equipment. We got the best furniture, granite, and books. Lots of books. Not that we had a tonne of time to enjoy them, but we got them. It was a magical time.

About three years in, one Friday afternoon in winter, I said goodbye to my last patient of the day, looking forward to a bike ride home over the causeway. Even in the snow I loved to ride the lakeshore past what later became Gordon Downey Pier. My Cannondale was brand new and needed breaking in.

Our renovations were complete. The plan was to surprise Grace with charcuterie by the fire. She was 'post-call' and not due back at the hospital until the next morning.

But my Blackberry buzzed in my pocket and our plans had to change.

An Army doctor practices medicine, yes, but that's about half of what the job entails. The rest might be lumped into the category of 'soldiering'. As part of any Army unit, you need to understand your greater context, where you fit into the brigade, division, and Army, to do your job effectively. To appreciate all that we 'exercised' frequently and I found that work exhilarating. It was familiar, given my experience in the reserves, and a whole lot of fun.

The buzz in my pocket was a text from Jill, our Operations Officer (OpsO). It read, "Exercise, Exercise," and I felt that familiar excitement bloom. A 'warning order' followed with the where and when that I had been anticipating for weeks. We had been sitting on 'one-hour-notice-to-move' and that text was our starting gun. We were required in the briefing room, prepared to deploy anywhere in the world.

Charcuterie by the fire would have to wait.

My kit was packed upstairs in my office and, being the last to leave clinic, I'd be first to arrive, which was great. It was good to be first. Made you look prepared and keen.

I clicked the lock on my bike and went back inside.

Grace would understand. She always understood. I was her soldier. She knew I was still enamoured with the Army machine and found meaning in my work.

"Sorry babe. Ex just started," I texted.

She ghosted. I could see she'd read it, but she didn't respond, for the rest of the weekend.

That was fine. Her medical journals would keep her occupied. She preferred reading journals to listening to my philosophizing anyway.

She's the one who married a soldier, I thought as I climbed the stairs to the briefing room. *She loves being married to a soldier*. She jokes with her friends about the *danger* of my work even though these exercises are all on paper. But you never really know how someone truly feels.

Our conversation the night before had been about destiny. We often talked about things like that back then. I was reading the Greek tragedies, out loud, as she drifted to sleep each night. She said my voice was soothing. The night before, I remember, I had finished the Myth of Sisyphus. That's the tragic story of a hero condemned by the gods to eternally push a rock up a hill and watch as it rolls back down each night. Over and over for all eternity he pushes it up again, and again, and takes a dark joy in his fate.

I had stopped reading and mumbled through the last few parts sensing she was drifting to sleep but she stirred and turned. I could see she was awake and we started talking about destiny.

"I like that one," she said sleepily.

"Me too… Do you believe every person has what they need inside of them to reach their full potential? Or do you think it develops through the choices they make? That somehow our choices determine our potential?"

"Like Sisyphus choosing to keep pushing that rock?" She pulled the covers up and closed her eyes.

"Well, yeah. If we choose to take on a mission, or feel a sense of duty to something, do you think that's how we become who we are? By choosing those things. Or, do you think we are who we are despite what we choose?"

"Or maybe, the universe conspires to choose for us?"

"Ha. Maybe. But don't you think our choices matter?" I was rubbing the stippled pattern on the back cover of that old book. It was torn and falling off.

"Jack, I'm sleepy and you're doing it again. Just go to sleep."

"I think we need to choose... That's how we connect with higher meaning. Don't you think? When we pick something hard to do, we move closer to our higher purpose. That's what I think. Like med school and residency. That was hard. And it changed us." I set the book down, clicked off the lamp, and snuggled in. "You know this better than most. You're the hardest working person I've ever known, my love." I wrapped my arms around her and kissed her shoulder.

"Well, if the rock keeps rolling down for all eternity... that sounds like the definition of frustration." She smiled, then flipped onto her back and pulled the duvet up to her chin, "I wouldn't wish that on my worst enemy—condemned to pointless work for eternity. That's a nightmare."

"I suppose. But what if it's also a metaphor. Maybe the rock represents his purpose. It's hard work, and seems futile, but maybe lifting heavy objects is the entire point. The point of living..." I was having a hard time articulating what I was feeling about the story. She'd seen me like that before and sometimes cut through and helped me explain, but it was late, and she was tired, and drifting to sleep. Her breathing was getting steady. I left it.

We hadn't finished that conversation. But I knew she'd understand when she saw my text. I had to go to work. The exercise was meaningful. It was part of my choice to work hard and see where my choices led. I was a proud Canadian soldier, proud of what that represented, and proud of the work we did in the world.

I was the first one back to the briefing room.

Jill and the Base Surgeon were keeping tabs up front.

"Good job, Jack," Jill said quietly with a subtle thumbs up. I sat down in the front row with my 'junior general kit', an Army green notepad protector. Pen at the ready.

Jill was a nursing officer by trade, heavy-set, and strong willed. She was one of those officers who quoted directly from the 'Queen's Regulations and Orders' from memory.

Commanders trusted her judgement, and more often than not, she got the job done. The exercise was mostly her design.

Sitting down I watched them finishing final preparations and thought about the other person in the room. Our Base Surgeon, Brad. He represented the new Army to me. He was back from his training for the next rotation into Afghanistan. He was being deployed as commander of the role one medical contingency in Kandahar, and instead of going to the Bahamas or Jamaica on his two weeks off (which is probably what I would have done) he was with us, running an exercise. Everyone knew he was scheduled to be 'in theatre' in less than a month. That alone was awe-inspiring.

Brad was one of those guys who went all in, worked flat out at everything he did, and his concentrated effort was focused on the Army, the medical branch, and his career. He was the definition of dedication and sacrifice. Everyone knew he was going to make it. People talked about a short list of future Surgeons General; he was at the top of that list, at his rank, hands down.

Most of us have no idea what that's like. We never figure out what we could become because we never dedicate our lives to something the way he did. Like Sidney Crosby, or Tiger Woods, or Serena Williams. The Army defined him. You have to know, somehow, all that sacrifice will be worth it in the end. But how can you? Well, Major Brad Ridgeway was going to find out. You knew that the moment you met him.

"Good afternoon Jack," he said without turning around.

"Sir," checking my arms was a force of habit around him, "I thought you were on your way to Afghanistan?"

"I am. I'm not here," he joked. "Ready for a fun weekend?"

"Stoked, sir," I said, meaning it.

He studied the map. He was not moving, but I could feel his kinetic energy. Efficient and confident. The kind of guy you want to be around.

'Base Surgeon' was his title, not his profession. He was not a surgeon the way you're thinking. The same way the Surgeon General is not necessarily a surgeon. He was the doctor in charge of the base hospital and that's what we call the person in that job: a holdover from the British aristocracy or something. Brad was an emerg doc, like me, but more seasoned and experienced. I went to him often with difficult cases and he invariably set me straight. He was reassuring. His uniform was crisp. His boots always polished and tidy. A stethoscope poked from the cargo pocket of his desert pattern fatigues. His role this weekend would be to grade our performance and relay results to his own task masters in Ottawa.

Within twenty minutes the crowd settled in. A few stragglers were taking seats at the back as Jill began her operation order. We took notes, focused on our tasks, customarily holding questions to the end. For the next two days we didn't leave that building, nor did we perform any actual medical care, but the agenda made us feel like we had.

Every step was relevant and related to exactly what was happening on the ground in Afghanistan right then. Brad made sure of that.

All in all, it was surprisingly effective. I learned it was unfair to deride officers from the ranks (we used to call that type of exercise a "PENIS" – "Practical Exercise Not Involving Soldiers"), but I learned to appreciate how the machine works to prepare us at every level. By Sunday afternoon we were tired, but had successfully banished the Fantasian Hordes, and funnelled 1200 injured through our pipeline. Major Ridgeway had taught us a great deal and we were better for it.

Our pride swelled, and the beer tasted great.

Everything about the Army back then seemed useful. Always moving in a positive direction. Grace would have to understand that missing one weekend together was a small price to pay. And she would love to hear my stories.

She always made me feel like she loved to hear my stories. I was part of something bigger than myself. And she could see how important that was to me.

———

On my way home, cycling through downtown, I passed a cathedral on Chapel Street, and thought about my sister again.

She was always lamenting the lack of beauty in our Canadian churches. And how the architecture was weak compared to the old world. I would have to show her that one: a big gothic number with eight spires and stone golems. The beauty there touched the transcendent.

My sister is an Anglican priest. She told me stories from the Bible ever since we were little kids running around the base. I don't remember a time before she told me stories from the Bible; often about sacrifice and suffering. I was thinking about that, pounding my pedals through the snow.

I never understood why sacrifice, in the Bible, always involved baby goats or lambs being slaughtered. I pictured serious men in beards grabbing baby lambs from flocks and killing them, and burning them in sacrifice, and that never quite made sense to me. I suppose there's a metaphor there somewhere, but it sounded like they really did kill baby lambs all the time.

I could not imagine ever being that serious about anything. I tried to take my job seriously, but imagine being so serious you go out and take a baby lamb and slit its throat over a rock and drain its blood and burn it. Even if you think the ritual will somehow bring God's favour on your tribe. That would be hard. It's impossible to know for sure if they really did that as much as the Bible makes it seem, but if they did, you can't deny that's serious business, and those must have been some serious men.

Maybe they knew something we don't know anymore. Something lost about who we are or what we're built for.

Maybe life is supposed to be about doing serious things and maybe that's all that matters. Maybe we're supposed to keep doing the most serious things and that's how we make sure everything works itself out around us.

That's what I was thinking, as I cycled through the cold wind going home. My tires hummed rhythmically on the crunching snow.

Grace and I had sacrificed an evening of charcuterie by the fire, and a weekend together, and that seemed worth it to me.

I couldn't explain all that Bible stuff to her because it never sounded right when I tried. She would say I'm being *that way* again and we might laugh a little but I'd lose my train of thought as I do. So, I kept those things to myself.

"I'm home," I said, closing the door.

The house was quiet and the lights in the kitchen were off.

On the table, I found a note:

> *Gone to the hospital. Leftovers in fridge.*
>
> *Love, Grace.*

I opened a beer and started a fire.

She knew my work was serious and that I was serious about my work. She knew those exercises were useful and that I saw Canada as a beacon for peace in the world.

We debated how Lester Pearson's Nobel Prize defined us internationally and whether peacekeeping was still the most quintessentially Canadian thing, but it was Grace who asked me, "When's the last time you heard that word?" And I couldn't remember.

But she knew I believed in the Canada of my youth and the great things our Army was capable of doing in the world. Or at least I hoped she knew that.

The war in Afghanistan was happening after all and I was a soldier who needed to be prepared to go if it came down to it. But my obligatory service was ending, and she had started hinting about life after the Army.

"We can open a practice downtown," she'd say. "We can work at the University."

She always made the next life seem so glorious. "I can't wait to settle down and have kids with you, for real, Jack. I know they'll come," she said, "I know we'll have a family someday. I know it."

But it always made me feel like she thought my Army service was a phase. Like I was only playing a game for a while. And the game was coming to an end.

I love Grace dearly. But how I felt about being a soldier then was hard for me to explain. My identity was tied up in it. I never felt she could truly understand that.

I opened another beer.

She was doing important things right then. Delivering a baby. Obstetrics is a bloody business if there ever was one. Things go bad in a hurry all the time in obstetrics. They usually go well, but when they go bad, they go bad quickly. She was on her game for that. She had to be. That was what she did.

She had to understand, we both had serious work to do. Mine was different, and maybe seemed to her unnecessary, but both were serious.

I had trouble sleeping when she was away in the night. I knew I would toss and turn waiting for her to come home. So, eventually, tired from the exercise, and the cycling in the snow, and my third beer, I passed out on the couch by the fire. And dreamed of Sisyphus pushing that rock.

I was helping him. But he looked like Schwarzenegger in Conan and didn't need my help so I ran up and watched from the top. Then I grabbed a shovel and tried to make an impression in the mountain to stop the rock from rolling down. But the hillside was granite or diamond or something glittery. I drove the shovel hard trying to make a dent, but couldn't. I was swinging a pickaxe at a glint in the rock which seemed the easy place to make a dent, but I kept missing. Sparks flew all around. Sisyphus and the rock were closing in, and the axe wasn't working. I adjusted my aim but couldn't make a dent. Then the rock was there, and I stepped back and tried to help hold it, but it wobbled out, and rolled down, past us both, to the bottom where children at a school were running for their lives. Afghan school girls screaming and running in the sunlight, but they couldn't get away. It mowed them down and destroyed their school.

I awoke with an overwhelming sense of despair and self-contempt, feeling responsible for the death and carnage of the dream. I was alone in the heat of the fire, sweating. An unbearable weight of helplessness and an uncomfortable sense of self-loathing washed over me. I swallowed it down.

What replaced it was a need to try. A need that made my jaw clench and chest tighten. A need to try that was palpable. A need that would linger in the weeks to come.

I put the fire out and staggered upstairs to bed.

Chapter Five

Intubation

The next morning Grace was home in our bed looking peaceful. I tiptoed out and unlocked my bike from the rail. A light dusting of snow covered the ground as I raced the morning sun across town to the base hospital. A brand new brick and glass building across from the rifle ranges. Sergeant Jimmy Sheffield met me out front and held the door.

"Morning Doc, glad you're here. We need you in trauma one."

Jimmy was the senior med tech. He beckoned me to the trauma bay. Hidden in the back just beyond the rattle of the ambulance bay doors. Bright and stark, smelling of antiseptic and urgency. On the way we passed a few doctors standing around prepping for clinic. Jimmy had passed them on his way to get me. I noticed that immediately. It wasn't subtle. It meant he'd sought me out for this and snubbed them. His confidence in my skills was greater than my own and, if I'm being honest, that felt great.

At this point, a few years into my career, I was at the peak of my powers. Close enough to residency to recall everything I'd learned, and seasoned enough to know how much I didn't know. "One of the JTF2 guys fell off the rappel tower," Jimmy said.

It appeared I was in for some real medicine. A welcome change from the paper-patients over the weekend.

"Really? What happened?"

"Sounds like someone pushed him. Maybe a lover's quarrel," he joked, "I don't know. He's in trauma one."

The JTF2 was the "Joint Task Force", one of the Kingston area's largest units. Special ops. Super high tempo. Tasked with black ops and secret squirrel stuff that we never heard about. All we knew was they trained hard, and we hardly ever saw them at the base hospital. Accidents were exceedingly rare. It was a bit unusual that he was here.

Entering the bay, I dropped my bag and surveyed the scene.

A soldier on a stretcher in combat fatigues surrounded by four others: Nurse Lara, at the crash cart arranging kit for venipuncture. Junior medic Sam, applying pressure to a head wound. Jimmy, heading for the monitors. And a bystander, the patient's buddy, a sergeant with "Jones" embroidered on his chest.

I scanned the patient quickly.

His eyes were closed and his limbs were still. *Not localizing obvious pain. Less than eight on the Glasgow Coma Scale—Classical teaching says "less than eight" means "intubate".*

He needed airway protection.

Spine awareness is key. Handled, for now. Collar in place protecting c-spine—that would make intubation interesting. Need to ask Jimmy to grab the video glidescope.

The laceration to his left scalp had a skin flap that was still bleeding. The medic, Sam, was applying pressure with a handful of gauze. A field-expedient splint, on his right arm, would need replacing. *Bone visible, blood seeping—compound fracture—needs prophylactic antibiotics, stat.* The other arm, across his body, had a deep sulcus sign below the acromion—*dislocated shoulder. Looks like that might have been missed at the scene.*

Pelvis looks stable. *Probably. Legs straight. No obvious leg-length-discrepancy. Still need to check his pelvis.*

That took about four seconds. I was ready. I was confident and capable and still loving the rush. "Morning team. Nice way to start the week. What do we have?" I said, taking charge as I felt for a radial pulse, which he had. Brisk and regular.

I stepped back and threw on gloves and a gown.

"Twenty-four-year-old private fell from a tower about fifteen minutes ago," said Lara. She was a nursing officer. Captain. Competent and helpful.

"Thank you. We need a pressure and a sat right away. And Jimmy, when you're done monitors, please bring the advanced airway cart to the bedside. Lara, thank you, yes, we'll need two large bore IVs. Please send off a basic panel and start a litre of ringers from the warmer on a slow drip, and a gram of Ancef. Let me know when that's done."

They moved like clockwork. Closed loop communication.

"Sure thing boss. Glad you're here," said Jimmy.

"Good to be here, Jim. Looks like he hit his head on the way down?" The scalp laceration. "Did anyone see the fall?"

"I did." This was Jones.

He looked composed. A tall man with broad shoulders and plain features. Brown hair. Blue eyes. Strong jawline. Fit. "He fell thirty feet and hit a stanchion on the way. Landed in the sand. He hasn't moved much. Is he gonna die?"

"He's not dead yet, and we're going to do everything we can to prevent that, but we've got work to do. Why don't you sit outside." By this point I had taken my place at the head of the bed and was examining and positioning for intubation.

"Sam, please show the Sergeant out."

"Sure thing boss."

Pupils equal and reactive. A good sign. White parietal bone beneath the wound. Intact. No skull fracture. No reaction to pain. Moaning. Confirms GCS 8. Monitors: strong heart rhythm. Tachy but not dangerously so. Breathing and saturating well at ninety-eight percent on room air.

This was a very fit soldier at baseline.

Fingers flexing. And releasing. A good sign.

"Line is in."

"Thank you, Lara. Everyone, presume spinal fractures until proven otherwise. Let's be gentle," I said. *He's going to survive this. Need to check his spine and get imaging.*

Then the patient retched.

"Tilt on three," I braced his head and neck. *Decision made. Intubate for airway protection.*

Lara expertly glided to the patient's left next to Jimmy. Their arms overlapped. On three we tilted, gently, and I swept his mouth free of breakfast. *Scrambled eggs.* I suctioned his mouth clear and ran my hand down his spine feeling for steps and deformities. We lowered him flat.

"Let's prep for intubation." His vitals looked good. I preoxygenated with a bag valve mask. On my order Lara pushed a dose of sedative and lidocaine followed by rocuronium to paralyze. I swept his tongue with the blade and glided an endotracheal tube in place.

We watched on the glidescope display as the tube passed the chords. There was a rush of relief when it went in. I inflated the cuff and listened over his chest to confirm placement. *That was slick.* I thought. But out loud I said, "Still not an expert," and Jim and Lara smiled.

In medical emergencies imminent disasters are always looming. Intubations go badly from time to time. It's easy to miss them, to not get the tube in the right place, and then you've got a patient whom you've paralyzed, and have to breathe for. And sometimes it goes so badly that a cricothyrotomy is required. No one wants that. Cutting into windpipes is not an ideal solution when a tube down the trachea, through the mouth, is much, much safer.

But the legend says you're not an 'expert' until you've failed a few times. It's a catch 22. The law of averages. You have to have a lot of cases that go well under your belt before the bad ones find you. You think you're good, until you fail miserably—and that's when you're an expert.

Terrible outcomes happen. And they matter. But it's a bit of a trial by fire. I'd been in practice for about three years, working in various emergency rooms and trying to gain the experience needed to feel confident and capable. I'd run into my fair share of intubations, but none that I could not perform. Yet. And with not a lot of medical failures under my belt, not even little ones, the dark side was still looming: like an anvil.

I felt like I could do no wrong, but I knew I wasn't an expert. And after another perfect intubation my mind screamed, *I might be really good at this.* When you avoid disasters long enough, you begin to imagine it's because your skills are genuinely great. But you always know 'pride cometh before the fall'.

In those days—*before I left for Afghanistan*—I thought I might be pretty good at emergency medicine.

"You're just that good, Doc," said Jimmy, reading my mind, and that made me smile.

We rolled the patient and took the time to check his spine from another angle and his sphincter tone for spinal integrity. His pelvis was stable and the remainder of the secondary survey seemed okay. We cleaned his wounds and braced his arms.

"He's pretty stable, let's get him to imaging," I said, moving to the side table to complete the chart. "I'll whip-stitch that wound and set his shoulder when he gets back."

"Oh yeah... His shoulder is out..." said Jimmy examining it closer, "I didn't see that!"

I smiled sidelong and shrugged.

Things were under control. Jim and Lara could handle things from there, and Jones was waiting outside. I sat next to him in the hall.

"He's going to pull through," I said.

Jones, startled, looked up from his notes, "Thanks, Doc."

He had his nose in a pile of scattered papers. It looked important. Mission planning. Maps and aerial photographs. I caught the words, "Situation", and "Mission". It looked like a half written operational order. He gathered up the papers and leaned back.

"How are you doing?" I asked, resting the back of my head against the wall and stretching out.

"I'm good. That was hard to watch though. Bad fall," he said, clearly a little shaken up. Probably still seeing his friend tumble.

"We're running some tests. But he's stable." I didn't know what else to say. I summoned all my doctorly persona, trying to provide that empathetic 'reassurance' that I could never quite muster, "We'll know better soon. He seems strong..." I trailed off. The outcome was still up in the air, and that head injury was quite severe.

He was shaking his head. So, I changed the subject.

"Looks like your unit is up to something interesting," referencing his work.

"Ah... The usual shit. More work-up training. We're heading back to Afghanistan next month." He leaned back and stared off to the line of windows at the end of the hall. "We've got a line on this Taliban asshole who's been using kids as weapons... rounding up orphans... strapping suicide vests on them. We tracked him to a village South of Kandahar in the Panjwai district. The intel coming in is quite horrible... You do *not* want to see the pictures... We are going to take him out, and I hope to be the one pulling the fucking trig—"

He stopped abruptly, and looked sheepish. "You have clearance for this don't you, Doc?"

"I mean, security clearance, yes, can't work here without one. But the details of what you guys do out there, always been a bit of a mystery to the rest of us," I smiled.

"Right. Sorry. I'm just... Suppose I shouldn't be talking about this guy... our missions... I'm a little more shaken up than I realized... It's just... this one hits a little close to home... You got kids, Doc?"

"No... Not yet... We're working on it though..."

"Well... I have a baby girl at home... and some of this... horrible what this guy's doing."

"I can't imagine… How old is your girl?" I asked trying to change the subject.

"She's four… going on twelve… Ain't nothing better… She's the apple of my eye."

I watched him smile thinking about his daughter and a familiar sting returned. Like iodine on an open wound. A longing for fatherhood lingered under the surface of my life. Having never had a father to tell me how to live or let me watch him do it, it was hard to understand that longing, but I knew I wanted kids. Grace would make a wonderful mother. We had been trying for years and been close a few times, but those were the final stars that had yet to align for us.

The first miscarriage was hard. After the third we knew something was wrong. Grace had an obstetrician friend who sat us down and gave us the bad news. We were sad together for many months but lost ourselves in work, and found our meaning and purpose there. We had each other, and grew to understand. And maybe, we just weren't ready yet. The universe had other plans for us, and there were other things we needed to do. But our love grew stronger for it. The suffering together tempered our bond. We found our happiness, despite the pain of disappointment, which withered slowly, but inevitably, and becoming less immediate, less searing, with time. It only returned in moments like those, seeing Jones in reverie about his daughter, and his fatherhood.

"You're a good man, Jones. Sounds like you've got a tough job," I paused for a moment before standing then added, "I hope you get that fucker."

"Ha... Yeah, me too... Thanks for what you do too, Doc, and thanks for taking care of Brendan," he said. "His mom is on her way from town. I'll tell her to ask for you."

"That's fine. The front desk will know where to find me."

"Thanks again." We shook hands as he stood to go.

"Jones, if you ever need to talk to someone, you know where to find me. Your job is tough and we don't see enough of you guys around here. I'm happy to help in whatever way I can."

"Thanks, Doc."

"And try not to worry. We'll take care of your friend. I'll look out for his mom."

Chapter Six

The Call

Back in residency I saw a plaque, at Sunnybrook, that said, "If you Want to Be a Surgeon, Follow an Army." It was on the wall behind the desk of a big-shot trauma surgeon named Dr. Harry Chan and it resonated truth. That trauma rotation was amazing and he was a great teacher but that plaque set me moving.

"If you really want to learn trauma, you gotta go to war," Dr. Chan would say. He'd been there at least seven times and I'm convinced that's what made him great.

As a junior resident on the trauma service though, you mostly care for patients on the wards. You run around answering pages and writing orders for Tylenol and crap at all hours of the day and night, but for your efforts you get to help with all the fresh trauma.

I put my hands on every trauma that came through the doors that month. I stole a few hours, here and there, in a call room for sleeping, but, in case I ever did go to war, I wanted to learn from the best and see as many traumatically injured patients as possibly. The Army needed well-trained docs so that's what I was aiming to be.

Dr. Chan guided my hands as I placed chest tubes, packed wounds, and set bones. And he told me stories from the war. Unfortunately, in a trauma rotation in Toronto, you mostly see car accidents. Mostly blunt trauma, only the odd knife wound, and a rare gunshot (not like what happens in Panjwai).

The worst case I saw was probably that "skidoo vs tree" that came in (spoiler alert: trees win, every time), but there were a lot of other crazy cases too. Like this one guy who got stabbed with a ceremonial sword through his liver. He was stuck to his front lawn by his neighbour's wife. She grabbed it off their front hall display when she saw them fighting on the lawn and impaled the guy. Stuck him right to the ground trying to stop him pounding her husband. It worked. Ironically, as I recall, they were fighting over a snow shovel. Only in Canada.

Another young lady was beaten by her father. Her CT showed a knife *in situ* right across her skull above her eyes. That was a wonder. It must have bounced right along her orbital bones below the frontal lobes of her brain. She came in alive with that knife sticking out of the side of her head. People can be really shitty to one another. Dr. Chan said, "Penetrating trauma to the cranium, that crosses the midline, is universally fatal." I'll never forget that. We took her to the operating room and I helped pull the knife out. She lived a couple weeks. I was fascinated by her. But he was correct. In the end she succumbed alone on a Tuesday. I filled the boxes of her death certificate at her bedside.

That's the way it is in medicine, too many of those lonely quiet moments.

The gunshots were rare in Toronto but I learned how to handle them. We didn't see many explosive injuries, but we knew we'd be dealing with them overseas, so Dr. Chan made sure we knew the basics, "Improvised Explosive Devices (IEDs) are the insurgent's 'weapon of choice'," he'd say. "They like to bury pressure plates on the pathways and roads linked to makeshift bombs with the power to destroy trucks like putty."

You don't see a lot of those injuries in Toronto, but Dr. Chan laid out the approach. It was a great elective. I learned how to manage trauma like the pros in the most advanced trauma centre in our country. And when I saw that plaque, I wondered if my real education might happen overseas… if I ever went to war.

That is why when Major Ridgeway, home on another two-week vacation from Kandahar, invited Grace and I to dinner on a Saturday night, I was stoked. I wanted to get to know him better, and very much wanted to hear stories from the front. I was hoping to learn a thing or two about trauma and war medicine on the modern battlefield.

———

Brad and his wife Katie, lived in a swanky apartment overlooking the lake with a bellhop and a valet. Grace and I dreamed of living like that someday. We were excited to see their place and looking forward to the meal.

They put on a spread fit for royalty. It was next-level amazing. The duck confit tasted like Swiss Chalet Chicken and the wine was delicious and fancy. Katie said it was a 'new world' Cabernet Sauvignon from Prince Edward County. They served it with savoury butternut squash soup, locally grown herb roasted potatoes, and asparagus with blackened almonds. The cloth napkins and candelabra with bright white candles blazing over the piano set the mood. Eating like that, up in the sky, overlooking the marina—felt like we'd arrived.

The sunset filled the sky over the windmills on Wolfe Island as we settled in. Grace and Katie hit it off immediately. At one point they were talking about the duck, or maybe us soldiers, leaning into each other on the couch, laughing uncontrollably, and pushing on each other like they were old friends.

Brad and I smiled at that, but we were not that close.

It was a great night. After dinner Grace and Katie went out on the terrace to admire the stars over the lake, and Brad waved me into his study.

The wainscotting was dark and polished. He poured two glasses of whiskey from a crystal decanter, "A Rocky Mountain Glenfarclas 25", he said as he lit a cigar and settled into his plush leather chair. I relaxed into another with brass carpet tacks on the arms and turned the ice in a heavy tumbler. It smelled like dried fruit and honey, and leather, and fresh ground coffee, all at the same time.

"Whiskey smells great," I said. "Too bad it tastes like poison." I smiled and sipped it slowly as he chuckled, "I could do without that cigar stench too," I added.

"Ahh, you don't want one?" He sucked and puffed a perfect ring that floated above him. Then he flipped a switch on a tray and we watched the smoke draw down through the filter.

He was Churchill at his desk.

We bantered back and forth about sports and the exercise and recent news for a time, and then, as I was about to ask him about Afghanistan, he began...

"As you know, Jack, I am commanding the role one contingent in Kandahar." He leaned back and his chair creaked.

"Yes," I said, excited to hear more, "What's that like?"

"I want you there," he said simply and took another puff.

I didn't catch it right away.

I was staring at the books on the shelf to his right.

But when I ran it back in my mind *chills* went down my spine.

"I'm sorry?"

"I've been impressed with your work. You excelled on that exercise and I need a doc I can count on outside the wire.

I was stunned.

"There's a TAV (a Technical Assistant Visit) coming up. I'm hoping you'll take it. We need a physician with your skills to backfill medical stations at our FOBs in Panjwai. Our PA's need to take some leave."

It was slowly dawning on me what he needed.

He wants me in Afghanistan, at the Forward Operating Bases, while the physician assistants go on leave... on a TAV... while he is still there.

That sounded soon.

"I'm sorry. When?" I took a gulp of whiskey and didn't taste it.

"You'll leave in two weeks. We'll need you for about four months, maybe five. You'll bounce around leading trauma teams. Nothing new for you, except... it'll be in Taliban country. A little more *shooty-killy* than Kingston." He chuckled again.

This is exactly what I've been dreaming about.

I rolled the ice cubes and watched the amber liquid catch light. He was saying something else, "...suspect you'll want to run it by Grace, but a TAV is a great opportunity and you should take it."

I took another gulp.

I'd been asking the universe for that very thing. And there it was, suddenly glimmering before me. What do you do in moments like that?

You freeze.

I drew a breath trying to settle the butterflies in my stomach. I was beginning to think maybe I wasn't wanting the right thing all this time. Maybe it was patently stupid to want a thing like that. Then overwhelmingly: Yes, it is a stupid thing to want. Of course it is.

What was I thinking?!

"You seem hesitant, Jack. I thought you wanted this?"

"I do... Yes... I do... I just wasn't expecting it so soon."

"People of strong character take action without second-guessing themselves... Do you believe that?"

I was suppressing an impulse to stand up and leave. It took me a moment to process what he said..., "I suppose so... Yes," I agreed.

"You're a thinker, Jack. That's why I want you there. But, if you think too long and hard you'll find lots of reasons not to go. Trust your gut. If your gut says you're the right man for this job, trust it. You're needed over there. Kids are being blown up and shot and we need people like you, skilled emerg docs, out at the front."

"I get that. Yes," I said. But I was thinking, "I'm pretty sure my father was a truck driver. Maybe I should go be a truck driver."

He puffed on his cigar.

"I know what you're thinking: Who willingly enters a war zone when they don't have to? You've got a comfortable life, a beautiful wife, and a happy home... But, Jack, sometimes we need a will to stupidity..."

"I'm sorry? ...A will to stupidity?"

"Yes! The courage to jump in and stop trying to make too many counter arguments. Even when they may, in fact, be good arguments." He laughed another deep hearty laugh, "I went through the same damn thing before my first tour. I'm sure you'll come up with a thousand reasons why you shouldn't go, but it's only the few good ones that

matter. And mostly the fact that it's the right thing to do…
In fact, that might be the only thing that matters. At least
that's what matters most to me."

Out the window the moon was bright in the sky.

*Maybe I should go somewhere and wait for a better idea
to come along... Maybe I should quit medicine altogether... A
carpenter... I'd make a good carpenter...*

I was thinking that, but instead I said, "I suppose if you
keep second guessing yourself you might never do anything
at all..."

He clapped his hands. "You got that right. And if you
wait around for the perfect idea, how would you recognize
it when it punched you in the face?"

Then he held his glass across the desk, "Here's to being
the lucky few who never have to worry about that."

I smiled. "I'll drink to that," I said, as our glasses
clinked.

I usually trusted my gut. My gut led me into soldiering.
And I was good at it. That had to be worth something.
This had felt like the right path all along. If I stepped out
of my current moment of hesitation and confusion I still
felt like a soldier. A Canadian soldier. And that made me
feel prideful. The Army suited me. It felt right. It made me
part of something bigger than myself. I was experienced
and trained to do complex things in support of complex
operations.

I would be useful over there.

And then my mind wandered to the desert. And I started
to think about the point of our intervention there. The

Taliban and 9/11 and harbouring terrorism—and more—why Canada was there. The Taliban were bad people. Or, at least that was my impression. Helping Canada. Bringing peace to the world. It felt like why I existed back then. Protecting innocents from bad actors, and that's—I was spinning.

"What's it really like over there?" I finally settled my mind enough to ask. In an effort to ground myself.

"I'm hoping you'll find out soon enough."

"Right… but… what about the Taliban? Do you see them? All I know about them is what we get from the news."

"Don't concern yourself with the bad guys too much. You'll be there only to do medicine. That's it. What I can tell you is they're thugs. Oppressive and violent. Especially to little girls."

I knew that. It sounded bad. But it wasn't much of an insight...

How does he know? What influences his narrative?

I had seen a recent news report about a girl getting acid thrown in her face for trying to go to school, and wondered why that was the story we were shown. Why did the powers that be choose to show us that one? It felt somehow contrived. Horrible, but contrived. We never seemed to see the other side, and I was hoping someone could show me something real about the other side. Their motives. Something endearing about them that justified so many followers. But I couldn't find it. That felt like I was being manipulated.

But Jones had talked about a bad man using little girls... And that was real... Wasn't it?

"Do you get intelligence briefings? I mean, I'm interested in motivations... I don't quite understand."

"Don't overthink it, Jack. The Taliban is an umbrella term for a loosely connected group of thugs. They are locally commanded and disorganized. Like street gangs. Our Coalition of forces is trying to stabilize the South so the Afghan administration in the North can establish institutions down there. We are training the Afghanistan National Army (ANA) to take over security. It's not complicated. The bad guys don't like it. They want the entire place under Sharia Law so they can oppress little girls. They don't like what we're doing. They're planting bombs and recruiting suicide bombers, and blowing people up... Bottom line, we need good docs. It's that simple. Best not to overthink it."

That seemed reasonable. I had to believe if Canada was behind this mission, the mission had to be just. Our country had always been a beacon for peace in the world, and outsourcing Canadian values seemed fundamentally a good idea.

It had to be that simple.

I simply wasn't expecting the opportunity so soon.

But Grace wasn't ready.

The offer to chat with Grace sounded reasonable, and he seemed to be asking and not telling. So that was good... He was saying something about the OpsO...

"...Jill will arrange to DAG you green so it won't be an issue when it's time to go."

DAG is short for Departure Assistance Group, which doesn't matter. We were always helping soldiers "DAG medically" at the clinic. I'd been DAG'd in the past, but not recently. This would be the first time I'd be DAG'd for a war zone. But I did need to update a few qualifications. Outdated soldier stuff: gas hut drills, personal weapons testing, things like that.

He was saying something else...

"...outside the wire they're getting hit pretty hard. We need good docs, Jack. The medics out there are good, but they need our support. Your level of expertise will be invaluable. And it will only be a few months..."

Then he paused and smiled and took another puff of his cigar.

"I should talk to Grace," I said.

"Sure. I'll give you the weekend," he said as he tapped his knuckles on the desk and stood.

————

The valet brought the car around and opened the door for Grace. She looked beautiful in the wind off the water with her flowing dress pushed tight around her legs. I started the car and glided into traffic.

"That was a lovely evening. I really like her," she said.

"Yes. It was. You two hit it off." I was staring straight ahead and gripping the wheel a little too tightly.

"So, what did you two chat about?" she asked.

Two weeks.

I didn't speak.

"Jack? What's wrong?" She could tell. She could always tell. She turned down the music.

A war zone. I never expected it to have to tell her this... But here it was—happening.

"He asked me to go."

"Where?"

"There... Over there. With him."

She looked down at the clutch purse on her lap and played with the zipper... "Afghanistan?"

"Yeah. He asked me to help him with the current Roto. They need a doc for a few months. On a Technical Assistance Visit... A TAV."

"To do what?"

"Backfill. When others take leave, I guess. It would be sort of... a short duration trip."

She was silent.

I didn't like the silence.

"Canadians are being blown up and dying over there, babe, and I can help."

She stared out the window at the passing cars.

"I know this was never on your radar... I know we talked about my Army days coming to an end soon... But this seems like a good opportunity for us... and my career."

The Animals were playing quietly on the radio. She clicked it off, "How is that a good opportunity for us? I thought you were submitting your release next year?"

"I will. I mean, I was going to—"

"Is he asking or *telling* you to go?"

"It sounds like he's asking—for now."

"Well that's easy then. The answer is no, right?"

I let that linger, clutching the wheel.

"Who would volunteer for a thing like that?"

"It's my job."

"No, your job is seeing patients at the base hospital and coming home to me. Your job is being my husband. And hopefully, a father to our unborn children..." She was holding back tears. "...not fighting in some God-forsaken hell hole half way across the world."

Her eyes were glistening.

I needed to let her be upset, but I was frustrated.

"Kids are dying over there."

"I know. That's a good reason not to go."

"But this is what I've dreamed of my whole life... Watching M*A*S*H with mom... I could be your 'Hawkeye Pierce' for reals..." I tried, smiling in her direction.

"It's not funny... You're not Hawkeye fucking Pierce."

The last part was a little too loud and a little too sharp, and she was not smiling.

"No. I know. I'm not... But this might be the closest I'll ever get. Remember that plaque I told you about at Sunnybrook?"

"You're not a surgeon either, Jack."

"I know. But this is my job. And he asked nicely... It could be the experience of a lifetime... And maybe next time he won't be asking."

There was more silence for moment.

The only sound the sweep of tires and quiet hum of the electric engine. Then, when I couldn't stand the silence any longer, I spoke... "Next time, I could get dinged for a full roto and be gone for a full year or more. At least this way we decide. A short TAV is better... It's better this way."

"But, that's just it. He's asking. Not ordering. You can say no to this and by the time the next one comes around you'll be closer to your release date, and maybe you can get out instead."

I didn't respond. There were things in my head about soldiering that Grace could never understand. Things I loved about the job that I couldn't articulate. She couldn't understand the part of me that didn't want a release just yet, maybe never wanted a release. I was a soldier to my core. I felt like a soldier then, and wanted to keep feeling like a soldier for a while longer. This might be my one shot, my only opportunity, to make something of this life and accomplish something truly important. The thing that might fill the void. Make me feel worthy of this life. I wanted to be more complete, more whole... Like her.

She didn't have to worry about any of that. She couldn't understand that feeling. And I couldn't say it.

"For mc, Jack. Please say no for now."

I could only hope it might be the wine talking.

"It's not that simple."

"It sounds that simple."

We pulled into our driveway and made our way inside. The house was quiet as we trundled up to bed; alone with our thoughts. I didn't read to her that night. She slipped out of her dress and under the covers and turned her back. She was asleep in moments. I lay awake watching her for a while, until her breathing steadied and she began to snore.

Grace's snore is not really a snore at all. Not the kind of snore you might imagine. You can barely hear it; unless the house is quiet and you listen close. It's the quietest, tiniest snore you'll ever hear. A tiny catch at the back of her throat when she inhales.

She knows how I feel about the Canadian Army and about the war. She knew my stories and above all she knew I was searching for meaning and purpose and answers.

This could be my chance to find out who I really am.

I wasn't even certain I was someone who could handle going to war. I thought I was. I was trained to be someone who could handle going to war. I needed to find out. As a human male. Would she even respect me if I shied away from my responsibility? If I dodged; if I declined.

Underneath, I knew that she knew I couldn't. The Army needed my support, and my skills, and had earned my dedication. The Army was the reason I had these skills. They paid for my medical training. Our troops deserved good care. If not me then who?

But she was scared.

The unknown is always scary.

And she had said, "...for me, Jack."

If I decided to go, she would be left at home holding the fort, not knowing anything about where I was or what I was doing and that would be extremely difficult for her.

The fact I could get hurt, or worse, was something that would hurt Grace and I loved her so deeply I couldn't want anything that might hurt her in any way.

I watched her sleep trying to imagine not being able to watch her sleep. I listened to that tiny snore and the thought of not being able to hear that tiny snore made me sad.

So I decided. It was worth trying to say, "no".

The house was deathly still when I finally fell asleep.

But I fell asleep ready to tell him no.

Chapter Seven

Squirrels in the Attic

Grace was writing an academic article that Sunday. That was her thing. She lost herself in writing sometimes. When she got called to the hospital for a delivery before dinner it meant we wouldn't get a chance to talk about my leaving before the week began.

Monday morning, I was on the range.

I loved range days; out in the open air, under the sun, being paid to shoot a well-oiled C7 rifle. What could be better?

My mother bought my first BB gun when I was eight years old so I'd been shooting most my life. After my dad left mom joined the Air Force to make ends meet. The base housing was so cheap back then, which was helpful for us, but those places were all the same: drafty, war-time, monopoly homes with parquet flooring, baseboard heating, and squirrels in the attic. The scratching and scrabbling up there kept us awake at night for years, so the first thing she did, after handing me that BB gun, was send me up the attic ladder to kill squirrels.

And I was happy to do it. I was the man of the house, and it felt good to be useful.

And it didn't take long to get darn good at shooting.

I remember lining up glass bottles on the back fence and picked them off from upstairs. My sister never liked me killing those squirrels, or rabbits, but I found they made the best sport. The faster the better. I could hit one running at fifty feet by the time I was ten.

So, learning to shoot a military rifle was a bit of a joke.

There were more troops on the range that Monday morning than usual. Range days tend to be 'unit-based', so you normally know everyone there, but that day we were surprised to find a slew of JTF2 troops milling about. For the most part, those guys trained on their own. We figured in secret, so it was odd to see them shooting with us medical folks. But the Army had added an extra qualification in the wake of the war. The "PWT-3"; a slightly more advanced personal weapons test (PWT). So we figured it had something to do with all the new requirements. We all had to qualify shooting from farther back, and complete some 'run-downs'. Instead of shooting only from our bellies at 100 and 200 metres, we also had to be running around with loaded weapons.

Our targets were the same "person-shaped Figure 11's" that I'd been shooting since my early days in the reserves.

"Good old 'Herman the German' I said when I saw it." And the corporal running the stores truck looked at me sideways.

"I'm sorry, sir?"

"Herman the German," I said, pointing to a stack of paper targets splayed out on a six-foot table.

"Oh... We don't call them that anymore..." she said.

"Oh. Right. Sorry."

Fewer and fewer troops remembered that we once called them Herman. We always had for as long as I could remember, but I suppose with the Germans being our Allies maybe that change made sense. Strange how some things about the Army shift slowly, while others disappear fast. I imagined they were called that since the forties, or maybe even since the first Great War. Probably the same shape the entire time (the shadow of that helmet was decidedly WWII German if you asked me), but no one called them Herman anymore.

The run-downs were different. Running down a range with loaded weapons all around, not knowing if the guy beside you has his safety clicked, can be interesting. Weapons bouncing around muzzles swinging right at you sometimes. That's fun. But the point is to get up on the berm, drop down, take up a firing position, and finish off old Herman, with a five-round grouping at his centre of mass, as quick as you can. Before the target drops.

Shooting with your heart rate elevated and your breathing heavy is a little more difficult, but not too bad. I was surprisingly good at it. I got on the berm early and shot a perfect grouping every time. It's apparently embarrassing for special ops JTF2 super soldiers to be beaten by a medical doctor. So that was fun too.

After my shoot I sat with the others on the dry grass and opened a box lunch. The sun was high and it was cool in the shade of the ammo truck.

A Lieutenant-Colonel I'd never seen before came over and sat to my left. He was fit. Brown hair. Brown eyes. Nothing distinguishing about his face. Wouldn't call him handsome. Rugged. Maybe, ruddy. But he was pleasant and articulate.

"Good morning, Doctor Henry. That was some nice shooting," he began.

"Thank you, sir." I figured he'd read my name-tag and assumed my profession from the 'medical' inscribed on the slip-on over the epaulette on my chest. They had announced the scores, and I was one of the few who finished with a perfect one-sixty.

"You made my troops look bad," he said.

"Sorry about that, sir." I smiled. "Not sure I've seen you around. Have we met?"

"No, I don't believe we have. I'm Clark. Lieutenant-Colonel John Clark," he said, reaching out a meaty hand.

I shook it. Firm. Friendly. He was wearing a fleece over his uniform. "Nice to meet you... Jack," I said.

"Well, Jack. You've obviously used one of those before. Where'd you learn to shoot?"

"I was in the reserves before med school. How'd you do, sir?" I asked.

"I re-qualified. Which is all that matters." He smiled.

"Of course." I went to work on my lunch: tuna sandwich, juice box, single serving cheese, and an apple.

"Have you heard about any good TAV opportunities in Panjwai?" said the Colonel.

That surprised me.

"Yes, I did, sir. The Base Surgeon mentioned one the other day... Why do you ask?"

"Beautiful country over there, Jack. A short TAV might be a good career move for a doc. In and out. You gonna take it?"

"I'm still thinking about it." His directness seemed out of place. I started wondering if he might have sought me out.

"A TAV performance evaluation is how I got promoted," he said. "Performance evaluations recorded in the presence of an armed enemy are great for that. You don't get a lot of opportunities for those. They tend to be right-justified, if you know what I mean."

He was being chatty.

"Is that so? I was not aware of that."

"Yep. If you're in theatre for ninety days. They'll write you up a 'tour PER' and your next promotion is virtually guaranteed... As long as you don't screw the pooch in theatre... Ha." He smiled brightly. "Imagine mistakes in your trade have a few more 'life and death consequences' than most."

"Not more than most." I grinned.

"Not a lot of docs stepping up to go... The danger pay is great, too. You know that? You don't pay income tax over there. Lots of good reasons to go, you should think about it."

His Blackberry buzzed. Glancing at the display, he said, "I gotta run." He stood and strode away answering the phone.

I gathered my trash and dropped it in a garbage bag being ferried around by an industrious corporal, and when I looked up he was gone.

The range is an open space with a long road with a few trucks and people milling about. It was a strange feeling that he disappeared. I wanted to ask more about tour evals and taxes, but he was gone.

The range safety officer barked a command that got us up and moving. I formed up on the road with others and began the march down range to the butts. That stretched the legs and felt good in the open sun.

Maybe Grace would appreciate the financial incentives.

Maybe going on a TAV wasn't such a terrible idea after all.

Chapter Eight

Destiny

I played intersection hockey on Tuesdays. Major Ridgeway had slipped away until later that week delaying our conversation. The week was passing uneventfully, so a good hockey game would do me some good.

I played right wing on the second line of a decent intersection team. We had a good game: 3-1 victory. Our goalie, Mike, stood on his head.

"Nice game," I said, tapping his pads.

"Thanks, Doc. Nice goal." Throwing his water bottle in his glove as he skated with me to the gate.

"Dean's pass across the middle was incredible," I said smiling. Trying to be humble, but thinking about my sweet dangle and quick backhand over the glove. The empty netter at the end sealed the win, but that second goal was the game winner.

Snipe. No celly. Act like you've been there. (It really was a sweet dangle though.)

"You heading home after this? The guys are stopping by the mess for wings. You should come," he said. There were a bunch of junior officers on that team. I should have joined them more often.

"Can't man, gotta get home. Grace is waiting."

"Happy wife, happy life... Hey, isn't your obligatory service up this year?"

"Early next year, yeah. Why do you ask?"

"When are you releasing then? Wondering about the team. I assume you'll get out as soon as you can?"

"What? No way, man. You can't get rid of me that easy." I sat down at my hockey bag in the corner, "I'm gonna be your Surgeon General one day, bud!"

"Oh man, you've got to be kidding."

"What?" I opened my hockey bag and threw in my jersey and elbow pads. The smell was ripe.

"Dude, you're a doctor. How many doctors stick around past obligatory service? Can't you make like two or three times on civie street?"

"I don't know about that. But so what? Who would give up the chance to care for you fuckers?"

"You're nuts. If I was a doc, and had a wife like yours, there's no way I'd be sticking around here. Especially with this war going on."

Dean agreed, "Frigging right man—your wife is hot!" he said, standing up, wrapping a towel. Flashing a glimpse in the process. There's always one guy. They were all laughing now. "What? It's true. You got a golden ticket. Why risk this shit?" he quipped on his way to the showers.

The whole thing took me off guard. I was being a little facetious, but their opinions were completely unexpected.

For them to be open about what they thought of my future and my career, and what they would do in my shoes...

"You think any of us would stick around, Jack?" Mike continued. "Who here wouldn't walk in a heartbeat? No more chicken shit bullshit. No more shit postings to Shilo, Manitoba." He said, nodding towards Arne who was posted to Shilo in the spring, and not particularly pleased about it.

Arne added, "It's true, Doc. We love having you on the team, and God knows we need good docs around here, but you're nuts. I'd pull pin." Then he added, "But your wife *is* hot." As he too climbed out of his hockey pants and headed for the showers.

"Boys. Listen. I'm not going anywhere. This is the way for me. I was just talking to Grace about M*A*S*H*. I'm Hawkeye Pierce, man. You can't get rid of me..."

I trailed off, and they moved on, rolling their eyes, and making fun of Arne.

I was thinking about being a colonel up in Ottawa, writing white papers, fixing the Army Medical Branch... That wouldn't be so bad... The pension, and benefits; nothing like that for doctors on civie street. And the Army is in my bones. And soldiers are good company, and they deserve the best doctors, or at least ones who really care and know what it's like...

The showers were hot and the water pressure was great. In the mirror I glanced at the maple leaf tattooed on my chest. What they were saying made some sense, but the Army had been a part of my life for as long as I could remember. Even that leaf had been there since I was eighteen years old. Six guys from my first platoon got the same one. Each of them had gone off and wore blue berets around the world as Peacekeepers in Golan, Cyprus, Bosnia, and Rwanda. Places I never got the chance to go. I was focussed on my education, on becoming a physician. While those guys made a real difference in the world. I stayed home studying. But now I had a chance to do something. Being a doctor for the Canadian Army had so far been the best job I could think of. Why would I ever leave?

I was last to leave the dressing room that night. Wasting time on contemplation again.

The Army was good for me; the structure, the uniform sensibility, the camaraderie, and promotions. Always reaching for that next brass ring. Christ, we even sewed our brass rings on our sleeves. The 'attaboys' and promotions felt great. How could I leave all that behind. Life after the Army wouldn't have any of that. And that was an uncomfortable thought.

———————

After Hockey, Grace warmed some leftover lasagna and served us each a small plate. She poured a glass of Cabernet from the cellar and had a splash. She mostly drank Perrier. I finished the bottle. We chatted about the future all night.

It was wonderful. One of those evenings. That woman. She makes my world grand. She draws out parts of me that I don't understand. We hadn't discussed the TAV since the night at Brad's but we each had had some time to think and process. I was starting to see my life with her in a clearer light.

She was sitting on my lap with her tweezers. I have one freaky follicle that grows a hair at a rapid pace out of my right forehead. She loves to pluck it when she sees it. The wordless way she smiles and approaches with the tweezers, every few months. It's painful, but it's beautiful. One of the increasingly intimate rituals that mark the collapse into oneness that is our marriage.

Wiping the tear that inevitably follows the pluck, she smiles at me. "Grace. I love you. I love our life. I see how your practice is thriving, and I've heard the things you said. I've tried to think deeply about all this Afghanistan business... The guys at hockey seem to think I should get out."

"There is more to life than the Army, my love." She put the tweezers down and slid a little closer. She kissed my temple, cheek, and ear.

"This TAV seems like a great opportunity for so many reasons, but you're right. I'm not being ordered to go. I can say, "No thank you, sir.""

"Oh babe. I see you're torn. It's important you make this decision yourself. It's your life. It's your decision. I don't want you to feel like I'm pressuring you." She smiled and began to unbutton the top three buttons of her blouse. "If it's important to you to go, then you need to go." She stood and finished the unbuttoning and smiled. "This decision is a big one, and it has to be all yours." She straddled my chair, hugged my face. I kissed her skin and stood with her in my arms and we made our way upstairs.

She was right, the guys were right. We'd worked too hard to get through med school and get to this place in our lives where everything seemed to be going our way. My obligatory service was almost done. I'd paid my dues and sold my time for a medical degree, and this future.

The TAV would be great opportunity for a military career, but that would be a thing of the past soon enough. Grace had her work at Queen's, her practice was well established, and I could join her there, or pick up more emerg shifts. I still loved emerg work. We could buy a lake house, settle down, and kids would come. They had to come. It wasn't impossible. The OB had said 'unlikely' is all. And if it didn't work out, we could always adopt. We knew we both wanted children. It was the final piece of this perfect life and we both knew it would happen. Eventually. And we had begun to discuss adoption. Grace brought home a few pamphlets from the hospital and we had some websites bookmarked. It seemed such a beautiful thing. There were so many children needing good homes. And we could give them one.

Going to Afghanistan was a silly idea.

I remember that evening as perfect. By the time I switched off our bedside lamp, it was abundantly clear the TAV was a bad idea. I would chat with Brad in the morning. My mind was made up. I would say, "no, sir."

Sometimes, in my quietest moments, that's the night I'd go back to. If they ever figure out that flux capacitor thing, I'd buy a DeLorean, and choose that day.

———

Brad was not around when I arrived at work the next morning. When my morning clinic ended, I noticed a disturbing quiet in the hall. Normally people would have been milling about completing clinical tasks, but the doors were shut, and the hall was silent.

Then a noise from the team-room drew my attention and I wondered if I had forgotten a lunch-and-learn. I quickly made my way there and opened the door, and was immediately greeted with a resounding chorus of, "Surprise!"

The entire unit was there, but I noticed Grace first.

She was at the front in her grey wool power dress with the clean lines and smooth collar. Brad and the leadership team were beside her.

I was at first confused, then noticed the plaque in his hand with a Canadian Decoration Insignia. I was due, but I wasn't expecting my clasp for a while. Someone must have indented for it exactly on time for it to be here already.

"Come on up here, Jack," the Base Surgeon said.

I waded through to the front, people smiling, clapping my back.

"Ladies and Gentlemen," he began as the crowd quieted, "The traditional joke here is to complain about someone being improperly dressed." This was met with your standard few snickers. He continued, "As you know our good Doctor Henry has been working diligently with us for these past three years. You may not be aware he had a former life in the Army Reserves." Someone in the back yelled, "LET's GO, JACK!" and the crowd took another moment to settle. "He's been a great addition to our team. He's hard working, and good at what he does." That felt uncomfortable, but people kept saying it.

"Front and centre Captain Henry."

I came to attention at the front, as you do.

"Let me be the first to congratulate you." He shook my hand; someone was preparing to snap a photo. "With your combined twenty-two years of meritorious service, it is my pleasure to award the Canadian Decoration, First Clasp." He smiled and handed me the open box with my new medal. I shook his hand and smiled for the camera. "Twenty-two years of undetected crime," he joked and the crowd laughed. "This clasp represents a life of service. We're lucky to have you."

I was beaming and Grace kissed my cheek.

"What are you doing here?" I whispered, smiling.

"I wouldn't miss your big award, silly." She grinned.

Then the crowd started chanting, "Speech. Speech." I held up my hands and began, stumbling at first, "Well. I guess I'm a big deal now." They laughed.

"BIG DEEEAAALLL," Jimmy yelled from the back.

"Thanks everyone," I began again. "Umm. Sir, it's been a pleasure learning and growing under your leadership.

This is a great team. All of you. Thank you for your support and encouragement these past few years." Then turning, "Grace, thank you for being here, I know your schedule, it means a great deal. Thanks for keeping me going every day. Thanks so much for this. Everyone. I look forward to continuing our work together. Thank you."

Major Ridgeway took it from there, "Cake and coffee at the back. Enjoy. Back to work at one. Cheers, everyone." Then he turned to Grace and I and beckoned us to follow. We exited a side door and followed him up the stairs to his office.

Nice place. Large wooden desk. Nothing like his condo in the sky, but reasonable, for government work. We sat in cloth chairs and stared past him at the diplomas and certificates lining his wall.

"Have you discussed the TAV?" he started, sitting down.

I looked at Grace. I knew what she wanted. I knew what Brad wanted. I knew what we'd discussed. But my stomach was turning somersaults...

And then, there on the wall behind him... that same plaque:

If you Want to Be a Surgeon, Follow an Army.

My head was spinning.

All I could see was the opportunity of a lifetime shining before me. Going to war! Fulfilling a lifelong dream. The award I just received the first of many. I saw myself sitting on the other side of that big Base Surgeon desk with the arc of my life leading from promotion to promotion and back to Ottawa and a glorious home on the river. Children in private schools and summers at the lake... The TAV seemed like the only thing… the beginning of so many important things.

I glanced around at the photos lining the walls, marking time.

One with Brad shaking hands with the Prime Minister. One with him on a hill in Afghanistan. Him pulling a stretcher up the ramp of a plane. Him saluting at a ramp ceremony...

And then, in the corner of that one I recognized a face. An old friend from my first platoon with a solemn look on his face. A friend, with the same tattoo as mine. A pall bearer at that ramp ceremony.

I had never seen that photo.

I stood and walked over to get a closer look.

"Look, Grace. That's Jason Pearson."

"Where?" She came to my side.

"Right there. Holding the coffin."

"It is, too! That's weird."

"You know that guy?" asked Brad. Brad was in the foreground, but that was definitely Jason with the coffin.

"He's an old friend."

"He must have been close to the deceased... only the closest friends carry caskets," he said.

I thought back to that summer in the park. Jason and I sitting in the shade. A solemn man in a blue jacket, beside us. His war stories ringing in our ears.

"Do you think you could do it, Jack?" Jason had asked.

"I don't know, J, I hope so… If the time ever comes, I hope to be ready to take up the torch, you know."

What would Jason say if he found out I turned down a chance to serve… to go to war… To see if I could handle going to war…

I was being asked to go, on a short TAV, in support… Not to the front… Not to fight a raging German war machine…

What would Jason say if I turned this down? What would all the guys say?

Grace couldn't understand. I never gave her the opportunity to understand. We'd been too busy learning medicine and building this life. She had barely met my old friends, at the wedding. And I'd lost touch with most of them. In that moment, that made me sad, and with Jason's solemn picture staring back at me.

Grace only knows Jason from my stories.

To her, I was a doctor, married to a doctor, surprised in unexpected ways to have this vocation, and salary, and privileges. She didn't understand my soldier side. She couldn't have. And it was my fault she couldn't. I never showed her. She couldn't understand how I'd never dreamed about any of the things we had downtown. And for me, going to war had an inevitability to it, that she could never appreciate.

I had dreamed of being Hawkeye Pierce and this was my one true opportunity. Maybe I was supposed to be a truck driver like my father before me. My mother had always told me he was a truck driver. But I wasn't a truck driver. I was a soldier. A Canadian Army soldier. Who'd shot for the stars and got himself into medical school.

So, yeah, a doctor too.

But I saw my star glimmering before me right then...

"We have, sir," I said, as I sat down...

"I have decided to go, sir."

I stared straight ahead and noticed Grace shifting in her chair. To her credit, she didn't react more than that. She didn't deny. She didn't speak out. She played the role of the supporting spouse. She smiled and nodded.

But she was gripping the arm of her chair a little tighter.

I saw her knuckles blanch out of the corner of my eye.

"That's wonderful news," Brad said, "You are going to do amazing work over there. The boys we send need your help. They deserve your help. We're lucky to have you," and to Grace, "Thank you for giving us your husband for a time. We'll do our best to get him back to you in one piece."

That was probably not the best choice of words, but that's what he said. He stood and gestured to the door, "I'll have the OpsO set up your final training runs for next week. You leave two weeks from Sunday."

———

We walked out of his office and down the stairs in silence. I followed her to the car and sat briefly in the passenger seat as she started the engine and gripped the wheel. She knew

I had patients waiting inside, and she had to be back for hers soon as well. So we sat. In silence for beat. And then she spoke. And her tone was soft, and calm.

"I thought you were going to say no."

"I thought so too. I did. I really did."

"But you said yes."

"I couldn't… I think of those kids, being injured and killed, and coming home in boxes. What are my skills for? If not to help them? …If I don't go, Grace, who will?"

"They'll find someone."

"But I'm here. I'm trained. And I can go. I was offered the TAV."

"I don't want you to go."

"I need to."

"But I don't know if I can handle it."

"I know, my love. But it will be good for us, I promise. I don't pay income tax over there, that's huge, and danger pay—it's a huge step financially. It makes sense."

"I don't care about money."

"I know you don't… But I have to go."

She paused for a moment. Then took my hands and turned and looked into my eyes. "I know you do. I'm not angry. I see you… And if you feel you're moving in the right direction, keep moving."

That made me smile. She was not smiling when she said it. But it made me feel like she understood. Like she was still on my side. 'If you feel like you're moving in the right direction, keep moving.' That was something we said now and then; a line from a books we'd read together. What I heard, was her seeing how important this was to me, and that, despite all our fears and trepidation, she had my back.

She always had my back.

But just then my Blackberry buzzed: "First patient in a room," was the text from Lara.

"I gotta go, Grace."

"Of course, Jack. I know. Congratulations on your award, Captain Henry," she said.

I saw a glint in her eyes that might have been a tear, but I ignored it, "Thanks, babe. We can talk tonight. This is exciting." I kissed her cheek and stepped out, "I'll see you tonight, my love," I said to myself as she pulled away.

That was the last we spoke about it.

We spent the next two weeks circling one another never digging below the surface of our fears. We could sense the enormity of the chasm beneath. It was too uncomfortable, and scary to go there. The decision was made, the dominos were falling. Our human forms are soft and small and finite and it hurts to think too deeply sometimes. If we shine too bright a light, it frightens us, and we have to turn away. We each sensed that in those few weeks. We both had our worries, about the TAV, about the future, but it was not something we said aloud. We didn't want the veneer to shatter. If it crumbled, everything might have crumbled. We might have crumbled.

We didn't talk about it.

Part Two:
Tests, Allies, and Enemies

Chapter Nine

OBUA

You've probably heard of Delta Force or SEAL Team 6 or the British SAS. In the Special Operations community they call those, "special mission units" or "SMUs". They are the elite of the elites. You may not be too familiar with ours, but Canada has them as well. The Joint Task Force (JTF2) is our top tier, and some say they're the best of the best of all of them around the globe, but it's as Canadian as maple syrup and poutine to not toot our horns about it. And we don't have a 'Hollywood North' out there raving about our guys.

So I'll do it for them.

Our Canadians are so good, the SEALS, and Delta, and SAS love to come train with us. From what I hear, our guys are the model for shooting, planning, and thinking about special operations. If you are an American you probably think I'm being boastful or stretching the truth about that, but if you're SOF, you know it's true. Our guys are the best.

And part of what makes them so awesome is how humble they are. Our snipers are unbelievable. Their tactics so clean. Only the most mentally tough, efficient, and accomplished get there. They punch well above their weight in every category. Those are facts. But we're not supposed to talk about it. And we usually don't, because we're Canadian, but I can't help myself, because of what happened after I said yes to the TAV.

Everyone in the Army knows the JTF2 are tier one SOF, an elite SMU, so when I heard I was going behind the looking glass—that I would be one of the lucky few to see behind the curtain and possibly even train with those guys—I was as excited as a pig in shit.

I needed a few boxes checked quickly, and as it turned out, the only unit doing that sort of training at that moment in time was the JTF2.

It felt like I'd won the lottery.

There's a component of workup training called OBUA. That's 'Operations in Built Up Areas' that every soldier going over needs to qualify on. The Army is nothing if not thorough. I tried to imagine a scenario where things went so completely off the rails that the doctor needed to be kicking down doors. It seemed ridiculous. But I wasn't complaining. They said I needed OBUA checked off, so I went and got it checked off. I loved that soldier stuff.

I was smiling ear to ear as I parked at the OBUA range and walked to the hut.

"Morning. You must be Doc Henry." A young soldier with clear eyes and tanned skin and a scruffy beard greeted me. "Grab your kit," he said, pointing. "That should be everything you need."

He was dressed in desert pattern fatigues and wearing a Kevlar vest and the muscles of his forearms rippled as he cleared a C8-A3 Carbine Rifle, and showed me the empty breach.

"Clear," I said, as one does.

He handed me the rifle and directed me to a table in the corner. Next to a placard with my name was a Kevlar vest, matching web gear, and a helmet that fit surprisingly well. Four magazines loaded with 5.56x45mm standard NATO rounds: Live, ball rounds. The deadly kind.

That was the first time I'd held one of those short rifles. And I'd never put on a Kevlar vest before. They were heavier than I'd imagined, but I guess you need the weight to stop bullets. The guy gave me a hand with the Velcro and I got the impression he wasn't too pleased with having me there.

"We'll start with a series of short lectures then get into drills." He was wearing no identifying data on his uniform. He directed me next door to a small lecture hall. Concrete floor. Six-foot folding table with a projector. A single chair. It looked like I was the only pupil.

Then, standing at the podium, fiddling with a Toughbook laptop, I recognized Jones.

"Come on in Doc," he said, then, under his breath, "Don't mind Lester, he's not too happy that we have to add you in today but I don't mind. It's good to see you."

"You too, Jones. How's your buddy doing? I heard he was discharged from ICU."

"Yes, he sure was. He's going to make a full recovery thanks to you. Thanks for caring for him."

"No problem. It's what we do. And that's great news. So, you're gonna train me up on OBUA?"

"Sure am. Don't worry it's not rocket surgery." He smiled. "The team you're joining knows all of this. They're inside starting their drills. I'll run you through the basics then take you through a few scenarios."

He proceeded with his lecture. I grasped the overall concept quickly; the details of positioning, efficiencies of team behaviour. He was a good instructor. He asked questions to confirm I was engaged and picking it up. It was vaguely familiar from recruit phase. He had to double back a couple times, but soon we were heading out onto the range.

"As long as you don't kill anyone, or screw it up completely, we'll sign you off."

"Sounds good to me."

That was a great day. I'm not being hyperbolic when I say those guys are the best soldiers in the world. And I have a theory why that is. I think it's our numbers. You'd think having more troops to choose from would be an advantage, but it's not. From the very beginning every Canadian soldier is taught more concepts than most. We can't afford to specialize too early. Big Armies don't need as many generalists. For us, it's an economy of effort. If you've got one million soldiers, you don't need them all to be good at every part of soldiering. There's redundancy. But we don't have that luxury in Canada. Our soldiers need to be able to do all of the things. We learn multiple weapons, various pieces of communications equipment, tactical combat casualty care, navigation, etc, etc, etc.

Countries with much larger forces have enough soldiers specializing in any one of those things. I have a feeling that lack of redundancy has a paradoxical benefit to our special forces. It's just a theory, but I figure we have a much more advanced recruiting pool to draw from. Troops selected from lower tiers have more skills to begin with. Like infanteers in your basic rifle company try out for SOF, and only the best of them are selected. Then the entry level SOF guys try out for the next higher tier, and so on, drawing from the best of the best all the way up, but starting from a more solid foundation. Despite our lower numbers to begin with we end up with a better product. They don't waste resources training specialists to be generalists.

That's my theory. But I'm pretty sure Jones told me some of that. He liked to say, "It's like our hockey system. Your average Canadian triple-A hockey team beats any team, from any country, at any age level, hands down. So, when you pick the best of the best from those teams you quickly end up with an unstoppable force. JTF2 is like Team Canada." I'm pretty sure he said exactly that with a smile.

All that to say, I got to work with the smartest, fittest, most dependable, laser-focused troops I'd ever seen that day. And that's the truth.

But all grey men too. Non-distinct. Never trying to stand out in a crowd. You could tell they were smart and pleasant, but you would only notice the paucity of effort in their movement, the world class strength and endurance, if you were paying close attention. And despite clearly not being excited about me being there, and having to train me that day, they never grumbled. Never complained.

I expect any one of them could be sitting next to you on a bus right now, and you wouldn't even know it. And they seemed to me to be totally selfless too. From what I've heard, that is the key difference that distinguishes that top tier. The final piece that gets them into that top tier of the game is selflessness. You'd never make it to the highest levels if you weren't that. I got the impression they'd die for one another, and just might fight over who got to fall on the grenade.

And I got to spend a day with them.

Watching them, I learned how to move through OBUA ranges.

It was impressive how they supported one other, and learned from one another. They discussed each error openly, and reviewed feedback from every angle. But rarely, if ever, did they miss a shot.

"Slow is smooth, and smooth is fast," was the refrain. The instructors kept repeating that as we drilled, over and over. I learned how to kick doors, stack in, hit the targets, and shoot to kill... centre of mass... Not the kind of training a doctor usually gets, but I wasn't complaining. I needed my paper signed.

That was a bucket list day for an Army nerd like me.

We started with a requal on the Browning 9mm hand gun. I was familiar with that weapon and proud of my pumpkin-sized groupings from distance. But that day, the instructors adjusted my grip, "Apply more pressure at your palms. Let your fingers relax. Squeeze the trigger. Like an orange. Don't pull or jerk. Gentle. Focus on your breathing." They fixed my sight picture and stance too. I'd been firing that weapon for over twenty years and never shot a grouping smaller than six inches, but in that one single afternoon they had me down to a toonie. Those steel plates, twenty-five meters downrange, never stood a chance.

Later, I was paired with Jones and his team. Our scenario involved a Fantasian stronghold. Two bad guys with hostages. Stockpiles of bombs and weapons. Dead of night. Bad guys presumably sleeping. Plan to go in hard. Flash bangs. Kicking doors. Stacked approach. First man react, second counter, third high, fourth low, etc... We practiced over and over. I accidentally shot a few hostages. We would enter too quickly, and I would shoot when the targets popped and kept killing a hostage.

They didn't mind though. All part of the learning curve. "Collateral Damage," they'd say. "It's all right Doc, you gotta fail to succeed."

The plastic pop-ups didn't mind. We were training for battlefield conditions. Slow is smooth and smooth is fast.

I was pleased when I finally got it right. It was long and tiring day, but I qualified. By the time I got to home, Grace was delivering another baby at the hospital, so I settled into bed still spinning and glowing from working with those guys. It felt like everything was going my way. I wasn't sure if any of that training would matter, but I didn't mind the need to do it. That was a great day. Those SOF guys know what they're doing.

Chapter Ten

The Approach

The day before I left for Afghanistan, Grace and I were still circling one another. We hadn't talked about the TAV since the day in Brad's office. I continued reading stories as she rested her head on my shoulder, but we tried not to think too deeply about my going to a war zone in a few days. She was busy at work with deliveries and teaching and we chose, silently, not to wallow in the inevitable.

I was determined, and felt ready. She never spoke of how she felt. She seemed trepidatious, but could sense my resolve. She never questioned my decision. Her love was always around me. Not so much in words, but little things. She made my eggs the way I loved them in the morning. She brought my lunch to the door when I forgot. My towel was always fresh by the shower. She did little things for love and I tried to do the same. When I was searching for something, she always knew what for and where to find it.

My flight out of Kingston was at 0437hrs on a Sunday morning. That night we climbed the stairs together. I remember holding her hand and undressing her slowly and seeing her in the moonlight through the high window in the loft. We lay naked in each other's arms for a time and made love in a frantic, searching kind of way. I kissed her hands and neck and thighs and she was soft and smooth and powerful and the most important thing in the world. We moved together and pulled on each other as though we would tear a piece off and keep it, even as we held each other whole by the moving.

She fell asleep in my arms, and I watched her there for a time and didn't sleep for a long while. I woke before my alarm and turned it off and took a moment to leave a note. I tried to fill that note with hope and sacrifice and purpose. But mostly it said, "I love you".

I left my final will and testament under my pillow where she would find it. With directions to open "only in the event of my death".

It was all so very serious after that. Cloak and dagger. Jill drove me to the airport. She felt it was her duty, as OpsO, to send off the troops heading overseas. She was good like that. Her pickup rolled to a stop at our curb. It was dark and quiet and the stars were shining. Grace was sleeping as I threw my case in the bed of that truck. I looked up at the dark window as I climbed in.

I had my army duffle folded inside my civilian luggage and left my rucksack and web gear at home. I was to be passing through the United Arab Emirates, and my orders were to not advertise my military status. Civilian attire only. Our presence was not widely known and the Emirati government preferred to keep it that way.

Uniforms were to remain packed. Army kit would be issued at Camp Mirage. I had packed three sets of combat fatigues, boxer briefs, socks, a shave kit, and a stethoscope. I had a few paperbacks in my carry-on, but that was about it.

The ride to the airport was quick. Jill didn't say much. She was tired and somber.

"Stay safe, Jack," was all, as we pulled up to departures.

It happened fast. I checked through security and sat watching the commuter plane that would take me to Toronto. When my flight was called, I walked across the tarmac, up the stairs, and settled in my seat. As I buckled, the pit of my stomach was churning.

My Grace was probably still sleeping and I wanted to be home with her.

I called home on a layover, "Hey. I'm in London. I miss you already."

"Hey babe, great to hear your voice. I'm sorry but I'm just on my way into a delivery and she's crowning. I can't talk. Have a great flight, stay safe, and call me when you can."

"I'll try, babe. I love you," I said.

"Remember, if it feels like the right direction, keep going," she said. "Take care of yourself."

And she was gone.

———

I flew Air Emirates out of London. Somehow, the lovely clerk in Kingston had finagled an upgrade to business class for that final leg. It was a pleasant surprise. I could lie completely flat. I made a mental note to thank her if I ever saw her again.

The stewardess was an attractive young lady with a beige, red trimmed uniform. She brought two papers, a lovely meal with asparagus, eggs, and cheese, silverware, ceramic salt and pepper shakers, and a leather-bound shave kit, which I was allowed to keep.

Business class is the only way to fly.

Customs in the United Arab Emirates was another story. I waited a nerve-wracking hour for my bags on the other side. When they finally arrived, I was standing near the baggage claim in a soaring concourse completely devoid of passengers. A young man in an impossibly clean white robe with a flowing headdress, a dark band cinching it to his head, approached. He had a tightly trimmed beard, a handsome olive complexion, a pleasant demeanour, and a few pointed questions.

I told the truth. What choice did I have?

I'm a doctor deploying to Afghanistan with the Canadian Army. Yes, that's my name. Yes, those are my combat fatigues. I knew I wasn't supposed to advertise my military status, but no one had said I'd be stopped at customs. I had no compass. No idea what secrets to keep. It was a strange feeling, not knowing. But my reflex, as always, was to trust the system, and be honest.

Eventually he handed back my green passport and suitcase, which had been emptied and re-packed haphazardly, and sent me on my way.

My orders were to meet a driver holding a placard with the letters 'HLTA' in bold blue letters. No idea what that meant. I later learned that HLTA stood for "Home Leave Travel Assistance" and was commonly used as the Canadian equivalent of the American "R&R". Soldiers came and went on HLTA, mid tour, quite frequently. Since I was off-cycle and not travelling with the contingent, the system treated me like those returning to the area from vacation. As if I should know how all this worked. As if it was not my first time travelling into a warzone, alone and confused.

I found the man with the sign by the exit. He was an olive-skinned welterweight in a navy-blue buttoned-down shirt, khaki pants, and a clean, tightly wrapped turban.

"Good morning. Doctor Henry?" he asked, in heavily accented English.

"Ah. Yes. Hi," I said.

"May I take your things?"

"Sure, yes. Call me Jack, please. Are you taking me to Mirage?"

"Yes. But we don't speak of it here." He grinned at this and I couldn't tell if he was joking.

"Oh. Sorry."

"I am Abbud," he said as we stepped outside. The hot air struck my face like a wall. I took a moment to acclimatize, as he loaded my luggage into the trunk of a mid-sized sedan. Grey, late model, clean. The loading zone was busy yet surprisingly spacious and modern.

"How long is the drive?" I asked. I had heard Camp Mirage was a small airfield near the gulf, but never saw it on any map. I had no idea where I was going but, again, trusted the system to get me there.

"Long drive. You may sleep. If you wish."

"Thank you. It's okay. I had a nap on the plane."

I settled into the air conditioning on the passenger side. "I've never been to Dubai. It's quite beautiful. Are you from around here?" I was making small talk and he was happy to oblige. We sunk into plush seats as we pulled away. The glare-reducing blue strip across the windshield was dark and familiar, as was the pine scent and faux wood panelling.

As we drove through the airport traffic and out onto the highway, he spoke of his home and family and how he came to be a driver for Canadian soldiers. His pride in working with a kind and gentle people was humbling. Everything about that day felt right. I was moving in the right direction.

Dubai must be considered a masterpiece of urban planning. Its soaring architecture juts from the desert like some Ridley Scott alien landscape. Lush green patches of grass seem out of place against the stark clean desert sand. Sprinklers cast rainbows inspiring a charming sense of wonder. Those manicured patches of green were mesmerizing; islands of grass between perfect asphalt highways, set where no one, except possibly a road crew or gardener, might ever step, yet perfectly maintained as if a world cup match was about to be played. The infrastructure and constant vigilance required was awe-inspiring. The highways themselves were perfectly smooth and dark. I thought of Kingston, how the frost heaves split our highways; old and dreary in comparison.

Abbud was talking and the hum of tires on those smooth roads was soothing. I had a lot of trust in that kind stranger. He matched the description, had the sign, and knew my name. That was enough. I went with it. But I have to admit, there were moments on that trip across the UAE where I worried. Maybe he got my name from the customs official and he's taking me to some political prison? This could be the start of an international incident: Doctor Captured in Protest to Canada's Presence in Dubai.

I was relieved when we turned off the road and Abbud waved an arm, smiled and said, "Behold, Camp Mirage."

Ahead were small buildings and an airstrip. Two military planes could be seen taxiing in the distance. A standard air traffic control tower with an octagonal room of glass hovered above. Across the road, a film played on a suspended sheet with Canadian soldiers gathered in lawn chairs all around. It looked inviting. But first, on the road in, we had a checkpoint to clear.

"They will need your ID at the gate," said Abbud.

I had not prepared for that.

"My passport and wallet are in the side zipper of my carry-on... It's in the trunk," I said as he pulled to a stop by the guardhouse.

The Emirati guards approaching were heavily armed.

I don't think he heard me.

"Abbud, I need to get in the trunk for my ID."

Then he looked at me with a disappointed and stern face, breathed a sigh, gripped the wheel, and stepped out of the car.

The guards were local and very serious. They didn't like him getting out. He spoke quickly and they conversed, and when I got out, they trained their weapons on me. I rounded the car and Abbud popped the trunk. Behind me, I heard two clicks: one from each rifle. They were disengaging the safety mechanisms on their weapons.

I'm not sure why I found that amusing.

The sun was setting over the airfield and the purple sky was beautiful. I was in the middle of nowhere, far from anything and anyone I had ever known with two strangers, a finger twitch away from ending my life, and I felt lighthearted and calm. Abbud might have known of danger. He might have been sweating on my behalf. But I thought it was funny.

That might be the definition of over-confidence.

I lifted the lid and reached into the boot pulling my carry-on forward.

I imagined, for fun, that my life was in real danger. That I was a spy in a movie, hiding a pistol in that trunk. I imagined what it might be like to pull it out quickly, depress the safety (which always sticks), turn on those two strangers, cock the mechanism (which is heavy and needs to be gripped overhand most of the time), load a round into the chamber, and shoot one, then the other guard... and have them be surprised by my swift actions.

With rifles trained on my back.

Before either could flex a trigger finger.

In the movies those things seem easy. In reality, the pistol would get caught on a zipper. Like my wallet did just then, and I laughed out loud.

They looked bemused. I showed them my CAFIB20 Military ID. Thankfully my picture was much the same as my face, having been recently renewed. They lowered their weapons and waved us through. I got back in the car and Abbud pulled ahead, through the gate.

"Why were you laughing?" he asked.

"Just tired I guess."

"I like Canadians," he said. "All so happy and friendly. But sometimes I don't understand. Those men do not work for you. They are Emirati and not happy you are here."

"I'm sorry, I wasn't aware of that."

"I hope you have a good trip in my country."

"Thank you," I said. He pulled up in front of the main building beneath the control tower without another word. On our right was a hangar and a few administrative buildings. Across the road was that shabby theatre outside a barracks, and a small mess hall. He removed my bags from the trunk, deposited them on the asphalt and, with no more formalities, he drove away.

And just like that I was standing under the open sky alone in a foreign country.

I could make out the dialogue from the movie across the road. They were playing "Three Kings" and the soundtrack reached me. George Clooney was saying, "You're scared right? …The way it works is you do the thing you're scared shitless of, and you get the courage after you do it, not before you do it…" And the other guy says… "That's a dumbass way to work, should be the other way around…"

And I laughed again.

Standing there alone. I felt happy and content. The evening breeze was cool and the sky was full of stars. The adventure was beginning and it felt right.

If you're moving in the right direction, keep going.

I grabbed my things and walked to the nearest building to see what I could find. The clerks were expecting me. They had a room ready in the barracks and a meal card. My flight into Kandahar was eighteen hours away.

I found my room, dropped my bags on the creaky cot, and wandered over to the lawn chairs. I passed a few arcade games and a pool table under a gazebo near a barbecue. It looked like a nice place to spend some time.

Then that thing the universe and the Army does sometimes, happened again. You can't be alone in the Army for too long. There's always a familiar face around the corner…

"Rolly?" I said.

He stopped. "Jack? What the—JACK! When'd you get here?" He stood from his lawn chair and came over for a hug. I obliged.

There's nothing like that back slap. No words I can use to describe how that feels. Nothing I can say, unless you've met an old high school buddy, across the world, in a hostile foreign land, after being accosted by customs officials and strangers at a guard post, wondering if you'd make it—you can't know how that felt.

"I literally just got here," I said.

"I haven't seen you in, what, ten years? How have you been, man?"

Rolly was an old friend. We joined the Army Reserves together in Ottawa many years before, when we were still young and dumb. We did our recruit training together and shared the same maple leaf tattoo. He had gone off and got married and joined the Air Force around the same time I went to med school. We'd lost touch. And in that moment, I couldn't imagine why. "Good, man. It's so nice to see you. Have you been here long?"

"Almost two months this time. This has been my second home for about five years. We're in and out. Three-month roto's, maintaining the planes. What are you up to? I heard you got into med school?"

"Yeah, man. That's why I'm here. Fully trained Army doc for about three years now. Just like the plan."

"Get the F out of here. Dude, that's amazing. Good for you. You always said you were going to do that. I'm not sure we ever believed it... Ha... I'm glad it worked out for ya. That's great, man.... Is this your first time over here?"

"Yes. First time."

"You're a good man. It's getting hairy in there. The air field isn't very secure. They can't seem to kick out the insurgents from the surrounding hills. We keep patching bullet holes in our planes."

"Well, that's reassuring. Thanks for that. My flight's tomorrow."

"Well as long as you stay out of Panjwai, you'll be fine. I assume you'll be at the role three hospital in Kandahar?"

"Ummm. Nope. I'm heading outside the wire—into, ahhh, Panjwai."

"Oh shit, Buddy. Sorry about that," he said with a sheepish grin. "The troops have been coming out talking about that place lately. Helmond province was the hotbed earlier, but seems all about Panjwai now. Lots of IEDs and suicide bombers. Guy last week said there's young girls being martyred up. So that's new... Watch your back, man."

"I heard about that. I will try."

"Listen. Let's have a near-beer and talk about the old days. I've seen this movie."

The mess was next door. It was brightly lit with fluorescence and white paint. It was a dry camp but the 'near beer' was cold. "Remember the time at Ross the Boss's cottage when Steve fell down the stairs? That was fucking hilarious." "Or how 'bout Chartswell wiping out on that hill in Petawawa? I think his knee is still fucked up." "Or the time you threw Styles over the balcony into that snowbank." "My heart pumps purple piss," we said in unison.

Those old stories came flooding back. Rolly was off until morning and we stayed late talking about old times. About a time in my life when I knew who I was and what I wanted. Rolly reminded me of that. Six years of med school, and the three years since, with all the pursuing and acquiring shiny objects, slipped away that night. I was glad to live in those memories at a time I needed the soldier in me present, front and centre, for a while.

In the United Arab Emirates, I slept one blissful night in a secret Camp on the Gulf of Yemen with a full belly and a feeling that the universe wanted me there.

In the morning I was shaken awake by the vibration of the building as an aircraft landed less than two hundred yards from my pillow.

Reality check. Here we go. I love you Grace.

Chapter Eleven

Threshold

It was nice to see Rolly at breakfast. He was finishing up as I sat down.

"Are you coming to the ramp ceremony?" he asked.

"What ramp ceremony?"

"Two medics came in this morning, killed by a roadside bomb in Panjwai couple days ago. I thought you knew, sorry."

I needed a moment to process that.

"Their ramp ceremony is in about twenty minutes. We gotta transfer their caskets to the strat air platform."

I hadn't heard of medics dying in theatre.

"Are you sure they were medics?" I whispered, knowing he wouldn't have said it if it wasn't true. The words caught in my throat. I braced myself against the table.

"Oh yeah. Two of them. It destroyed their amb. Brutal. I didn't get all the details but they're here now and heading home tonight."

"Canadians?"

"Yep."

"Wow... Of course, I'll be at the ramp ceremony. Show me where."

Rolly waited while I scarfed down my meal, then we dropped our trays and headed to the flight line. I was dressed in uniform and had transferred my kit into a single army duffle. The rest of my luggage would be staying there in storage.

We approached a group of troops forming up at the end of an aircraft. Soldiers came naturally to attention as the ceremony began. Two coffins emerged and moved down the ramp at slow march. An honour guard lined the red carpet that marked their path to the 'air-port-shuttle-turned-hearse' that would transport them across the tarmac to an awaiting C17 Globemaster.

I stood in a small crowd at a distance, Rolly at my side, his headdress at his chest. It was a brief, solemn ceremony. No speeches. No music. Only the silence of a crowd of introspective soldiers. When the doors closed and the hearse drove off, the conversations began again where they'd left off.

"That was quick," I said.

"We're used to it."

Turns out I was heading into Kandahar on the same plane that brought out two dead medics. Heroes. But the crew needed a few hours to turn it around, so Rolly and I made plans to stay in touch back home and said our goodbyes, and he headed off for work at the hangar.

I spent the day reading in my room, trying not to contemplate the reality of my situation, and returned to the flight-line an hour before my flight, as directed. There were twenty or so troops waiting in an open hangar. I didn't recognize any of them. There were no customs to clear, but we waited in lineups for weapons issue. As an officer, I received both a C7 Rifle and a Browning 9mm.

It felt like I was back in the Army reserves preparing for a weekend exercise: Load magazines, place in the web gear pockets, sling weapons, strap on leg holster. Hurry up and wait. We sat on our kit in that hanger for two hours. When the C130 Hercules finally taxied around and stopped out front it arrived with a sense of relief and trepidation.

The ramp came down towards us and crew started loading pallets with a forklift. Once secured, they waved us over and divided us randomly into two files. I went to the right. As we shuffled up the ramp, pushing our way toward the front, I had a feeling we were cattle heading to the slaughter.

I couldn't shake that feeling. It lingered long after we were in the air.

We were arrayed on nylon mesh benches facing the pallets in the centre. Our kit was at our feet, or underneath. The benches were comfortable enough. I reclined, relaxing. The guy next to me sat on his helmet and gestured for me to do the same. Looking around I saw others doing it, so I placed my helmet beneath my butt, on my duffle.

If there were bullets, they'd come from below, so we sat on helmets.

I cared for a guy later who had been shot through the wall of a plane. He barely touched ground in Afghanistan and was heading home.

It must have been pretty harrowing for the aircrew. They were all very serious. The last hour or so was 'contour flying' into Kandahar. Weaving through mountains, using evasive maneuvers, or avoiding turbulence. It felt overdone, but they knew what they were doing. Rolly had said they needed to avoid small arms fire, but that didn't make it easy. It wasn't particularly fun back there. If you've been on the Zipper at the Toronto Exhibition you know the feeling: hard turns, ups and downs, tough on the stomach. And the noise in the back of one of those planes is impressive. The engine hum eats up all the sound. My foam ear defenders did basically nothing. You could feel the hum in your bones. At one point I tried to speak to the guy beside me and nothing seemed to come out of my mouth. I could barely hear my own voice inside my head. You could yell at the top of your lungs and not make a sound over that hum.

I was luggage. There were no ceramic salt and pepper shakers, no friendly stewardesses, and no drink carts. So, I pulled out my iPhone and played a few levels of a mindless game then deleted the app.

Later, ignoring my queasiness, I remembered Grace had downloaded books on my phone. Yes, my 'book app' was full. I smiled. She was still looking out for me. She knew what I needed before I knew I needed it. I had a couple of paperbacks in my duffle but she had downloaded ten onto my iPhone. Always one step ahead. I smiled at that, and clicked open "The Collected Works of Sir Arthur Conan Doyle'.

I settled in. The first story: A Study in Scarlet.

The opening scene: 1881, Doctor Watson, a physician, having recently returned to London from the war in Afghanistan... recovering from a bullet wound to his leg...

Nope.

That hit a little too close to home.

I switched it off and looked around. As my eyes adjusted, I could see through a slit of a window near the back ramp. The horizon was rising and falling, and a sliver of light was flashing in and out, up and down.

I wondered what Grace was doing right then.

She would say, "Live in the moment. Focus on the task at hand. Do good work." She was probably waking for the day. Standing and stretching. Her t-shirt lifting, revealing skin at her waist above her plaid cotton pants. I'd have to find a way to call her soon.

She'd get a kick out of Rolly. "She's going to like Rolly," I thought.

The landing was slick but it came with a jolt and the screech of tires. While the plane taxied, the loadmaster got us up and moving. As the ramp came down, over the heads of those weary soldiers filing out, I caught my first glimpse of Kandahar across the tarmac.

Through the heat waves I could make out a few buildings, concrete stanchions, and some green canvas tents. A military airfield like nothing I'd ever seen before. Crowded sea containers stacked, shading an outdoor gym.

A basketball court behind a red brick building with soldiers in shirts and skins running, their rifles leaning on an adjacent wall. Beyond the hangars and airfield buildings, the hints of a city. Beyond that, in the distance, jagged, sand-covered hills and a bright blue sky in every direction, all the way to the horizon.

We were ushered into line at the fence. Stepping away from the aircraft with my ears buzzing, the first thing I noticed was the smell.

"What is that?" I said to the soldier in line in front of me.

"First time here, sir?"

"Yes."

"That's the poo pond."

"I'm sorry?"

"There's a lake of sewage on the edge of town we affectionately call the 'poo pond'. You're smelling the festering waste of 30,000 people," he said with a grin.

"That is grim," I scrunched my nose reflexively.

"It's not so bad from here. You should smell it up close."

"We're not in Kansas anymore," I said, while thinking, I'm not in Kingston anymore.

But despite my disgust, I had a good feeling. That soldier's laughter, the hot sun, moving my feet; this was the beginning of another grand adventure.

The smell marked an indisputable change though. The heat was stifling. I would need time to acclimatize, but it felt right.

I pulled out my passport and followed the line through 'customs'—if you can call it that.

We placed our rifles, pistols, and ammo on a conveyor belt and watched them go through scanners. *Scanning for what?* We stepped through a rusted arch of metal that appeared devoid of power, and picked up our weapons on the other side.

The irony of that exercise seemed lost on everyone. I strapped my holster back on my belt and around my leg and looked around for someone else to get the joke. But no one seemed to recognize a shred of the hilarity.

Everyone was so serious. For a second I thought I might be the crazy one. I was suppressing a giggle when I heard another familiar voice behind me.

"Jack Henry. Welcome to Kandahar airfield, our wretched hive of scum and villainy."

———

"Obi Wan?" I said, turning around. Recognizing the line from *Star Wars*. My suppressed smile took over my face, and I turned to find, smiling back, another old friend who came in for a hug.

"Good to see you, Jack."

"Ian. I heard you might be here. I was hoping we might cross paths."

I met Ian in med school at one of those provincial gatherings for Army students. He was hilarious and smart and we had become fast friends. The Army was good like that. Lots of familiar faces when you need them.

"How was the flight?" he asked.

"A little rough. But we made it. I didn't puke!" I gestured back at the rusted metal detector and people walking through with weapons. "What is with this?" I said.

"Yep," he nodded, "Welcome to the third world."

He picked up my duffle and slung it over his shoulder. "They told me you'd be on the previous flight. What happened? It's not like you to make me wait."

"I took the scenic route."

"Thought you might have turned around and gone home."

"I thought about it."

"Well, I'll be your cruise director for this boarding phase," He smiled and handed me a bottle of water and took a sip of his own. "First thing, you gotta check out the old role three. It's being decommissioned as we speak. You won't want to miss it. Then I'll show you the barracks."

"Sounds great." We stepped onto the street. There were no sidewalks or traffic lights, but you could call it a road because that's where the vehicles were converging at odd angles. Mostly military pattern, a few civilian pickups and motorcycles, but it was not jammed with traffic. This was the airfield after all. Not the main city. Kandahar itself was a few kilometers to the north. Ian had a truck and driver waiting, but he sent them away. We could walk.

We ducked through a crowd and around the side of a building where I caught my first glimpse of the new role three up close. The red brick building I'd seen from the plane; large and square and brand new. It seemed out of place against mud and concrete, clean and red. Not enough windows. We walked past the entrance and across the lot toward a collection of tents.

"This is the original role three," Ian said.

"Now that's what I'm talking about!" I said. Ahead was a haphazard collection of canvas with wooden doors reminiscent of M*A*S*H*. My sense of arrival was palpable. All my childhood dreams manifesting. I couldn't wait to get inside.

"You like that?"

"Of course. That's the field hospital, right?" I said.

"Yes, sir. It is—or rather, it was." He gestured to the brick monstrosity behind us. "That's the new one. We work there now, but this place was glorious."

"How long have you been here?"

"About two months. Since the tour started. Don't worry, you get used to the smell."

"You're role three then?" I asked.

"Yep. We occasionally pop over to the role one clinic, to see how the other half lives though. It's up the road, over there." He pointed to a white building at the end of an alley in the distance; the only other two-storey building in the vicinity. "They are looking forward to having you... I hear the clinics are getting busy."

"That sounds like work," I said, looking around. I was not feeling like seeing patients right then.

We were approaching the double plywood doors when an air raid siren sounded: loud and rolling. I looked at Ian as he shrugged and looked around. Then he walked calmly over to a concrete structure with three sides and a roof, a little wider than a sea container, and stepped inside.

I followed. "What's happening?"

"Oh you're gonna love it here, man. Trip of a lifetime." He nudged me with his arm from the side. "Rocket attack," he said looking up through the opening. "They happen."

He was a little nonchalant for my liking, "What? We're being attacked?"

"Yeah. Just wait here, under cover for a few minutes. They'll sound the all clear shortly… Insurgents in the hills lob artillery or mortars into the city pretty much all the time."

I peered out the opening and looked to the sky, "How do they know they're coming?"

"Radar. They warn the city with these alarms and we hunker down for a minute. Sometimes I wonder if it's concrete suppliers lobbing those bombs."

"What?"

"Well, I've never seen them hit anything meaningful. And whoever sells concrete around here is making a mint."

"Ha. Right," I couldn't help smiling again.

The hot sun and smells were becoming familiar already, and I hardly noticed my weapons. "So, you're basically Hawkeye Pierce," I said.

"Basically, yeah!"

"Is there a clerk around here with super human hearing?"

"Ha. No. I wish. No Radar O'Reilly. But we do have air raid sirens."

The all clear sounded and he pointed up with a grin. We picked up walking where we left off. On the way we passed a Blackhawk helicopter on the edge of the airfield.

"As you remember from your training," he began as though we weren't just cowering in a bunker, "...the role three is our tertiary care centre on the battlefield." I let him carry on with his mock lecture, to see where he'd take it. The springs on the door creaked as we stepped into a double-wide tent. It was arrayed with decommissioned trauma bays. Wires dangled from tent poles, empty med carts and wheeled stretchers were strewn about, looking tired.

"This is where the magic happens, or rather, happened," he said, grinning.

The *M*A*S*H** vibe was overwhelming. I'd been on the ground in a war zone for less than half an hour and already standing on a *M*A*S*H** set.

Like the alchemist following his legend, it was almost too perfect.

"You must have seen some real trauma here."

"Tons. Place looked awesome before they stripped it. Blood products at every bedside. Teams circling like well-oiled machines. The past few roto's really pushed the edge of trauma here. This is where our massive transfusion protocols were developed, and honed."

He seemed as much in awe of the place as I was. He moving around the place like a dancer. "The medics and nurses are so good too, Jack. I barely have to think an order before it happens. Battlefield medicine. They hit these doors, they live. Period."

"That's awesome, Ian." I was getting *the* tour.

A couple of troops packing boxes in the next room recognized Ian and stood to attention. He set them at ease as they chatted and I saw the serious officer he had become. His voice deepening almost imperceptibly. More stern and commanding than with me. It worked for him. You could tell he was a good boss, and a great physician. They clearly respected him.

It was calm and quiet down the hall.

"I heard you're heading outside the wire," he said.

"I think so. Brad said something about FOBs and Panjwai. But I have no idea."

"Oh man, you're going to be deep in the shit." He stopped for a moment and looked at me. I said nothing and looked around.

"Have you been out?"

"No way, man. I mean... the role three needs me at the role three. You know."

"Right," I said, frowning and nodding.

"No. I do envy you though… going to the pointy end. Right there, putting them on choppers, sending them here. They land right over there," he said, gesturing in the direction of the helipad. "I hear it's pretty intense out there. Limited resources. No surgeons. Man!"

"I'll let you know," I said, not knowing what to make of all that.

We stopped as we passed 'Radiology'. "What's imaging like? How's the scanner?" I asked, pushing the door and peaking inside.

"Top of the line four-slice CT," he said, laughing.

A CT scanner draped in a tarp sat in the room, wires hanging out the middle.

"That thing gives decent pictures, but there's a brand new 128-slice in the new hospital... Not sure what the plan is for this one."

Down from radiology another sign read "Kandahar Institute of Surgical Sciences" in pointed letters. We snapped a selfie under that and went through into the Operating Room.

"You should have seen the surgery in this room, Jack." He opened his arms wide and spun. "This OR did not stop. Feels eerily quiet right now... damage control surgery... therapeutic amputations... craniotomies... you name it!"

"Intense." I said, "did you scrub-in a lot?"

"Sometimes, yeah. Mostly trauma team lead. But sometimes."

I was beginning to contemplate sending patients from the front for 'damage control surgery' and 'amputations', but stopped myself.

"I heard the success rate is impressive," I added. "Something like ninety-eight percent survival?" I had read that somewhere.

"That sounds about right," he said looking thoughtful.

Then he turned and stopped and said, "The truth is, Jack. It's the role one who saves those lives. We get all the credit, but it's the medics out there, at the front, who deserve it. These troops survive if your guys get them here. If a soldier makes it off the battlefield that's nine-tenths of the way home."

He seemed quite solemn and serious about that.

"Nine-tenths, eh?" I said, "Only nine-tenths? ...I thought the success rate was ninety-eight percent?" I was trying to lighten the mood. Ian had a tendency to brood sometimes. "So you're saying, all this extra equipment and CT Scanners and crap is for eight points?"

"Ha. Yeah. I guess."

"I'm looking forward to it."

"I hear it's pretty cushy... They say there's ice cream."

"Seriously? Is that a joke?"

"No. I mean it. They've got freezers packed with single serve cups... All you can eat."

I could not tell if he was joking.

———

When we finally stepped out from under canvas into the bright light of a Kandahar street I had only two things on my mind: Paul Newman and a ride home.

No. Not true.

I was thinking about Grace again, and about my place in the universe.

I breathed the stench and puffed my chest.

Hawkeye would do the same.

My cog fit here.

I was grateful for the tour.

"Thanks for showing me around, Ian."

"No problem. I knew you'd like that."

We walked across the street dodging a US MRAP – mine resistant ambush protected – light military vehicle, all that armour made the driver basically blind. We walked between some concrete stanchions. People in various uniforms passed. We opened our waters and sipped as I followed Ian, taking it all in: mostly grey and sand and uniforms.

"The trauma is always brutal, Jack," he started, slowing his pace as he said it, his feet kicking dust and stones. I could sense more brooding coming, "You'll never see anything like it back home... We have a guy in ICU right now who lost both his arms and legs... All four... In an IED blast... it's unbelievable he survived. We've kept him in a coma for days... We usually don't wake them, and send them off to Germany right away, but he's being delayed, and needs to be woken up tomorrow."

"That's hard... Are you… going to be there?"

"Yeah. I suspect it will be hard… But the point is, the tactical combat casualty care is unbelievable. His buddies threw on tourniquets, stopped his massive hemorrhage immediately. Saved his life."

"Sounds like he's lucky his friends were there. Lucky the Army taught them what to do... Sounds like he'll make it home to his family."

"But he's got no arms and no legs, Jack. I have to tell him that when he wakes up. I don't even know how to process it. Can you imagine? …Sometimes I wonder. The pain and suffering… war is hell, man… that's a long road home for him, you know."

I took a swig of water, "Dude, I just got here. Enough of this heavy shit. Aren't you supposed to be the event coordinator for my cruise line? Take me to the barracks or lose me forever."

"Sure, Jack," he said with a smirk, "It just wears on you."

"And if it didn't, you wouldn't be human. It's okay, Ian."

He smiled and I nudged his shoulder and kept walking. We passed a high wall of concrete, a motorcycle buzzed by kicking up dust.

"Hey, what's the guy's name?" I asked with a big shit-eating grin. He was smart and witty and caught exactly where I was going with that.

"No. Don't…" he said, but his suppressed laugh was obvious.

"What?"

"Just don't. It's too soon."

He shook his head, but smiled, crookedly. His glasses slipped down his nose and he pushed them up. I waited until mid-sip before continuing.

"Your friend 'BOB' probably won't be a strong swimmer." His classic spit take was perfect. Exactly what I was hoping for.

"Jack!" he said, trying hard to compose himself. "You can't do that. That's all wrong on so many levels."

"I'm sorry."

We continued for a moment in silence. Then, as I was taking a sip, "They found him in a ditch..." I could see what was coming and swallowed hard,

"—PHIL. We've been calling him Phil."

"No, you didn't," I laughed, "Really? Clearly. You had no choice. But I wonder if there were leaves in the ditch..."

"RUSTLE," we said in unison. We laughed the rest of the way to the barracks.

"If my officer commanding heard me joke like that... or that poor kid... my God... I can't believe... It's mortifying Jack. I don't know what it is about you..."

"I don't know either Ian." All I knew was that I liked Ian and preferred him laughing. Even if it was harsh and inappropriate, he seemed to need it. We both would have been mortified if anyone had heard us. God forbid someone related to that poor man, but we needed a laugh. Ian needed a laugh. And sometimes medicine survives on dark humour. It seemed tenfold in a war zone. I found that out quickly.

———

Our barracks reminded me of the back of an eighteen-wheeler, without the wheels. Three or four lined up end-to-end, welded together with doors and air conditioning vents cut in the side. The space between the rows was covered in plywood. Little makeshift plywood hallways. Each block divided into tiny spaces big enough for two bunkbeds, one taking up the end wall, another on the side. Across the road was a two-storey structure with a Canadian Flag and 'Canada House' painted above the entrance.

"Good luck with PHIL tomorrow," I said, "Hope it goes well."

"Thanks. His wife and parents have flown to Germany to wait for him. I hope that wasn't the wrong call. Hope he's okay, and gets to see them soon."

He dropped my duffle by the door and handed me an envelope. Inside was the room key, a clearance card, a meal card, and a note from Brad:

Jack, Welcome to the show. Ian will guide you through in-clearance. Meet me at the role one at 0700hrs tomorrow morning, Brad.

I opened the door to my new room. Cool air washed over us. The air conditioning was cranked. We stepped inside the refreshing cold.

"Looks like I'm clearing in today? And off for the evening. What do you do for fun around here?"

"You hungry?"

"I could eat."

"Perfect. We'll start at the mess, then clear you in this aft. Then tonight I'll take you on an old-fashioned evening stroll."

"Evening stroll, eh? Sounds good to me."

"Kandahar airfield is a great place for an evening stroll when the mortars aren't falling. This area of the world is a crossroads full of history if you know where to look." Ian was a history buff.

The other bunk in my small room was claimed by a Warrant Officer Baker who was not there. His name was on a barrack box and above mine on the door. I dropped my kit on the free bunk.

I was looking forward to spending some leisure time with Ian. But we had logistics to get through first. And I was beginning to feel anxious to hear Grace's voice.

"I'd like to call home if I can," I said.

"That might have to wait. There are some sat phones at the role one, but not many, and they are constantly in use. But they're worth waiting for. A little piece of home goes a long way." He sat down on the bunk by the door and took a deep breath that sounded like a sigh, "It's good having you here, Jack. I missed laughing."

"You gotta laugh," I said, not completely appreciating how difficult it could become.

———

We slung our rifles and stepped outside.

"Let's get'r done," I said, "lead the way."

"Do you know about Kandahar, Jack?"

"Just what I got from trip advisor, and the glossy pamphlets at the travel agency," I joked.

"Right. Well, let me regale you."

We came out of the barrack block at an intersection. A few army green planes were parked along a fence-line in the distance. The people passing kept their distance. No smiling. No waving. "Control of this region gave access to the entire ancient world," he began. "You are standing on roads that run West to Iran, South and East to Pakistan and India, and North through Kabul to Asia. Empires have clashed here for centuries," he said.

"Really? I said. It looks like a makeshift airfield to me."

"Well, I take it on good authority that Alexander the Great died right here on this very spot." He pointed to a boulder at the corner of the intersection.

"Are you serious?"

"Serious as a heart attack."

"Right there? How do they know that?" I said staring at the non-descript boulder, searching for a plaque or something distinguishing.

"Well. Not, right there, dummy. But it sounds better that way."

"What? ...Did he die here or not?"

"He did... In Afghanistan... Somewhere. Yes."

"Right."

The thought of Alexander the Great dying right there, or anywhere nearby, was not particularly reassuring, "Wasn't he the greatest conqueror in history? Didn't he conquer the entire world at one point?"

"Yes. The known world. At the time. He did."

"And then he died—here."

"Yes. Fighting a war of conquest—"

"Great. So, we're fighting the same war the greatest conqueror in the history of mankind died fighting. Is that what you're telling me?"

"Pretty much. Yes—It's best not to overthink it."

We laughed and kept moving, chatting more about home and family. Ian knew his history. And despite the smell, that turned out to be a pleasant afternoon. I was looking forward to more, out of the hot sun, that evening.

————

The mess-hall reminded me of a high school cafeteria, with more pressboard, canvas and guns. All the doors were spring-loaded plywood that slapped shut behind you. My meal card functioned, which was good. I slopped on some breaded mystery meat with brown sauce and a scoop of rice. Unfortunately, I didn't see the excellent salad bar until my plate was full.

We gravitated to the Canadian corner where Ian introduced me to a slew of nurses, medics, and administrators. I recognized a few. The only other doctor was Dylan Chamberlain. He was at the end of the first table and caught my eye.

"Jack, I didn't know you'd be coming," he said.

"Well, if I knew you'd be here, I would have passed," I said. And noticed a few knowing smirks of others at the table. Dylan was a morose, frumpy little man, almost always ill-informed, but possessed of an impressively logical brain. In short, he was a dick. He rubbed virtually everyone the wrong way at some point or another. He'd been my instructor on a career course a few years back, and not a particularly good one.

"Congratulations on making it to the show," he said.

"Thanks, Dylan," I nodded, and moved on as quickly as I could. Having the same rank, and not having to call him 'sir' or 'staff' was satisfying though.

We made our way to a distant table and found space to sit. Ian sat across, and to my right. Next to me was a kindly Afghan with a shaggy, endearing beard and bright eyes. He was wearing Canadian fatigues.

I bumped into him as I sat and apologized, "Sorry about that."

"No worries, sir," he said smiling brightly.

"Our translators don't usually eat here with us, they have their own Deefacs (dining facilities) on the other side, but we make an exception for Lucky… Lucky is the best translator in the Coalition." Ian said by way of introduction.

"Is that so?"

"Well, I humbly try to do my best, every day." His voice was clear, soothing and confident.

"This is Doctor Henry," said Ian.

"Nice to meet you Doctor, my name is Achmed Yazdani, but people call me, Lucky." He smiled with his entire face as we shook hands. I liked him right away.

"Nice to meet you, Lucky. Please, call me Jack."

We had interrupted a conversation he was having when we sat, so he diplomatically extricated himself and turned back. I heard them speaking about President Karzai and some Mullah in Panjwai, but nothing specific.

Ian and I made a plan for the afternoon. He had a map. We plotted a route to touch all points and finish back at the mess for dinner. We finished our meals, dropped the dishes in the bins, and headed out.

"Stores, I.T. Security, and then the finance office."

"I was told 'danger pay' doesn't start to accrue on the system until we clear in," I said. "Maybe we should go to finance first."

"Suck it up, buttercup. You've waited this long."

We had some laughs. Everything that day told me this was right for me. It felt purposeful and real. The extra funds would go a long way back home. My heart was full, but I was done with the heat by the time my card was stamped.

We passed the role one on our way back, "Brad, has an office on the second floor," Ian said. "I suppose you'll be working in the clinic until you head outside the wire."

I cupped my hand on the window and peered inside. It was a standard clinic occupying the entire main floor. It was hopping with patients and nurses and medics moving in and out of curtains. Reminded me of a busy emergency ward in small town Ontario. But it looked like work in there, and I didn't feel like going to work just yet.

"Let's *not* go in, Ian. I'll be back first thing tomorrow." There was also, seemingly, a great deal of activity on the second floor, and I sensed not being seen yet was better.

"I'm good with that," he said, and we headed back to the mess.

For dinner I had a salad and afterward went back to the barracks for a shower, in preparation for our evening stroll. I was clean, settled, and had a full belly when we met outside the barracks.

We bumped into Lucky and he joined us.

In the late summer, in Kandahar, when the sun goes down, the heat floats away and it becomes a little more bearable. The conversation was light. Lucky talked history with Ian, and I mostly listened. They spoke of empires clashing as we toured the sites within walking distance. Most of the buildings recently erected by the Coalition, but we found a few old factories and a mausoleum.

When I rested my head on my bunk that first night in Kandahar, sleep came easily. I had a much deeper appreciation for the place, and understood better where I fit in the Coalition. My mattress and pillow were clean and comfortable.

That night I dreamed of a battle with Persian soldiers, Turks and Mongols, fighting under Khan's, storming that intersection with bows, and charging horses, swords drawn, scimitars flashing. The souls of the fallen, swirling in the dust, trapped in the billowing eddies, confined to spiritual prison for all eternity as temporal punishment for the sins of their commanders.

I awoke in the night in a cold sweat, shivering and turned the air conditioning down. I sat on the edge of my bunk and pulled out my journal and wrote a note to Grace.

At first about my trip through Dubai, and meeting Rolly, and my day with Ian and Lucky, and the tour of the role three, and then, at the end, I wrote this:

Kandahar is not like London or Jerusalem or Rome, my love. Those places show their age in architecture and antiquities. Kandahar air field feels more ancient than any of them. The oldest mud structures make the architecture of European cities seem brand new. But my barracks, and most of the buildings around here, are new.

Remember Paris? The Louvre and the cathedrals? There's no beautiful architecture like that here. But between the concrete stanchions and new plywood, there's a feeling of ancientness that wraps around you, and sits heavy in your bones.

My room is cold tonight, my love. The air conditioning was on too high today. Air conditioning and trucks and soldiers seem out of place here. Like they're not wanted. It feels like Kandahar is biding her time, tolerating, but wanting to be left alone...

But I feel my purpose is here, my love. It's going to be okay... What Kandahar wants doesn't matter... The universe needs me here right now... I don't know how I know that. But I feel it.

I miss you, and love you, and hope you're not too upset I did this. I will try to find a phone tomorrow. Can't wait to hear your voice.

Love, Jack

Chapter Twelve

The Role One

I met Brad, on time, the next morning. He was standing in the hall outside his office on the second floor, "Good to see you, Jack." He was brief. "We will get you out to the FOB soon enough. For now, go see patients in the clinic and we'll touch base about next steps in a couple of days."

That's all I got. He was a busy man. In charge. In his element. He exuded the military acumen and confidence of command. Even the soldiers around him seemed more competent when he was there.

I caught a glimpse of the activity through the door. A map on the wall with pins and strings, comms equipment chirping, a table full of notes and op orders in piles. I left him to it and walked down the stairs to the clinic.

For a clinic at an airfield in a war zone, it was surprisingly familiar. It reminded me of the base hospital in Kingston; similar reception, same white walls, same charts and curtains between gurneys, and the patients were Canadian soldiers, except these ones had a baseline healthiness that justified deployment to a war zone.

Having nothing else to do, awaiting my logistical stars to align, I draped my stethoscope over my shoulders and went to work. I worked there for about a week seeing minor injuries, bumps and bruises, and a few mental health concerns. Nothing that might get one sent home. I was where and when the system needed me to be. A cog in the wheel, spinning. A doctor, with necessary skills, seeing patients.

One of my first patients in Kandahar was a young lady complaining of toe pain. A Master Corporal, clerk-type, with an ingrown toenail.

Ingrown toenails, also known as onychocryptosis, happens a lot in the Army. That doesn't change in a war zone. Even working a desk job it's hard to concentrate with toe pain like that. It's distracting and debilitating. Army docs are proficient at cutting those out. It had been a while since I'd done one, but that wasn't about to stop me.

Toenail resection requires a small rubber tourniquet around the base of the toe, a needle and syringe for the digital nerve block, sharp scissors to cut the nail, and forceps to yank it out. Once you cut and pull the offending nail, you dab phenol on the matrix to ablate the bed. Simple.

At home I always used phenol. It stops the nail from growing back. But I looked around the clinic, and asked, and couldn't find any phenol. Maybe they didn't have any. Maybe I couldn't find the person who knew the person who knew where to look. Or, maybe I was just wearing my man goggles, as Grace would say, but I couldn't find any phenol.

Then I had a thought. A super confident, you're the man kind of thought. There at the bedside, like a beacon, was a tube of silver nitrate sticks. I was certain I had definitely read somewhere that silver nitrate can be used, instead of phenol, to ablate the nail bed. So, I decided, in my infinite wisdom, to use silver nitrate instead.

I didn't stop to look it up. I didn't read about it. I simply went ahead and dabbed it in the wound to ablate the bed—deep in the wound.

That might sound bad, if you wonder if that is something that might cause harm, but silver nitrate is used on wounds of all stripes all the time. It helps with clotting. I may have been using it for something else entirely, but I was sure it was fine. It wasn't going to hurt. I may have been over-confident, but I wasn't a monster.

I couldn't find any phenol, that was all. And I was sure I was correct.

Turns out I wasn't.

Silver nitrate tattoos the upper dermis.

That was my first of many lessons in Kandahar.

That Master Corporal clerk-type came back days later with a toe that looked like it'd been slammed in a door. It was black and blue, and looked ischemic, as if it was about to fall off. And, just my luck, on that return visit, Doctor Dylan Chamberlain picked up her chart.

"What the hell happened here?" I heard him say through the curtain. It sounded bad. Not a lot of equanimity in that. That was part of the reason I hated that guy, his tendency to jump to conclusions and say negative shit about other physicians. He was always putting people down. He never debased himself with any 'there, but by the grace of God, go I' sentimentality.

"Captain Henry come over here please," he commanded. We stepped into a side room for privacy. At least he showed me that courtesy, "Listen, Jack. You think you're hot shit, but you really eff'd up this time."

Yes. He said, "eff'd up."

Dylan had been there since the tour started, like Ian. He'd been working in that clinic for months and always acted like top dog. The nurses and medics were nice to me, which seemed to irk him. It was clear he wasn't happy with his life, and he wasn't happy with me just then.

I never did figure out why he didn't get sent outside the wire instead of me, but, I digress.

"What did I do?" I asked.

"That lady with the toe from the other day. She's in curtain four and it looks like she might need her toe amputated after what you did." When he said that the blood drained from my face and I felt queasy.

"Is she okay?"

"The nurse is removing her bandage. You should stay away. I will handle it," he said.

I ignored him and walked directly to curtain four. Dylan trailed. "Is everyone decent in there?" I took a deep breath and pulled back the curtain. The nice Master Corporal, clerk-type, was sitting up smiling. "Hey Doc," she said. "How you settling in?"

She looked fine. No wincing as the nurse removed the dressing.

That was a good start. I remained concerned though. The toe looked awful.

"How are you?" I asked. The nurse stepped aside and let me sit. I put on gloves and poked. She remained smiling, "Looks like crap, Doc, but feels alright," she said. "I can wear my boots for the first time in a while. It feels a lot better."

I took a closer look. An edge of black skin by the cuticle was peeling up. I picked at a corner, watching her face for signs of discomfort. None. I pulled more.

The skin rolled back and underneath was a shiny new pink layer. Healthy as a baby's bottom. The silver laced skin peeled away like schoolhouse glue.

I felt like Neo dodging bullets in *The Matrix*.

Some black skin remained, but it would fall off eventually. I looked over my shoulder at Dylan, who looked bemused.

"Listen. This looks okay to me," I said. "You should probably pop back in next week for a recheck. Dr. Chamberlain here will help you if I'm not around... I probably won't be here... I'm heading outside the wire."

"Well, thanks for fixing my foot. And, stay safe out there."

I smiled at her and stepped outside and leaned into Dylan, "Not dead. She's fine." I restrained myself from tacking on a "yeah dummy" at the end of that, but not before he saw that thought linger on my face.

"One of these days Jack your cowboy shit is going to get you," he said. "And I can't wait to see it."

"Not today, bud, not today," I said as he stormed off.

I watched the Master Corporal slip her boots on and walk away feeling joyful. She looked comfortable and had no hint of antalgia in her gait.

"Don't mind Dr. Chamberlain," said the nurse, removing her gloves and throwing them in the bin, "He's a bit of a windbag, but means well."

"Thanks," I said, and grabbed another chart.

"That's medicine. You gotta remember your mistakes and near misses," Ian said. We were sitting behind the barracks around what would have been a fire pit back home, but for the heat. Instead, it was a table with empty bottles of near-beer, which, again, tasted great. "Sometimes you gotta use what you've got to get the job done," he added.

"I thought silver nitrate was okay."

"It's fine," he said. "That's how I was trained. Apparently, phenol is the carcinogen. Silver nitrate is probably better."

"Well, there you go," I said, clinking his bottle.

"Sometimes you gotta do the thing you think is right even if it might be wrong because sometimes there's no one else around to ask or do things better."

"Damn straight. I'll drink to that," I said and took a sip.

"That's why I love being a doc," he said. "You use your wits and hope what you've learned and seen and done has taught you enough to give it a go. Sometimes it's what you decide in a moment that makes the difference between life or death."

"That's a little dramatic, but I'll drink to that too." I sipped again. "Sometimes doing nothing is best though," I added.

"Either way, it's a choice. And you need confidence to make that choice. Especially where you're heading, my friend."

"You're right. I don't need Dylan chipping away at my nerves right now." I was on my way outside the wire.

"Don't worry about him. He's insecure. Has to put everyone down. You'll be fine on your own. Completely alone. Out there. In the desert. Alone."

"Thanks, man."

"Don't worry. You're ready. You're one of the best docs I know. Trust yourself. Do the best medicine you can, and you'll be fine."

"I appreciate that. Thanks, man."

Ian knew I needed confidence: to trust my abilities without reservation. There were tough choices in my future, and second-guessing all the time would not make it easy.

"It's impossible to know everything and practice without mistakes," I said.

"Medicine is a science of uncertainty and an art of probability. If you can't trust your gut, you're done," he said.

I agreed. The toe was a near-miss but it was fine. Before bed, I reviewed the uses of silver nitrate and applications around toes and Ian was right. Doing something was better than doing nothing. My confidence almost took a blow, but it bloomed. My gut had not let me down.

I fell asleep believing everything I'd learned on the way to Afghanistan had prepared me for Afghanistan. I was on the right path. All the hoops I'd jumped through, the tests, patients, lectures, and scrutiny, it *had* been enough. I was trained to make good choices. The close calls and near-misses were par for the course.

My choices were sound.

I was ready.

Chapter Thirteen

Heart Attacks and Gunshots

First thing the next morning, a guy came into the clinic clutching his chest. He was in PT gear and sweating down the front of his grey t-shirt.

"Doc, I think I'm having a coronary," he said.

I dropped my chart and juked around the counter guiding him into the bed by the crash cart. "Over here, sir," I said as I watched Dylan juke the other way.

A couple of medics popped over to help.

Chest pain was in my wheelhouse. I was good at that. And I needed a win.

You don't mess around with chest pain. There are at least seven deadly causes. Not the least of which is heart attack. I started with a standard work up. History, Physical exam, basic bloods, and an EKG. Out there we used the old school troponin lab test. That was good, because I was more familiar with those. That's what we still used in the peripheral hospitals back home. The big centres had started using some new high-sensitivity test that I hadn't read up on yet. Again, the stars aligned.

With chest pain, it's all in the heart tracing. The EKG. That's where the money is. This guy's tracing had a funny blip, something I'd never seen before. It didn't look like the standard elevation or depression you worry about in heart attacks. But one segment was weird. It had an odd lump with a notch which made me think of another thing I'd heard some emerg docs talking about on a podcast. Something called a tombstone sign. I looked that up but couldn't find any images that fit. All I knew was his tracing looked a little tombstoney to me, and that wasn't normal. That segment was supposed to be flat, and the funny notch at the end didn't look right either.

I couldn't make heads nor tails of it, which was frightening. I woke up that morning believing I'd been well trained and prepared. I was certain my EKG knowledge was encyclopedic. Dubin's 'Rapid Interpretation of EKGs' was practically tattooed on my eyelids. I knew it. Cold. Inside and out. Cover to cover. I'd regurgitated it on multiple competency exams, and used that knowledge in real life emergencies, countless times, alone in peripheral hospital emergency rooms.

I was supposed to know those things.

But this one stumped me. Which was scary.

And after the near miss with the toe, I didn't need another hit to the ego.

The patient was an old corporal, in his late forties. I mistook him for a senior officer at first, because of his age and the fact he was in PT gear, not wearing a uniform.

Which doesn't matter. Doesn't change the doctor-patient relationship. But it did make me take interest in his story.

He'd joined the Army to go to war. Many were doing that in the aftermath of the Twin Towers. Many were wolves wanting to kill bad guys; some wanted to fix things, to be the change, to outsource Canadian values and all that, but all of them had a patriotic sense of duty that was laudable. He was no exception.

Unfortunately for him, when you're older, bad stuff is more likely to happen to your heart. All the heuristics were telling me to worry. His pain fit. His age fit. He was clearly a smoker from the nicotine stains on his fingers and moustache, but his vitals were good and he didn't look too bad. It was his EKG that confused me. And I didn't want to look bad. I was frustratingly at a loss.

So, I swallowed my pride and asked Dylan.

"What do you think of this tracing?" I asked in a quiet moment as he passed.

"All right, grasshopper, watch and learn," he started. Snatching it from my hand. What a nerd. "Rate, Rhythm, Axis, Intervals, P for every QRS, QRS for every P. Looks good... Except. That's an odd-looking ST segment. Only in the precordial leads. That's weird. And the notch?" He stopped. Then started again from the top. "...Rate, Rhythm, Axis..." ...Then he walked over to the desk and grabbed a ruler, scrutinized it further, measuring gaps, and comparing parts.

"Nope," he said finally, "I've never seen anything like that." And he tapped his knuckles over the EKG on the counter and walked away.

I stopped him. "Wait...," I said. "He's a fourty-six year-old smoker with central chest pain. It sounds a little like heartburn but it's central. And he used the word pressure. Does the role three have a cath lab?" I asked. "Do they do angio's? What do we do with cases like this?"

"Haven't had one…," he said. "You're on your own, hotshot."

"Dylan, come on," I pleaded.

"I suppose you do the same as you would back home… Phone a friend. They might be able to do something over there. I don't know," he said and walked away again. This time he grabbed the next chart in the rack and moved on to care for the next case.

The clerk at reception helped get the role three on the line. Happily, I got Ian on the phone and told him the story. "Sure, Jack, send him over. We don't have better tests and we don't have a cath lab but one of the ICU docs is a cardiologist. I'm sure he'd love to take a closer look."

I packaged the patient up and sent him over in the amb. I was worried, but he was stable—ish. Speaking to Ian later that night in the barracks he said the pink lady (a mixture of pepto-bismol and lidocaine and anti-inflammatories) I'd given him to drink had helped. But they were confused by the EKG as well. Even the cardiologist agreed it was funny looking. So they sent him to Germany on a plane. That made me feel better about not knowing.

I bumped into that old corporal much later out at the FOB. He told me he was in Germany for two weeks itching to get back the entire time. He had a million dollar work up with a scope and cardiac stress tests, and it turned out, after all that, it *was* just heartburn.

His EKG was strange at baseline, some genetic anomaly, channelopathy that we didn't know much about, but he was cleared to return to theater. He had a new prescription for antacid and a clean bill of health. They did, however, find some Barrett's esophagus, which is a pre-cancerous lesion near his stomach that needs monitoring every couple of years, so he was grateful for that.

I felt vindicated again. My skills were okay. I could continue to trust my gut. I had to believe if I thought something was odd or unusual it probably was.

Dylan and I had a chat about it later, before I left for the FOB. He actually thanked me for trusting him to look at that EKG, which must have been difficult for him. Turns out, he wasn't all bad. He jumped to conclusions sometimes, but he wasn't all bad.

Unfortunately, the man with the funny EKG died jumping a grape wall in Panjwai later that year. The bullets hit him in the centre of his chest. I watched him take his final breaths, and, while I zipped his body bag, I was thinking, "those bullets probably tore straight through his Barrett's esophagus." But that was later. At this point in this story things were still cruising along fine. I still felt great about helping him out. And being ready to help him out. Even though it took a few weeks, and a trip to Germany, to figure out he was fine, it turned out his heart had funny wiring and that was all. Even our cardiologists didn't know what to make of it. So I'd be fine. I was ready to go.

———

The next day before clinic, Ian suggested we pop over to the boardwalk for a Tim's. Dylan tagged along. It was my first glimpse of the strange and surreal Kandahar boardwalk, famous for its TGI Fridays and KFC. But it was the Tim Horton's Coffee that drew Canadians. The employees wore the same brown uniforms and yellow nametags and we ordered *honey crullers* and *maple dips* under the same counter displays as back home. It was strange having weapons in a Tim's, but the coffee was familiar and tasted great.

Aside from the lack of ocean, the boardwalk was vaguely reminiscent of Atlantic city. A raised platform walkway over soft sand. It made a massive rectangular oval. In the middle at one end there was a depression with a flat stone bottom. In fact, the shape demanded hockey. Some prior roto had set up boards and nets. Of course. You had to. There was a pickup game that morning, and most mornings, from what I was told.

The stalls and booths around the edges were selling trinkets and carpets and other wares. Through a window I glimpsed a rack of phone cards and I missed home sharply.

"Do you guys get to call home a lot?" I asked.

"Well not with one of those," Dylan said, noticing what I was staring at. "We use that rack of sat phones I told you about, upstairs in the headquarters. After hours you can ususually find one charged."

"I have to check them out," I said. But by the time we got back to clinic there was a lineup out the door. I powered through some sore throats, rashes, and sports injuries. I finally got to pop upstairs when we closed up shop.

Brad was at his desk. The place was frenetic. He was keeping an eye on the entire theatre of operations. We seemed to have medics at risk everywhere. But he was in his element. We were lucky to have him. I'm pretty sure he slept there. He waved me over.

"Jack! How've you been? Are you settling in?" he asked.

"Trying to. Yes, sir," I said. "We went to Tim's this morning. Sorry we didn't bring you one."

"No worries," he gestured to the wall behind his desk. "Look at this. This map shows the main road." He traced a black line running south out of Kandahar into Panjwai toward the red desert and Pakistan. "That's route Leopard. These FOBs here, here, and here, have been hit particularly hard lately. End of the week we're sending you here, to Sperwan Ghar. In a month or so we may need you here at Massum Ghar. Currently there are PA's in charge at the aid stations. You'll be the only doc out there. The PA's are being re-deployed so you won't have them either. It will be you and the medics. The transport plan is coming together. We were hoping to get you airborne, but you might need to go by road. You good with that?"

"Of course, boss," I said. "Whatever you need."

"Perfect, I'll let you know when the plan comes together. Touch base after clinic every day. We should know in a couple days." The comms chirped. He was needed and turned back.

The rack of sat phones was against the wall. I asked the clerk, "Can I call home with one of these?"

"You sure can, Doc. I'll show you. Find one that's charged and bring it outside." She grabbed her smokes and lit one on the way out the door. There was a quiet space at the top of the back stairs. She handed me a card, "These are the numbers you gotta press. Wait for a tone. Then press these. Then the area code and number."

"Thanks." It was like a sudoku puzzle but eventually the phone by our bedside in Kingston was ringing. Grace answered on the second ring. In my excitement I'd forgotten the time differential. We were eight and a half hours behind. It was after one in the morning for Grace.

"Hey sweets," I said through the static. "I found a phone."

"Jack! It's you. I was so—I mean, I love you. So nice to hear your voice."

"I miss you too, babe."

"I miss you, too," she repeated. I could hear her sitting up in bed. "How is it?"

"It's good. Everything's good. I'm working at the clinic at KAF. It's like home, but hotter. I'm sorry to wake you. I can call later." I'd have to remember to call in the morning Kandahar time.

"No. No. It's okay, hun. It's good to hear your voice. I'm awake," she said, sleepily. Then she added, "Jack—something—something—baby." Or at least I thought the last word was, baby? She might have said, maybe, or lately?

"I'm sorry?" I said. "I missed that—static."

"It's okay. It was nothing," she said, "How are you? Tell me about your trip."

I was at the top of a set of metal stairs pinned to the back wall, like a New York City fire escape, overlooking an alley and road that stretched toward the barracks. The buildings behind cast shadows on the alley below, but the sun beat hard on the role three, the airfield, and hills beyond. The sky was a crisp and sharp and pale blue.

"Are you sure? It sounded like you said something about a baby?"

"Yes, Jack. I do obstetrics, remember. It's not important. I want to hear about your trip."

"Oh, okay." Then I talked for too long about all I'd seen and done. I was excited to tell her everything I'd written. She asked lots of questions. Then, "I'm keeping a journal. I'm writing every day. I'm not sure how often I'll be able to call."

"It's okay, Jack. Call when you can. Things are good at home. My mom and sister are coming to stay for a while."

"That's wonderful. Give them my love. Can't wait to see you again. But this feels right, Grace. It feels like we're following our *personal legend*."

"Okay, Jack. Please be safe. And say you'll come home to me."

"I will."

"OK, babe."

"I miss you, sweets."

"Call when you can," she said, "Promise me."

An armoured vehicle drove into the alley and it's low-pitched rumble and metallic clanking cut us off. I stepped inside but the noise of the operations centre was distracting and people were listening and watching. "I will. I love you. Grace," I said.

But the line was cut, and she was gone.

———

We shut the clinic early that Wednesday. The role one was playing the role three in a grudge match. Ball hockey at the boardwalk. They asked if I'd play. I was glad to be invited. We raced around sweating for sixty minutes of running time. Three periods. It was a close game. Back and forth. Lots of goals. I don't remember who won. I do remember the rocket that sent us scrambling for cover at the end.

That was the only time I saw a rocket hit anything in KAF. It was a good distance away and didn't seem to destroy anything of importance. Most people were seasoned enough to saunter. Some new people, like me, still rushed. But there was a lot of cover to find, and we did. From the bunker we had a line of sight to where the rocket landed in the distance. There was a gap between the Tim's on the corner of the boardwalk and the next stall. There was a thud when it landed. It shook dust from the top of the bunker but seemed sad and small and ineffectual. Those that saw it, pointed it out. We mostly smirked and shrugged about it. But that was the end of our hockey game. When the all clear sounded we went for showers.

Sleep was easy that night.

———

Some of the engineers stayed in our barracks. I'd seen one at the clinic earlier and splinted his thumb. He recognized me coming in.

"Hey Doc, I didn't know you crashed here?" he said.

"Oh yeah. Home away from home!" I replied. "What do you have there?" He was inspecting and cleaning some equipment on a table out front. It was an impressive looking set of turtle shell armour for Explosive Ordinance Disposal.

"It's a brand new advanced bomb suit," he said. Then launched into a mini-lecture, "Designed to protect from fragmentation, overpressure, impact, heat, and flame," he recited, verbatim, clearly proud of his kit and his knowledge thereof. "Wanna try it on?"

Of course I did.

He had the entire get up. Full plate armour covered in tan fabric with a blast helmet and everything. Before I knew it, I was rocking the entire bomb suit. It was heavy. Restricting. Hard to imagine crawling up to a roadside bomb and trying to diffuse it wearing all that. But it certainly felt like it might save a life. He had me try some push ups and squats and laughed when I fell sideways against the wall. "Better help me out here," I said.

"Hey, you're from Kingston, right?" he said.

"Yeah, man. Posted there outta residency. Why do you ask?"

"My unit's moving to Kingston next year. I've been in and out of there. Have a house hunting trip planned for after my tour. It's a beautiful place. Do you sail?" he asked.

"We love it there but I haven't picked up sailing yet. I mean to. Maybe buy a boat with my tour money," I said.

"Hey, do you know a Lieutenant-Colonel Clark?" he interjected.

I remembered meeting a stranger on the range named Clark. "JTF2?" I asked.

"Yeah. That's him. He was asking about you at the mess the other day."

"Really? What did he want?"

"Not sure. I didn't know you at the time. But some of the guys at my table knew you from Kingston. He seemed to want more info on your character. Like, are you a good guy, and stuff like that. We all figured you might be trying out for special ops?"

"Not that I'm aware of... that's weird." I wasn't sure how to feel about that. I suppose doctors are of interest to people. Our special ops teams need good docs too. I don't know. Maybe he was just making small talk. "If you see him again tell him I work at the role one, for now. But I won't be there long. I'm heading outside the wire this week."

"Will do. Be safe out there."

Chapter Fourteen

The Queen Mary and the GIB

Brad was outside at the bottom of the stairs when I approached through the alley the next morning. He was smoking a cigar and speaking firmly into a sat phone, pacing on the gravel. His sleeves were not rolled and his boots were untied.

"We'll come to you for God's sake," he said. Then held up a finger for me to wait as I passed. "Tell them to leave an armoured LAV in the first bay for us. My guys will be there this morning to work on the amb conversion... Yes... Okay... Yes... We'll have something for you by tomorrow." He looked satisfied when he shut the phone. He pocketed it and turned to me.

"Come upstairs," he said. We climbed to his office. He moved quickly. He sat at his desk and rolled his sleeves. "We need you to run the clinic today. Dylan and the team are on another task."

"Sure thing, boss," I said. "What was that about?"

His face was like steel. His body was stiff. And he moved with more force than necessary as if he would do everything faster if he could but he couldn't, as if mired in something.

"Another convoy was hit this morning." He paused for a second and his breath caught, he looked defeated. "The amb was right there. They're targeting us, Jack," he said. "No medics died this time, but we've got another NS amb. The axle was destroyed. Thank God they're okay. I couldn't handle losing another."

The operations sergeant at the next desk was staring at Brad like a deer in headlights. I caught her staring out of the corner of my eye. It looked like she'd never seen him vulnerable in that way. He steeled his face and said, "That's why we're getting armour, Jack. We'll retrofit them as ambs and replace every one of those soft skin pieces of shit."

"Sounds like a good plan," I said.

The resolve beneath his pain was palpable. I couldn't imagine the stress he was under. He had sent medics to their deaths. He was the one who chose. Who ordered them out on those missions. And he'd nearly lost another crew that morning. He was carrying a weight that would crush a lesser man. I watched him for a moment, uncertain what to say. Knowing anything I said could never be enough.

"Can I help?" I finally asked.

"Yes. Run the clinic. Dylan and the medics are planning the armoured amb conversion. They will tear one apart today, and God willing, have them retrofitted by tomorrow." He started lacing his boots. "My medics need tanks, Jack. No more soft skin wheeled pieces of shit."

I nodded slowly and tightened my lips.

"And you will be going airborne out to the FOB. I'll make sure of that," he said.

"Thanks. I got the clinic today. No worries, sir."

He was turning tragedy into triumph in real time. He was bending the will of the new Army to his own. I've had many commanders over the years and only the best would have even tried. There is a saying: "The Queen Mary doesn't turn on a dime." But it seemed to me Major Ridgeway had the will to turn it. He had the reputation and conviction that would spin it like a top.

I popped down to clinic with a spring in my step.

———

There was a medic there I'd never seen before. She was limping around on a zimmer splint, rooming patients and populating charts. I wondered why she wasn't off resting, but I picked up a chart and started my day.

Later in the day I got her attention. "I'm not sure if it's my place," I said, "But shouldn't you be resting, with that leg?" I asked. She had bee non-stop since I walked in.

"It's not in my nature, sir. War doesn't stop for the wounded."

"Well okay, but I'm sure we can pick up some slack if you need a break."

"Thanks for the advice, Doc. But that's not happening. I'm good."

"What happened?"

"It's fine... just twisted my knee," she said abruptly and walked away to attend to her task of refilling the medication cart.

I moved on to the next patient. But throughout the day I noticed the nursing staff treating her with kid gloves: "You okay Joe?" and, "Do you need anything, Joe?" and wondered why.

At the end of clinic, as we were shutting down, she was still there straightening up and restocking shelves. I was in the corner completing my charts over an empty gurney when she finally sat down. In the chair across from me.

"You're new," she said. "When'd you get here, sir?"

"Last week. I'm here only this week. Heading out to Sperwan Ghar."

"Oh yeah? That's my crew. I'll see you there as soon as my knee heals up."

"Oh yeah? You'be been out there. What's it like? Is that where you twisted your knee?"

"Something like that, yes. It's great. You'll love it."

She looked a bit pensive there and we paused. I sensed there was more to the story.

In medical school they talk about those 'pregnant pauses'. Most people don't give the silence enough air to breath. Most medical students take too long to figure that out, but it becomes more natural after a while. That morning, I guess I let the silence linger just long enough... Because Joe told me her story.

She began a little matter of fact. "I was in that IED Blast that killed Gert and Chris." And it slowly dawned on me that I was hearing something that no one heard about back home.

Roadside bombs kill indiscriminately, but sometimes soldiers, inside the same vehicle as those who die, survive. In an amb crew there is a driver and team-lead up front, and a "GIB" (that's short for 'Guy In Back'), in the back.

Joe was the GIB when her friends died. GIB's sometimes get tossed around or scrambled back there, but sometimes, they get ejected through the top or out the back, and get a close-up view of the carnage. You never heard those stories back home.

Grace couldn't believe it when I told her.

Joe was a feisty, fit, twenty-something medic from Montreal with dark hair and blue eyes and steel in her spine. She could do thirty push-ups and run the mile-and-a-half in under nine minutes, when a twisted knee wasn't holding her back.

Sitting still was not in Joe's nature. Those medics (Gert and Chris) who came off the plane in Mirage as Rolly and I watched, were her amb crew.

She watched them die.

She didn't talk about it often, but she told me the story that day. At the end of a quiet clinic we sat, and she told her story. She was matter of fact about it, and I listened with as much equanimity as I could muster. She told me all the details, even the gory parts, which I won't repeat. Those parts were hers to keep, or tell, but she told me then, and it was an honour to hear it. Sometimes you need to get that stuff out.

I can only hope it helped her process her pain. Like those veterans on Major's Hill Park needed to tell their stories. It was fresh, and I was glad to help, in that small way.

But it was hard to hear. Her friend, the driver, had just finished telling a joke. She was frustrated that she could not remember the punch line.

"That knee is your ticket home," I said when she finished.

"I won't go," she said succinctly. And I knew there would be no debate on that point. She got up and began to finalize her task of changing the paper rolls on the gurneys.

As she worked and moved about the clinic, she called quietly over her shoulder, "Mission first, sir. My tour's not done."

Chapter Fifteen

Ramp Ceremonies

The ramp ceremonies seemed different in KAF, more intense, and they happened far too often. We showed the medical branch flag at every one. I went to my second that week, and it hit a little different than the first one in Mirage.

You've seen photos, and been to funerals, so I won't belabour the details: same red carpet, same green plane, same process. I didn't have an official role, so stood to attention in the ranks to one side. We watched pallbearers, stoic and silent, some sobbing, carry the caskets up the ramp.

I remember being distracted, and annoyed at some noises going on around us: a contractor cutting concrete. A shitter-truck sucking out the blue rockets to one side: allowing the damn doors to slam shut.

The war machine didn't stop for our funerals.

The hardest part for me was seeing Brad's tears. He didn't sob. He wasn't histrionic, but I saw him wipe his eyes at the end, and that got me.

After the ceremony I approached, "How are you, sir?"

"There's a Blackhawk heading to Sperwan Ghar tomorrow. You'll be on it. One of the medics will drive you to the flight line at 0730hrs. When you land, make your way directly to the UMS, your team will be expecting you."

"Sounds good. Anything else, sir? Anything else I need to know?"

"Yeah. Don't get killed," he said.

The rest of my day was spent preparing for departure. I went to the barracks and watched the walls sweat for a while then packed my kit and had a shower. Sometime around mid-afternoon Ian came around asking about a trip to the market before I left. I jumped up figuring I might find a nesting doll or some trinket for Grace. She'd appreciate that little memento.

We arrived in the heat of mid-afternoon and the market was bustling. There was a lineup four bodies wide and a hundred yards long. Locals and multinational soldiers from all over the world: Germans, Brits, Aussies, New Zealanders, others I didn't recognize, waiting to get into a roped-off corner of town with stalls selling wares. Exactly like you might imagine a bazaar to look like.

We walked around to get the lay of the land. In one back corner, some children were kicking a ball in the dust. The ball was flat, but they playcd it hard. One kid banged a goal and another threw him on his shoulders and circled the others laughing. The keeper jumped on them and knocked them to the ground. They fell hard and rolled in the dust. Laughing. Then the game started up again quickly. The fall looked violent, but they seemed unfazed. They looked nimble and strong and joyful.

When I turned back Ian had moved off in the distance. I wandered through the rows of stalls filled with hanging cloth, rugs, carpets, and fabrics of every colour, statuettes of horses and elephants, gold and silver clocks, globes and compasses, wind-chimes dangling in the wind. We had a plan to meet out front, so when I lost him completely, I didn't think much of it.

Some wares were made by local artisans; one of a kind. Others were clearly en masse from China, like something you'd find at a kiosk near battery park. I found a few things that would fit in my duffle: a nesting doll for Grace, some marble camels for her sister and mom, some small wooden crosses for my family.

It was fun bartering with artisans. I completed a purchase and was admiring the workmanship of a little wooden Jesus on that cross when a commotion began behind me.

A young father with a tight-cropped beard, his wife and children at his side, was arguing with one of the shopkeepers. He was yelling and pounded his fists on a table, and the shopkeeper was yelling back and shooing them away, but the father was determined about something.

The family stood solemnly by his side. Their clothes looked different than others. More colourful. They were clearly Afghan, but their dress was more formal than most. They might have been from up north, or going to a wedding or funeral or something. The boy and girl were holding their mother's *saree* and the girl was staring directly at me, her eyes shining gold in the sunlight.

I couldn't look away.

She was about seven or eight but seemed much older. Her clothing was that of an older child. She wore a long *chapan* shirt over pants and an iron blue *chodar* wrapped over the top of her head. Most small girls didn't cover their heads. She smiled and made a wave and I waved back transfixed by her eyes.

Then she let go of her mother and walked directly to me through the crowd. I took a sharp breath in as she reached up for my hand and took it. I stood there, in stunned silence, staring down at her, uncertain if I'd done something to invite her: maybe the way I'd waved or stared. Then she said, "KAA-NAA-DOO" and pointed to the flag on my sleeve.

I crouched and said, "Yes, CANADA."

She was very cute, bundled in her headdress with her eyes shining in the sun.

She repeated back more clearly, "KANADA."

That was my first interaction with an Afghan child and my heart reached out to her. She seemed innocent, but bold and powerful. In my breast pocket I had a booklet of English to Dari translations with common phrases. I handed it to her. She took it zestfully and turned the pages. Sitting on an overturned pot for sale in the next stall she began reading. I watched her in my crouch. Her eyes shone as she tracked the words.

Then her father yelled something in Dari or Farsi or Pashtun, I could never tell, directing his anger toward me. I stood and stared into his furrowed brow and dark eyes. His daughter suddenly looking scared and ran back to him abruptly, keeping the booklet.

He saw and grabbed her wrist and snatched the booklet from her hand and marched over to me. "Sir," he said, holding it out.

"No. You keep it. It's for her," I said.

He was angry now and thrust the book back. I had no inclination how it might be perceived; I simply held my palms up and did not take the book. I tried a smile, compelling him to keep it. "I want her to have it," I said.

But that was futile. He didn't understand. All I wanted was to gift the book to his girl but he was angry. He threw back his garment and revealed a knife at his belt. He pointed in my face and yelled aggressively and rapidly as I stumbled backward.

I thought about the pistol on my leg and how the holster was stiff and how the rifle slung over my shoulders hadn't deterred this man from accosting me.

My rifle wasn't *ready* anyway, and I wasn't about to draw my weapon. I'm a doctor. And a Canadian. Striking out in violence was not the way, and even if I could raise my weapon in self-defence that could lead to tragedy, and this was a busy market. I wasn't about to try.

He would probably draw his knife and kill me first anyway.

I tripped over the overturned pot and stumbled. I was alone and confused and wondered why I hadn't stuck close to Ian.

The man drew his knife and came forward as the crowd gathered beginning to close in.

Then another man stepped from the crowd and placed himself between me and the angry father. He was wearing a Canadian uniform, similar to mine, but worn badly. His pants were hanging loose over his boots and his sleeves were bunched, haphazardly rolled, only part way. His back was to me. I couldn't see his face but when he spoke, I recognized the voice.

It was Lucky.

Their exchange was rapid and the man quickly calmed down. Then the girl's father smiled toward me and it looked genuine. He held the book to his chest, then to his forehead, then slid it into his vest. Lucky had somehow turned his reluctance into gratitude. They spoke for a time as I brushed off and the crowd dispersed.

Then Lucky turned toward me as the family walked away. "You should be more careful who you upset, Doctor. That man was not happy."

"I didn't mean to offend him. I'm sorry."

"He said you lured his girl through the crowd. I told him you are a stupid foreigner but meant no harm. I hope it is okay I gave them your booklet."

"Of course. I wanted her to have it."

"Oh. I can't see the girl ever reading that book," he said. "But I promised her father you meant no harm, and offered the booklet as a gift for their trouble."

"Thank you, Lucky. You may have saved my life."

"Quite possibly," he said matter-of-fact with no trace of irony in his smile, "You should stay close to me now."

———

The rest of the day was uneventful. I spent some time writing a letter to Grace and arranging my kit for my flight outside the wire thinking about being part of a task force with a collective focus and common goals. It felt good. I slept well, woke early, and spent an hour in the gym. After breakfast I gathered my things and headed out.

On my way to the flight line, I met Lieutenant-Colonel Clark on the road. He was standing out the top hatch of a heavily armoured vehicle. He gestured to his driver to slow as they passed.

"Hey Doc." He smiled and waved pulling his bandana down so I could see his face.

I smiled and waved back.

"You keeping busy?" he yelled as they rolled by.

"Never a dull day in Kandahar," I tried.

"Maybe we'll catch you out there somewhere?" he asked gesturing to the great beyond outside the confines of Kandahar proper.

"Maybe. I'm on my way out to Sperwan Ghar now."

"Well, enjoy that. Try to come back with stories, not scars." He quipped as they sped away heading for the main gate and the road South.

There was a lightness to the moment. A levity in my step. It was a clear day full of purpose. I turned down the alley toward the clinic where my ride to the flight line was waiting.

Part Three:

Taliban Country

Chapter Sixteen

Sperwin Ghar

*"…The entire universe conspired to
help me find you."*

-The Alchemist

In my memory the timeline speeds up on that flight. There was no more fun and games at the FOB. The sensation arrived with a jolt as I buckled the lap belt and braced the straps over my shoulders. The Blackhawk had a small crew and a mission. I was their only passenger and a distraction. I found myself paying attention. My senses heightened.

The door gunner seemed joyous. Rounds, coiled in a box between his legs, led up the tripod of a 25mm canon on a chain of links to a long dark barrel with an aggressive flash suppressor. Those bullets looked like they wanted out; like they were jostling to be first through that barrel.

We were heading south into the foothills. A red desert stretched to the horizon, towards Pakistan. The terrain was like a scene from the Bible. Shepherds with herds of goats in the dust with crooks. Lush green lining the Helmand River: marijuana or opium or both. All else was muted yellow and brown sand and dust the colour of caramel candy. It filled the cracks between rocks and the sharp mounds of stone they called ghars.

Our flight traced a main road connecting villages and farms and grape fields. Field upon field of ancient stone grape walls supporting brown climbing vines.

This was Taliban country, where tribal leaders kept order via council meetings under Sharia law and the Afghanistan Ministry of Vice and Virtue was spoken of longingly in Pashtun.

We were simply tolerated. Unwanted but tolerated out here. Those who sought us harm were not banished or removed. They blended in.

I would only be there for a few short months but in that time I grew to respect the deeply proud and stalwart people. Their children were taught to obey, persevere, and work hard. Parents told stories of wise dervishes who never bowed to kings, of cunning wrestling teachers who would keep secrets from their students only to use those secrets, in the end, to prevail against the best of them.

Out there the desert people were the constant prevailing force.

They seemed content to wait for us to finish and go.

Like every other army had done and every army to come would do. Centuries upon centuries of armies.

———

The Blackhawk circled the FOB. From above it looked too small, too haphazard, and too new. Sperwan Ghar sat on the edge of a sprawling village surrounded by mud huts and grape farms and the occasional pomegranate tree. The only green was in the distance on the edge of a dry creek marked as the Helmand River on my map.

We did a final pass and swooped down landing abruptly. Two choppers, heavily armed, circled above us, protecting, watching the surrounding hills for insurgents, ready to strike at any threat.

The door gunner climbed down and turned to help me out. I jumped down onto the heavy gravel and pulled my duffle onto my shoulder. Large chunks of jagged stone beneath my feet had been packed tightly by a yellow steamroller to my right. I would later see them rolling the heliport daily to prevent particle entrainment and brownout. A light dust eddy surrounded us then. Beyond were sea-containers, a squat building of stone and particle board, a row of 105 Howitzers in the distance with sweaty soldiers rushing around and a jagged hill jutted from the desert at the centre of the FOB with a road that winded around to a tower at the top. A HESCO barrier, varied in height, walled us off from the surrounding village; merely a suggestion for the villagers not to pass.

I was greeted by Sergeant Collins in the downwash.

"Morning, Doc, nice to meet you—this way," he yelled. He held his helmet on his head, unstrapped, and beckoned me to follow. He wore desert pattern combat pants and a brown T-shirt. His rifle was slung and he squinted against the wind.

I had no idea who he was. He wore no identifiable rank or name tag but he knew who I was and it was clear I was needed in the trauma bay, post-haste.

My flight had been delayed an hour. The warrant officer I was replacing had shipped out by road that morning. They had been leaderless for a few hours. Medics out there were good—very, very good—but they loved having someone around trained at the next level.

They didn't need help. They wouldn't be there if they needed help. But they liked to play by the rules and there are certain 'advanced medic protocols' which require the presence of a licensed physician. It was my medical licence they found most helpful, not necessarily my know-how, or teaching. They could justify doing more when I was around and they liked that. They were experts at their craft and pushed the boundaries, but they loved the access to those advanced protocols that my presence afforded. Only in their most humble moments would they admit that having a doc around to make the toughest decisions was reassuring.

The helipad was closer to the unit medical station than it felt that day. We crunched between armour (a Bison or two and a few tracked vehicles) through a low stone headquarters, which had once been a small schoolhouse, up a dirt ramp to the unit medical station.

The UMS consisted of two converted sea containers set against a hillside covered in stone. A heavy metal door with a rotating latch kept the sand out. Outside was a rack for weapons. I placed my bags down and my C7 rifle in the rack and stepped inside.

A patrol had recently returned. Eight soldiers in varying stages of heat injury were there on the stretchers receiving fluids. The mood was jovial, which was a good sign.

"You must be the new doc. Welcome to the show!" said Corporal Higgins. He smiled and shook my hand as he increased the drip rate on an IV line.

He cut directly to the chase, "This all right by you, Doc? We've been doing IV saline drips when they get back from patrol. if they're wobbly enough," he said this to one of the haggard infanteers occupying the stretcher to his left, and they shared a chortle. "We keep the *hypertonic* for the field. Lower volume so we can carry more but back here we slam in cool *normal* saline, or ringers, whichever is most readily available." He opened the door to a small beer fridge which was stacked to the tits with bags of saline. "Don't worry, Doc, we know oral hydration is preferred, but they run out of water out there quickly, and sometimes get locked down longer than expected."

"Sounds like you know what you're doing. Oral hydration best... But, yeah, what are you giving them here? A litre each?" I asked, feeling like I should say something 'doctorly'.

"That usually does the trick," he said.

Heat stroke, if you don't know, has a ridiculously high mortality. Heat injury goes from heat exhaustion to heat stroke quickly, which may end in death more abruptly than you think. That is, if you're not vigilant. I was impressed at their vigilance. Soldiers out in that desert sun, with full kit, running, climbing walls, and fighting for too long could flip over that edge real fast.

I quickly reviewed their protocols and asked a few questions. Those medics were slick. They knew their stuff inside and out. They recognized signs and symptoms and knew what to do. And they did it—with bullets flying over their heads.

Dripping IV Saline was a daily routine in the desert. We needed constant resupply. The neatness of the stacks of IV bags and organized medical supplies on the shelves lining the place was astounding and reassuring and comforting.

Troops, out on patrol, wore camel-back canteens beneath their packs, and carried more water, and lugged extra twenty-litre jerry cans too. But a patrol can only carry so much. They always had miles to go, grape walls to climb, fields to cross, villages to traverse, and promises to keep. And the sun was relentless.

When they got back to the FOB their uniforms were always drenched and blotched with white salt stains.

I'm proud to say we never lost one to heat stroke.

"This all sounds appropriate. You're good to follow this practice anytime. Standing order." I said and caught a look of relief on Higgin's face.

"You're alright, Doc," he said.

He didn't know me yet, and technically had needed that order prior to placing those IVs, but he was correct, and probably saved lives that day.

The treated soldiers were sitting up on their stretchers ribbing each other. "When they start their comedy routine like this, we kick 'em out," he added.

Higgins was a good-looking lad from down east with a broad smile and dimples, pleasant and competent and morally grounded, even when he overstepped his training. I knew I'd have his back and immediately hoped he'd have mine.

A few of the bags were empty now so he pulled their IVs. The soldiers were relaxed and joking as they left for their barracks. The medics seemed to know them all by name, which gave the place a happy, hometown feel.

We few, we happy few.

Sergeant Collins introduced the members of the team who were 'on FOB' at the moment. A crowd gathered inside the UMS to feel out their new, short term, boss.

"Let's go around the room and introduce ourselves. I'll start. My name is John Collins, I'm a reservist from Toronto. I'm a paramedic back home and second-in-command out here. I make the rosters and keep these jokers in line. We're glad to have you, sir."

He was serious and set the tone. Brief and to the point. Clearly well respected, humble and kind. I found out quickly his skills were top notch. It was good to have an expert in pre-hospital medicine on the team.

"Sarge is our hero," said Higgins and the group laughed. Collins smiled. And Higgins continued, "I'm Wade Higgins, from Halifax. Joined the Army out of high school and never looked back. Currently posted to Pet, like the rest of these losers. Being a medic is the best job in the world. I'm looking forward to the next few months. It's exciting having a doc out here on the team. Not that our good Warrant Baker isn't awesome. Just having a full on Emerg Doc out here with us is pretty cool. Hoping to learn a lot from you, sir."

"Well, I'll see what I can do," I said. Then waited for the next few medics to make their introductions. There was Private Stacey Sullivan, a proud Newfoundlander and a fast talker who kept us laughing, even when we should have been crying. Corporal Steve Trollip always punched above his weight, like Higgins, occasionally overstepping, but rarely wrong.

There were five or six others, and more out on patrol or sleeping. They also mentioned Corporal Joe Bradley who I'd met at the clinic in Kandahar. They were happy to hear the leg was getting better, and that she was well on her way back out. None were surprised by that, but they became somber thinking about the team they'd lost.

And those two dead medics seemed to fill the room for a moment. An unprompted moment of silence lingered when Collins pointed out their pictures. The two of them hugging and laughing occupied a position of reverence, in a frame by the computer. I picked it up and stared.

"Listen, I can't know what you've been through out here. I can only say that I am sorry for your loss, and hope to help continue their work in a way that might make them proud."

The silence lingered for a moment longer before Collins finally spoke, "Thanks for that, Doc. Why don't you tell us about yourself?"

"Okay. I'm Jack Henry," I began. "I'm a doc from Kingston, Ontario. I was in the reserves in Ottawa for twelve years, a Sergeant, like you Collins, when I got into med school. That's when I transferred to the reg force and never looked back. I was posted to Kingston out of residency and I've been working at the base and moonlighting in the emerg in Napanee, Perth and Smith Falls. This is my first time in Afghanistan, and my first time at a FOB. Looking forward to getting to know you."

There was a bit of small talk after that, but I got the sense there was work to be done. As the crowd dispersed Sergeant Collins came over to chat. He asked a few more questions about the reserves and med school then showed me our barracks.

We bunked next door; part cave, part plywood panelled concrete hovel. Home away from home for the next few months. Out front, a fifteen-foot concrete wall was covered with little black choppers, one for every medevac had been spray-painted in little rows. An old ammo box full of stencils and spray paint sat at its base, ready to go.

A pressboard door on a spring slapped shut behind us as we stepped into the cramped living space. Three dusty faux-leather couches set in a 'U' surrounded a thirty-five-inch flatscreen television.

A Sony PlayStation was booting. Two medics had rushed back to start a game of 'Call of Duty'. The room itself was cool, dimly lit, and cozy. There was an air conditioner pumping refreshing air through a hole in the roof.

"I never got the hang of that game," I said.

"Don't worry we'll have you kicking ass in no time, sir," they said. I heard them whispering as we walked toward the bunnies in the back, but I didn't catch what they said. Could have been about their game, or about me, or something else entirely, but I remember hoping they liked me.

Our bunk-rooms lined the perimeter; set deeper into the hillside. Most had two bunk beds. Some had four. Collins directed me to a bottom bunk in an empty corner room. It wasn't much but it was quiet and private with a pleasant earthy smell. A heavy canvas sheet, pinned to the edge, made a private booth that was all mine. I dropped my duffle not knowing how much time I'd spend there in the coming months but feeling at home already. A tiny lamp hung from the planks above. It was a clean, well-lit place. Good for journaling.

Aside from meal time, there was not much of a routine. The injured arrived unscheduled. Some days were lighter than others but the work was constant and physical. Exactly what I needed, exactly what I had been yearning for, and exactly what I loved about the Army back then. You felt most alive doing busy work that had purpose. Like you were really living.

Those first few weeks went by in a blur. Every day became a Tuesday. Weekends were a distant memory. If we weren't dealing with incoming trauma, we were cleaning up afterward, or running clinics for Afghan nationals on the other side of the FOB. We went to the village on 'outreach' for the locals about once per week. Part of the plan for 'winning hearts and minds.'

We kept sane by lifting heavy objects in the gym behind the schoolhouse, or sleeping. But we could always use more sleep.

We had a satellite phone and I called Grace every chance I got.

"Sweetness, it's me," I said through the static and delay. I was sitting in my bunk, lying on a fluffed pillow in a clean, cotton cover.

"Oh babe, how are you? So nice to hear your voice. How are things going?"

"I'm at a FOB now. It's awesome, hun. The UMS is quaint. So tidy and organized. Just the way I like it. We have everything we need for major trauma—except most of the things, ha! We could use a CT scanner, and an Operating Room, and a surgeon... But the helipad is close. So that's good."

Grace knew. She had worked emerg in training, and seen some trauma.

"We have a portable ultrasound which I didn't expect, but it's always useful. And the team is great. They're competent and hard working."

I was trying not to think about how much I missed her.

"That's great babe. But, how are you? How is it?"

"I'm great! It's exactly what I imagined. Picture a rocky desert, now add more sand," I said, trying to be funny.

"Do you feel safe?"

"Oh yeah! Very safe babe. There's a lot of concrete around the clinic and the barracks. I'm under the side of a hill right now. It's fine, sweets. Don't worry." Saying *don't worry* felt cringey. Probably not helpful.

"I can't promise I won't worry. Please call when you can."

"I will try." I could hear her breath... and almost feel it. I was choking up. "—I miss you," I added.

"Me too, babe. I love you."

I choked back some tears and changed the subject, at risk of weeping uncontrollably, "Tell me more about home. What's happening in Kingston?"

Grace spoke about home and life and the hospital. Always busy with work and spending time with friends. Her sister and mother had been and gone.

I wandered outside for better reception as we chatted back and forth for about twenty minutes. When we finally said our goodbyes, I was standing next to a massive Canadian Flag made of painted stones set in the hillside next to our showers. A memorial I hadn't seen; built by previous teams. That big red flag looked like hope to me. Reading the plaque at the base and admiring the workmanship I stood a little taller and breathed a little deeper.

Home was far away but this was where I needed to be. I was following my personal legend and it seemed right. Grace was doing well. Grace was fine.

Chapter Seventeen
Shot Squirrels

As the doc at a FOB UMS you don't know much about the war going on around you. I mean, you have access to the headquarters and get to know the troops and their commanders but everyone knows you're there for one job— medicine. They give you some details of local operations if you might need to prepare, or if you're interested and ask, but mostly you don't ask. They prefer to see their doctor thinking about medicine and leaving them to do the soldiering.

It was clear the operational tempo was increasing though. The troops seemed more anxious and patrols were constantly rolling out at all hours. My medics went with them. But there wasn't anything I needed to do for them to go. All that exchange and movement happened without any input from me. They knew their jobs and did them well.

They were always absconded 'opcon'. Which meant "under operational control" of the patrol commanders. They'd leave with the infantry or armoured or engineers and return when they were done. Sometimes they disappeared for days and I'd be left with a handful of support troops and maybe a few medics if I was lucky. Other times they were all back at the FOB within hours and available to help with mass casualty events and other medical tasks: training Afghan National Army (ANA) soldiers, testing water samples, and inspecting lines for health and hygiene violations.

Most of the time soldiers were gathered in small semi-circles down the hill, hunched over maps and compasses or stripping and assembling weapons with the Afghan learners. There was constant work effort. It was impressive, awe inspiring, but it had little to do with me. I was focussed on the UMS and making sure it was ready to receive trauma.

Occasionally the guns rattled the walls. Out-going shells targeting insurgents in the hills. It felt like progress. Probably meant fewer bad guys shooting our way.

Our work in the UMS carried on both despite and because of all that violence.

Collins kept a rotating schedule to ensure I was never alone. But there were times when we handled events on a shoestring. There was one time I had a cook applying pressure to a head wound while I was sewing up a leg because that was the only help available that day.

Joe arrived sometime later; her knee had healed up. She immediately asked to go back into full rotation but Collins wouldn't allow it. He insisted she stay on FOB for a while and the entire team was on board with that. She was written into regular rotation at the UMS and stayed out of the leaguers and patrols. There were a ton of small jobs to do, like water testing and the like so it was good to have some consistency there. She made an already efficient system more so within a day of her arrival. She optimized. I liked that.

After what she'd been through, we were all determined to get her through this tour with no more scars. She would finish her tour, and be effective in unexpected ways. She got proficient with the radios, restocked the shelves, maintained our medical equipment, and kept the place clean and ready for trauma. I barely lifted a finger between cases because of her. And when I thought about some way to improve efficiency or something that would come in handy, she seemed to have already thought of it. Always one step ahead.

It was a slick operation and I felt at times like a cog in the works. I ran the daily clinics for the sick or injured; once a week for the ANA, and every few weeks in the village on outreach. And interspersed between was the occasional mass casualty event.

We were the node of convergence for all the horrible happenstance. I can't understate how correct that plaque at Sunnybrook had been. Despite the education I'd received, nothing could have prepared me for the reality of that war. You get very good at managing trauma out there.

And I certainly learned what an IED can do.

Those things were everywhere, killing indiscriminately: ANA, Coalition, locals, even insurgents slipped up and blew themselves up sometimes.

Our guys had electronic counter measures to block radio-wave detonation signals, but the pressure plates were unavoidable. By the end of my first few months out there I had managed too many limb amputations, and filled too many body bags. It was beginning to weigh on me.

Grace mentioned how the CBC spoke of Canadians being killed, and how our country mourned and kept count, but she never seemed to hear about the non-Canadians, and didn't seem to hear much about the humans being mutilated and injured, but living.

Maybe it was too much to contemplate. And might have filled the airways back home.

Kids were losing limbs at an alarming rate. And it all found its way to us. We cleaned it up and sent it back, and most of the time, if there was a medic around when it happened, they survived.

It wasn't only gunshot wounds and explosive injuries we were treating either. One day an artilleryman walked in with a Robertson screwdriver clean through his right hand.

What went through my head just then should have been a sign.

I immediately wondered if he was trying to pull a 'Corporal Klinger'. You know, that corporal from M*A*S*H* who was always trying to get a 'section eight' to prove he wasn't fit to serve and get sent home. For a moment I seriously wondered if he did it on purpose. I was clearly starting to lose my bearings. Imagine thinking someone drove a screwdriver through their own hand for a ticket home. Who would do such a thing? Who would think such a thing?

It turned out he'd fallen off a short ladder and by dumb luck the screwdriver bounced and ended directly under his bracing hand.

He was lucky it was just his hand.

Getting injured *will* get you sent home though. That guy had the option to stay or leave, and chose to stay. When I asked him later privately, he said it was for the danger pay.

Another young lady was bit by a viper on her hand while reaching into her boot one morning. I was worried about her. She had sprinted to the UMS and her arm was already swelling. We air evac'd her back to Kandahar 'pri alpha'. She returned a week later with a good story to tell her grandkids. I didn't see her much after that. I hope she gets to meet those grandkids.

We kept our heads down and did our jobs, bearing witness to the unexpected and horrible. In quiet moments, when things slowed, I began to wonder about the point of it all.

And that's where Lucky comes in.

Lucky was a learned man. He helped me understand some of the nuance and complexity of the geopolitics, providing a perspective missed in my intelligence briefings.

He popped into the UMS a few days after Joe got back, and it was nice to see him again.

Firstly, it is exceedingly difficult to practice clinical medicine when you cannot understand your patients. Trauma is one thing. But clinic can't be done without language. We call it veterinary medicine, and I don't know how veterinarians do it. There's a maxim: if you listen closely to your patient, they will tell you what is wrong. And it is true. Having a competent translator makes all the difference.

Lucky was a Godsend. He was perfectly fluent in all the dialects, as well as English, which was key (a lot of translators out there could not actually speak English).

I found him to be an exceptional translator, and one of the most interesting men I have ever met. In his prior life, he had studied political science and sociology at Oxford University, and still owned an apartment that he *lets* near Christ Church. He was in Panjwai, with my sorry ass, for the love of his homeland. He was born and raised in Kabul, desperate for his country to pull itself out of generations of turmoil and enter the first world, determined to do his part to help.

We were lucky to have him at our FOB.

His skills were in high demand. He could have chosen any of the Coalition Armies: US, UK, Aussies, Germans, or others, but he chose to work with Canadians. He said most translators choose Canada when they have a choice, "The Coalition Armies can be difficult," he said, "but we find Canadians tend to treat us Afghans with the most respect."

We were sitting at a quiet table near the kitchen where we often took our lunch, "I cannot abide racism in any form, and I see it rampant and unchecked out here," he said, "but your Canadian soldiers seem kindest. They seem to have been bred with a respect for humanity that is not prevalent elsewhere in the world."

I suspect he was trying to endear himself to me. His eyes were shining and his smile was infectious. It worked, and I agreed. I had seen many examples of troops behaving badly, and in general, he was right about Canadians.

"It must be bred in your snow?" he said.

"Ha. Maybe. I never thought about that. But yea, all that shovelling out for one another. The shared misery of it all. Our heavy snow might play a role there."

He smiled. "It does seem Canadians are more tolerant of others. It's a terrible thing when people are treated badly because of the colour of their skin, or the birthplace of their grandparents."

That was true. He was wise and kind and reminded me that out-sourcing Canada was worth risking life and limb for.

We discussed war, politics, and Coalition plans, and I grew to trust his thoughts and opinions.

A few engineers passed and waved to us on their way to lunch.

"The US troops can be the worst," he continued, "Degrading. I worked with them for a short time last year, but I never will again."

That reminded me of a story I'd heard, from one of those passing engineers, earlier in the day, "Did you hear about the attack on the US FOB in Helmand last night?"

"Yes. I'm not surprised. Probably a revenge killing."

"What do you mean? They launched an M-72 into the headquarters."

"I wouldn't be surprised if that young man was fed up with all the racism," he said.

"You mean he killed the commander and half the headquarters staff because they treated him badly? That doesn't sound right. That sounds psychopathic. Don't you think it was an act of war? Something planned by the Taliban?"

"Both are possible. But I suspect I am correct."

"That's ominous Lucky. Couldn't the Taliban infiltrate the Afghan National Army, or turn one of their soldiers, quite easily?"

"No. I don't think so. We have not seen anything like that before. It would be an evolution of tactics, and many of the Coalition forces incite great hatred in my countrymen. The American boys are less tolerant than your Canadians."

"Well, it would be an easy way to end all this don't you think? They could have people right here on this FOB right now. Planning an attack on us," I said looking around.

The shade of a concrete pillar cut across the sand at the edge of our table. It was mildly cooler there in the shade. A group of ANA soldiers were sitting on the nearby HESCO, looking out toward the village, talking on their cell phones.

"Unlikely. The Taliban have bigger plans for defeating this Coalition. They won't be trifling over FOBs. The work they are doing has been very effective."

"How do you mean?"

"I think," he continued. "Your Coalition misunderstands this insurgency. And it is at the heart of your problem. The reason you won't be successful. The Taliban are more coordinated and strategic than you believe. They are playing a long game. And playing it very well."

"I thought the Taliban was just an idea. Loosely connected. Disorganized tribes." I was drawing from what Brad had said, and my briefings. Although, lately those intelligence briefs were starting to blur together. They rarely pertained to me or my job so I'd stopped paying attention awhile back.

"No, no! The Taliban are organized and deeply opposed to the tribal system. They are using ethnic tensions in these southern provinces to create chaos and keep the elected government in the North de-stabilized. They want to create one Islamic Emirate, and they need the northern government to fall in order to do so. And they are gaining a foothold here in Panjwai, and building support. It seems more and more likely to me, that they will succeed."

"But that's why we are training the ANA."

"Yes, but what your Coalition is choosing to do with the ANA, hoping to create a security force, will not work. It is irrelevant busywork, and a waste of time."

"That's harsh, Lucky."

"It is my opinion. When your Coalition departs, the ANA will fall apart. Many of them will defect to the Taliban, as many have already done. The Taliban have too much support. This disgruntled soldier who shot up those Americans last night is one example. He is likely sitting with Taliban this very day. Didn't they say he simply walked away from the FOB?"

I had heard that, and nodded.

"They have many lines of exit and entry from the South. Your Coalition can't prevent them coming and going and building support. You don't have enough soldiers. I suspect they are succeeding in their goals despite your efforts."

"Well that's interesting, and disheartening, Lucky. I hope you are wrong." He was insightful and knowledgeable and I trusted his word. But I didn't like these ideas.

"I think I am right. The Afghan administration is run from afar, and marginalized down here. The tribes don't trust government and they see the Taliban shadow cabinet dispensing Sharia justice, collecting taxes, and supporting their insurgency. They see them claim many victories, like the one last night at the FOB. The tribal leaders see more and more insurgent victories. The Taliban propaganda machine co-opts them. Last night's violence will be seen as their own, and it will grow their influence. Their intelligence machine is more organized and efficient than your Coalition cares to believe."

"Wow, Lucky. I haven't heard it that way. Maybe you need to speak to our intelligence officers. Give a briefing."

"Not my place."

"What I don't understand is how the locals abide all the indiscriminate killing. How can they support an insurgency so violent and destructive to their own. You've seen with me, as many villagers come through the UMS as Coalition soldiers. How can they support that. They're being killed as often as we are?"

"Violence is a way of life down here. Suffering is not as difficult for desert peoples. What is clear to them is the insurgency and those that operate it, support them more than the Government in the North. And this seems to be getting worse."

"How can they see all the indiscriminate killing and not want it to end?"

"I imagine they do. But they also imagine a time when you are gone."

"I thought we were winning 'hearts and minds'."

"You may be, but I do not think it will be enough."

"So, you're saying our Coalition of Forces is doomed to fail?"

"I hope not. I hope we thwart the bullies. The Taliban should never hold power. That is why I go to the village daily, bring gifts, and teach the children. They need to see what awaits if the Taliban wins. I try to show them what is possible if they choose to rise above the oppression and build a strong democratic government. But it feels more and more futile."

I had seen Lucky mingling with locals and chatting with the Mullahs at our outreach clinics. I'd seen him in the village with children gathered around. He seemed well known and respected and deeply connected to the people. I was glad to have him on our side.

"But we are winning hearts and minds, right?" I asked again.

"Sure Jack. Canada yes. You have won my heart for certain."

"What about the smart people we have at the top? They are good at exploiting weakness and gathering knowledge. Maybe they'll surprise us? There is a Canadian in charge now! That's gotta mean something."

"The Taliban are adaptable. It is ill-advised to underestimate them."

I always enjoyed our conversations, but my understanding of the geopolitics was marginal, and I had no control over what the Coalition was doing.

I was there to patch wounds.

Lucky and I were walking back toward the UMS when the war reared its ugly head again. The ground shook from a distant explosion and we exchanged a knowing glance: another trauma was on its way.

———

An hour later, my chat with Lucky was a distant memory. I stepped out of the medical station and made my way over to the ridge that sheltered our armoured ambulance. I liked the view from there. On a clear day, you could see over the kitchen and helipad to the village and mountains in the distance. But not today. Today the sky was full of sand.

To my right the pressboard door to our barracks slapped and creaked on its hinge. To my left the cenotaph and makeshift memorial for our dead, fashioned from painted stones long before I arrived, protected me from the side and behind. I grabbed my rifle from the rack and stretched my back.

The medics had moved a couch here. A cozy corner overlooking the "FOB". It was my favourite spot for a quiet moment alone after the bad ones.

'Forward Operating Base' was a strange name. Forward in what way? The enemy was all around. Traditional army doctrine labelled the front as closest to the fighting, so I suppose that was us, but it didn't feel like the 'front' of a war. Our mission was hopeful, not destructive. Guiding, not forceful. We weren't trying to gain ground and push back with force the way the term front implied. It felt right to be there, but it didn't feel like the front of a war. FOB was a misnomer.

I was fighting the notion we were at the front of war. But outsourcing Canada was a good idea. Lucky reminded me of that. His raving about the kindness of our soldiers and their fidelity to goodness and hope was inspiring. Lucky said Canadians were different, and special, and I believed him. "It must be bred in the snow," he had said, and I agreed with him.

I was thinking about the collective misery of all our heaving. I thought about how helping our neighbours shovel out probably plays a part in making us. And my heart swelled when I thought about things like that.

I missed the snow.

Below, some soldiers were teaching Afghan boys how to soldier. Hunched over maps with compasses, dating lines. Helping them learn that those things mattered. They were learning to defend their nation against oppression. But bad guys were trying to stop us. That was it. There was something noble about that.

But so many people were bleeding on me.

And that was difficult to reconcile, despite Lucky's wisdom about Canadians.

Right then I was staring over the helipad and engineers' barracks because an entire family had driven over a pressure plate an hour before. That's what we heard as we walked up the hill.

The heavy door, closed behind me, was blocking my view of the carnage. Three dead humans I couldn't save.

Their care had been technically easy, as trauma usually was, but psychologically and emotionally impossible. We had done all we could, but it was too late from the moment of impact. That family had arrived beyond saving.

Only the girl, sheltered from the blast behind her brother and parents, survived. She was in Joe's arms just then; an orphan.

I think part of my brain was trying to protect me because I wasn't thinking about her at all.

I was thinking about the desert.

The sand in Panjwai is as fine as talc. I was thinking about the centuries of windstorms that made it that way: beating it relentlessly into superfine grains. The power and time to make sand like that was impossible to conceive. The physics implied by that handful of soft sand was almost too much to bear. Thoughts like those can overwhelm if you're not careful.

And the sand rose up that day. It blocked the sun.

When you think of sandstorms you probably picture whipping winds and violent gusts and some of them must have been that way for the grains to be so fine, but many are not. That day a silent wall of talcum powder dust stretched as far as the eye could see on either side, as high and wide as the sky from horizon to horizon. It rolled in over everything on a slow, hot summer breeze. We were in the middle of it by noon. Like a dry morning fog it had dropped our visibility to less than a hundred feet. It was deathly calm in there. Like a thick blanket. You could stare right at that painful dot of light slowly descending toward the HESCO barrier and barely even squint.

I was still wearing a blood-soaked gown.

I hadn't torn it off on my way out the door as I usually do.

My tan boots were blackened with prior blood spill but there were new distinct drops of red on one toe.

I was marvelling at their colour and wondering how I might get them cleaned or exchanged ...when the mortar landed.

Mortars do exactly what they're designed to do.

We use "Arty-Sims" in training and they say those have the explosive energy of a quarter stick of dynamite. When you pull the string and toss them, usually near recruits, they whistle for about four seconds then explode. Paper shrapnel scatters everywhere. Scary at first, but you can easily avoid getting hurt because of the whistle. The whistle gives you time to take cover.

The thing is, in real life, there's no whistle. There's no warning at all. One moment you're counting dots on your shoes in the quiet, the next, two boys are tumbling across the road like shot squirrels in the attic.

No whistle. No siren. No damn four seconds to take cover.

And the sound lingers. It rings in your ears. It hung in the sand that day as if commanding me to remember.

The shell had probably come from the northwest, somewhere on the hillside past the village, but I couldn't be sure. But a chunk of shrapnel flew past my ear and I didn't even flinch. I didn't have time. It was the strangest feeling. I stood there, took a deep breath, and thought, "Why the fuck am I even here?"

Then Grace was with me for a moment. I closed my eyes and felt her beside me. We were at home in our bed in the dark and I had turned in my sleep and her hair touched my face. I tried to remain deathly still to not wake her and held my breath to feel hers, sweet across my face. I basked in her warmth for one blissful moment trying desperately to hold on.

But the FOB burst to life.

Medics grabbed stretchers and raced down the hill. Two more casualties of war were heading back to Kandahar that day. Hopefully we'd spare them a pine box.

I set my rifle back in the rack and went inside to clear space.

That dead family needed to be moved out of the way.

Chapter Eighteen

Amalah

Inside Joe was sitting with a girl wrapped in a wool blanket resting on her lap with her head held serenely beneath Joe's chin. An orphan. Her entire family was there, beneath blood-soaked blankets, behind blue paper curtains, but gone.

The child held a power that was incongruent with her tiny frame. There was a calmness to her. There should have been hysterics. But there was not.

Stepping past that heavy door I found a wave of despair come over me. Despite the wounded on stretchers that were moving up the hill behind me. The girl was still. She blinked once. Then again, longer. Peaceful. Familiar. Like what my own child might become. Dark hair. Beautiful eyes that glinted gold.

Our eyes met briefly as she turned in Joe's arms. Then she drifted to sleep as we placed her family into mortuary bags.

The two unluckies made it up the hill quickly. They were in bad shape but they survived. You never know with mortars. Depends on how close and how much shrapnel hits you. We had some trauma work to do but Higgins called in the med-evac nine-liner and we got them out fast. Tourniquets in place, IVs going. They were both on a chopper within twenty minutes of the mortar.

Very slick. That team was something else.

I was proud to be a part of that crew.

Joe set up a low bed with cushions and pillows and blankets for the little one and she slept through it all.

"I wish I knew her name," I said as we mopped and cleaned the bays around her. We were constantly restocking and resetting.

"I've been calling her Aisha. She looks like an Aisha to me," said Joe as she knelt with a warm cloth to brush her hair and mop some dried blood off the girl's face.

The girl stirred and turned and smiled.

Her eyes opened and I caught a glint of gold shining from around her irises and suddenly I recognized her.

It hit me like a ton of bricks.

I suspect many doctors do this at mass casualty events. 'Mass Cas' is a fancy term for when there are more injured than care providers. Technically, we dealt with "mass casualty events" all the time. On days when there were three injured and only two of us, that was a 'mass cas' by definition, but the humanity behind the injuries is not particularly useful in emergent trauma; it's not your priority.

Not that you don't care. You do. But who the patient is rarely makes a difference in the management of trauma. Aside from age and gender and certain obvious comorbidity's, their individuality is secondary to their injuries. Your objective is to repair the injured flesh. We use basically the same approach every time. Technical skills fix trauma. Perform tasks in order: triage, massive hemorrhage, ABCs, vitals. I was good at that.

You don't look for a complete family history when you're in a 'mass cas' event.

I've spent hours with people sewing them up, and later haven't recognized them on the street. If that makes me aloof, so be it. It's the way it is. I have a job to do.

This one with the cavitated chest needs a chest tube. Middle aged man. Maybe the father.

This one, a woman, with a massive open belly wound and spinal disruption. Exsanguinated quickly. Maybe the mother.

I won't talk about the baby boy. That baby boy. Too much.

But the girl who lived... I recognized her.

Now that the melee was done. In a moment of calm, in the quiet centre of that storm, I remembered.

This was the family I'd met at the market.

Then I saw her book. The one I'd given the father. It was there among the tattered cloth cut from his ruined body. Torn and bloodied. I picked it up and leafed through.

There are moments from that time that stick. Even after all my exposure therapy. This family had found their way down into Panjwai. And met a tragic end.

I recalled Lucky saying they were here looking for an uncle.

I knelt beside the girl. She smiled. I removed my gloves and brushed hair off her face and smiled. She opened her eyes, and reached up to touch the flag on my sleeve.

"KA-NA-DA," she said. As clear as a bell.

That moment is burned in my soul. Her smile. The smell of the filthy bloody mop Higgins was slopping behind me. I wiped the book and handed it to her. She sat up. Grabbed it. And her eyes shone. She rubbed the front and turned it over and rubbed the side and turned it back. She smelled it. She flipped the pages then opened to the front and moved her fingers across the first words.

She looked like she was reading.

She looked too small to be reading, but she was reading.

Part of me never left that moment.

Part of me is still there.

———

The trauma of that day still haunts me. What happened to her brother, even with technical jargon is hard to put to paper. The boy inside of me receded after that. I was beginning to lose some innocence. It's easy to forget those parts. Even now I can't remember the person I was before as clearly. Time tends to steal memories away. Keeps the details for itself. But some things fill the crevasses and push a lot of the happy things out, leaving less room.

But I wasn't trying to remember my childhood then. We had too much to do. Two good sized trauma events back-to-back requires effort to report and organize. The bodies needed disposal. The two mortared troops were packaged for flights back to Kandahar. The bays were restocked and reset in prep for the next one which could arrive at any moment, or in three days. There was never any way to know. I found myself less worried about the neatness of the shelves.

A pressing issue was our need to find a plan for that girl.

Her only wound was a laceration to her flank and some bruises. I had whip stitched her flank earlier but now closed it neatly with a subcuticular stitch using an absorbable suture. She would need wound care and bandage changes but otherwise she was well. She didn't seem to have head trauma, despite likely being tossed a good distance.

She was a conundrum.

Social services were not a phone call away like back home. She was a problem that was not going to be solved quickly.

It struck me, how much we depend on our systems back home. We take them for granted. You notice them when they're gone.

I turned to Lucky for answers.

He knew the landscape and was aware of local customs.

The translator who was there in the UMS just then couldn't speak a word of English. None at all. I'm not sure how he got the job. I barked at him to go find Lucky, as I found myself doing quite frequently. He scrabbled away. That was pretty much all I ever said to that guy, "Go get Lucky."

When Lucky arrived, he was helpful, as usual.

"First, her name?"

After a short conversation, he turned back and said, "Amalah."

"Amalah. That's a beautiful name."

She looked about seven but acted more like nine or ten. That was the way with Afghan kids. You couldn't tell how old they were by their size. They all seemed to be built on tiny frames. They were small, but mighty.

Then Lucky helped me explain to her all that had happened to her family. She understood that she was orphaned and handled it admirably. There were no tears.

In truth, I never once saw histrionics from children in Afghanistan. Nothing like you see every day in emergency rooms back home.

Once, a boy repositioned a flap of skin on the side of his own head right in front of me and never made a sound nor shed a tear. He winced a tiny bit when I inserted the needle to freeze the wound edge, but that was all.

I don't know what to make of that. Afghans seem universally hard, quick, and resourceful. And their contentment with suffering blended with a feeling they were simply tolerating us in a curious way most of the time.

Amalah didn't cry. She was stoic. She was sad though and asked for time alone with her mother so we obliged. Mercifully, her mother's wounds were not to the head and neck. We draped her body as best we could. But Amalah asked for water and a cloth. We could only watch as she kneeled over the body and cleansed away the blood and sand. She was mumbling unintelligibly throughout. When we attempted to help, she brushed us aside. When she had finished cleansing her mother she rose and made her way back to Joe.

They sat together for a time holding hands. With arms rested around one another they looked up at me, "What's next boss?" Joe asked.

I was at a loss, bracing and holding back tears.

"Lucky? Do you have any ideas?"

"She tells me this was all of her family. Up North she is not aware of any others, they have all been killed in this war.

"I think they were looking for an uncle down here."

"She says nothing of this. But I will go to the village and ask for him."

"Thank you. That sounds like a good place to start. I'll inform my chain of command, and see if Brad has any ideas."

Amalah stayed with us for seven days. Brad liked the idea of seeing what Lucky could find, so we set up a cot for Amalah next to Joe.

She seemed happy. She played in the dirt and observed us a fair bit. She could be found by my side most often. We ate lunch with Lucky together every day. It was comforting having her there in a whimsical way, as if the war could wait.

And mostly it did that week. We called her our good luck charm because the major trauma seemed to cease while she was there.

We fashioned a checkerboard out of wood planks and rocks and, with Lucky's help, I taught her to play. Very soon she was able to win despite my competitive spirit and best efforts. Her wound stayed clean and dry and healed quickly.

She confided to Lucky that her mother had been teaching her to read in private and she showed us some words she could read in Farsi. Lucky helped her with some more English phrases.

Each night I read her stories from the tattered books from a shelf in the crumbling schoolhouse. There was an exchange library there, built on a whim by some past soldier. I left my copy of House of God by Samuel Shem, and picked out an anthology of short stories for her.

As many do, this one began with the story of Shaharazad and the Thousand and One Nights. She enjoyed those stories very much. She didn't understand all of the language but she seemed to laugh at all the right places.

Reading to her on those quiet evenings, in that cool desert cave, with the smell of gun oil and dried blood all around, felt strangely like home.

She brightened the gloom.

But we knew it couldn't last forever.

It wasn't long before Lucky found her uncle.

But by that time, I was worried I couldn't let her go.

Chapter Nineteen

The Uncle

Grabbing my rifle from the rack was a force of habit. Leaving it outside never felt quite right. I was from the school of soldiering that taught you to be within one arms-length of your personal weapon at all times. Disregarding that was a 'chargeable' offence in the Army reserves. Although all offences are technically 'chargeable'.

But these young soldiers, medical types, in a war zone, were trained in the 'new' army and had a habit of leaving their rifles lying all over the place.

It was like coming from a violent inner city to a small town where no one locks the front door and feeling like everyone around you had a bit of a screw loose. But maybe I was the crazy one.

There was another rule that I didn't find a great deal of comfort in: "No weapons allowed inside the medical station". That one was more antiquated. But it superseded others, so I didn't push it.

I was new, and that's the way it had been, so without debate we left our rifles outside, on a gun rack and it stopped feeling awkward after a while.

Soldiers from other nations left their rifles outside when they popped in, and never questioned it, so it began to feel normal. Everyone obeyed that rule, so it felt reasonable.

I suppose I could have changed it. It was probably my job to change it, as the person in charge, but I wasn't deployed for the entire tour and felt like an interloper, so I left well enough alone, and we left our rifles outside.

But I grabbed mine from the rack as soon as I left the building every time, and found myself checking on it a lot.

The truth is, having strangers popping in with loaded weapons might have been disturbing. And it seemed to add a sense of neutrality, and nobility to the medical station. A place outside of war where we patched all-comers, bad guys included, despite how others occasionally questioned the ethics of that.

Insurgents weren't only shooting up American headquarters and planting bombs in roads they also had a clear mandate to target red crescents and crosses. The order to remove those from our sleeves and ambulances had been carried out long before I got there.

———

One day there was a scuffle near the weapon rack. One of the locals who was being paid to suck out our shitters with his old sewage truck had walked over and picked up one of our rifles off the rack.

He was small and gyrated when he talked. He was probably hopped up on opium from the look of his pinpoint pupils, but his intentions were pretty clear. He cocked the weapon and pointed it toward the kitchen. Fortunately, he was tackled pretty quickly by a passing group of artillerymen. The gun went off and a full thirty rounds levelled harmlessly into the dirt, but he was folded up like a lawn chair and hauled off.

I never saw him again.

But that was when I started keeping my Browning, loaded, in my leg holster, and inside the UMS with me, at all times.

And no one said a word about that.

Eventually, Amalah's uncle arrived from the village. Lucky had found him. He got the story from a local farmer. Her uncle had a grove of pomegranate trees and had been waiting for his brother's family to help with the harvest. He hadn't heard about their accident and had figured they were delayed.

Lucky introduced us at the main gate. He would plan funeral arrangements and take the girl. He seemed grateful she could help with his harvest.

It all seemed reasonable. Despite our growing fondness for Amalah, we agreed she should be with her own remaining family.

The medics gathered around and said their goodbyes in the morning. She hugged each of us, one by one. Lucky wasn't around when that group of men in their white pickup truck—there were so many of those white pick-up trucks around—came to take her away.

That goodbye was hard, and made harder still because we couldn't understand her in those final moments. It seemed clear she didn't want to leave which was sweet and understandable. After all, we had books and candies and she liked it when Joe brushed her hair. She was fond of us, and the television, and she had her nose in a lot of our books.

Her uncle eventually manhandled her into the bed of his pickup. She was kicking and screaming but he placed her in the arms of another man who held her close. She seemed to settle in his arms as they drove away. But the unhappy look on her face was hard to watch. She seemed to be blaming me. She stared right at me. Her golden, sparkling eyes, and wet lashes, shining with tears.

Another one of the most unpleasant moments of my time in Afghanistan. I needed time alone in my bunk after that and I can't say I didn't shed a few tears.

———

When insurgents were captured, there was paperwork to be done and a medical examination was required to confirm 'status upon capture' and 'fitness for cells'. I performed too many of those medical exams down at the main gate.

The bad guys were rarely, if ever, hurt. Most were perfectly fit with a few scrapes and bruises, but we needed that status documented to dot the 'i's' and cross the 't's'.

I had no idea about the machinations of their capture or, frankly, how the good guys decided who was bad and who was good. I assumed they caught people in the act of some badness: shucking roads to bury bombs, or shooting at us, or something. I'm embarrassed to say they all looked similar to me: thin, strong, bearded Pashtun men in loose fitting linens and loosely wrapped turbans draped over their shoulders.

But late one afternoon they brought in someone different. Different in two ways: one, he was fat. Not morbidly obese, simply more meat on his bones than most Afghani men. He had a firm pot belly and jowls, which were rare in Panjwai. I never before, nor since, saw an Afghani man as well fed as that portly bad guy. And, secondly, his clothes were different. They were similar in styling but more expensive. The fabric was thick with intricate gold thread-work. The vest he wore was colourful, supple, and beautiful.

Most insurgents wore what Lucky called *'perahan tunban'*—traditional Pashtun garb. But this man's clothes were different. I figured him for a kingpin of some kind. Possibly a religious leader. I wondered if he might be one of the *Mullah's* Lucky said were coordinating the local Taliban activities.

But I was only there to document his wounds. That was it. It wasn't my place to speculate. And I didn't really care, if I'm being honest. I was still feeling bummed about Amalah leaving in the back of that truck. I found myself going through the motions. My mood was low when I began his examination.

He was strong. His arms writhed in the zap strap cuffs behind his back and his muscles rippled. He was mumbling something I couldn't understand and he smelled like cloves. We were inside a tent just to our side of the main gate. It was lit with electric bulbs strung around aluminum poles because the windows were down. That made it stifling, but it had a purpose. We were his captors, and we needed him in the dark to his location. I needed to remove his blindfold. The bandana covering his eyes covered a few key elements of the physical examine. Eye colour. Extra-ocular movements. Pupil diameter and reactivity. These speak to a patient's nervous system function and to the presence of any toxidrome (opium and cholinergics have opposite affects, for example).

As I lifted the bandana, he stopped mumbling clenched his eyes to adjust for a moment to the low light then looked me up and down with a scowl. He stared with a burning intensity and didn't speak. I examined his eyes and face and took note of his cauliflower ears. Probably a boxer or wrestler in his past. Pupils equal and reactive to light. He was staring at my eyes the entire time. And I looked away feeling likc I couldn't finish fast enough.

I was listening to his heart when a commotion outside interrupted. When I think back, I can convince myself I saw him smirk under his beard as I turned to the door.

Three Afghan men were yelling outside the gate.

This was unusual. The chorus of anger sounded urgent. It distracted the guard at the door and we both made the fateful decision to pop out and see what the yelling was about.

One of the three men might have been Amalah's uncle from that morning, but that was confusing. I couldn't be sure, but, for a second, I thought it might have something to do with Amalah. There was a translator nearby wearing Canadian fatigues yelling at them through the gate, but the exchange seemed confused.

I watched our guards in the tower above train their weapons down on the three men and shout a clear warning which seemed to fall on deaf ears because the men kept yelling. This distracted the guards who didn't notice that beyond, coming down the road they were tasked with guarding, in the distance, a white Toyota pickup was moving quickly in our direction.

There were boys playing soccer in the street outside the gate who noticed and scrambled into the field. The pickup kicked up dust between the last buildings on the edge of town and careened toward the gate moving fast and gaining speed.

Then the three men stopped yelling and ran suddenly away. They beelined for a grape hut. I saw them tumble through an opening and disappear into darkness moments before the Toyota sped into the open, moving swiftly toward us.

Then the soldier manning the 25mm cannon on the LAV at the gate made a decision. I didn't hear a warning.

Maybe there wasn't one. Maybe the rules of engagement were clear. This did appear to be a clear threat.

He opened fire.

There were stories about unfortunate kids joy-riding trucks and coming too close to FOBs and being shot to death inadvertently. But this didn't seem like joyriding kids.

I was grateful for those bullets. The chunk, chunk, of that 25mm, and the sound of shearing metal, sounded like victory. Those massive rounds shattered glass and metal and the flesh of that driver. It was ferocious.

The truck lolled to its right and bounced off the road into a dry mud wall in the field coming to an abrupt stop some forty yards outside the gate.

I was staring at that dead driver, his body slumping over the wheel, when the truck exploded. Shrapnel flew in every direction past where we stood. We felt the pressure wave and thudding as some of it embedded into the HESCO. It seemed more violent than I might have expected from a fuel tank, and when the dust settled the hole in the ground where the truck had been made that clear; this was a suicide attack.

Pandemonium erupted. Everyone seemed out of place. There was running and hollering and soldiers streaming in from seemingly everywhere. Mostly ANA, but also Canadians.

I was thankful to be standing behind the HESCO.

Those poor boys playing in the street were not so lucky.

We had work to do at the UMS that day.

I turned back toward the tent to grab a med bag. Trying to slow myself. *The first rule of any code is to check your own pulse.*

As I stepped through the opening, two soldiers with AK-47 assault rifles stopped me. I had not seen them before. They were Afghan, dressed in ANA uniforms.

The 'kingpin' I'd been examining sauntered out from behind them with his face uncovered and his hands loose.

He smiled at me. Then stepped between the two men and placed his hand on my shoulder. I was stunned and struck by the power seemingly emanating from him. We stood there in the shadow of the flapping canvas tent, with the hollering commotion going on behind me for a moment, and I was dumbstruck.

Then he spun quickly and with a sudden sweep of his leg, which seemed far too fast than he had any business being, knocked me off my feet. Then struck the back of my head with his elbow as the dust came up to meet my face.

I was dazed for a moment as they exited the tent behind me. When I finally scrabbled to my feet and followed in their direction, I watched helplessly as they climbed into a nearby pickup. I yelled for guards, but they were all attending victims of the explosion.

The window of the truck came down and I saw the muzzle of an assault rifle poke out toward me, so I dove for cover. Thankfully, no shots rang out behind me, or I would not be here to tell this tail. They had me dead to rights. I tried to reach for my Browning, to remove it from the holster but the clasp stuck and it took a moment. By the time I had it drawn, the truck had rolled comfortably away. With my pistol in hand, I followed it down the road. They were circling the FOB toward the far exit and no one was paying any attention to their escape.

I ran toward the guard tower. But no one was there. Everyone was tending to the soldiers and boys in the field. Then I saw the injured and realized I'd been hearing "medic" from various areas of the scene for the last few moments.

There were not enough of us to attend to all those injured that day. My job was not to stop an ANA truck nonchalantly winding its way through the FOB, away from all the commotion, even if a bad guy was getting away. I grabbed the first Canadian I saw, a corporal who seemed a little stunned at the carnage. "The prisoner is getting away," I said, pointing.

He glanced back, then down at the injured children, "I don't give a fuck, sir," he said slowly. And we surveyed the scene together. One boy with a head wound, another with a compound fracture of his femur, bleeding a little too profusely for my liking. Villagers running around us. Parents of children screaming. I grabbed my med bag from the tent and dropped in.

That was another bad day at the UMS.

Chapter Twenty

Pink Mist

In prehospital medicine the first hour after trauma is sometimes called the 'golden hour'. It's important. Lives are saved in that hour if everything is done well. Wounds packed. Hemorrhages stopped. Airways managed. All that became rote out there. I'm not sure there's anything particularly golden about that hour, but it certainly takes your mind off everything else for a while. We got through it quickly and saved some lives.

But I found out much later that no one had stopped that prisoner from escaping. They didn't even mount much of a chase.

I forgot about him pretty quickly after that. Not my circus. Not my monkeys.

We cleaned up after the events of the day and settled in for another quiet afternoon.

And it did get quiet. Eerily so. For a few days.

We settled into our daily routine.

I was watching Sergeant Collins conduct the daily water sample testing when a young Afghan man walked in with a belt tied around his arm. His entire right arm, distal to the tourniquet was black, ischemic, and dead. He was holding it up like a trophy.

It was something my former self would have certainly been shocked by, but I was past that by then. For a moment I wasn't even sure what I was seeing. I thought my senses were deceiving me, but that's exactly what it was. He had been bitten by a viper about a week prior, and had tied off the arm to prevent the spread of venom.

I was completely at a loss what to do.

The bite, I might have known what to do about, we had anti-venom. But self-inflicted limb ischemia was not something they taught much about in medical school. In fact, I can't imagine something like that ever happening in Canada.

I knew a little about 're-perfusion injury' and had a sense he probably needed amputation at this point, but I wasn't about to do that out there. I'd done enough crazy minor surgeries, many for the first time, but this one needed an operating room.

His arm was not coming back from that. I explained as much, through Lucky, and put him on a caravan heading north and he was smiling as he left on his way to the hospital in Kabul. Something about that young man reminded me of the moment at the gate, with the 'kingpin' who got away. They both seemed to revel in their own *intestinal fortitude*. It was astounding.

Alone in the desert that man had taken a band, wrapped it around his arm, willingly cut off his own blood supply, suffered unimaginable pain, watched his arm die over the coming hours and days, and never once removed the tourniquet. I cannot imagine ever doing that. I cannot imagine anyone ever doing that, and I met the man. It's unfathomable. Sometimes I think some of these things were made up in a dream. And the worst part, he probably might have been better off to suffer the venom. It's impossible to say. The entire thing was horrifying and tragic.

Not only the blackened, prosthetic-seeming tentacle he turned stiffly about to show me on all sides, but the look on his face as he held it up. I was used to suppressing shock and awe, prided myself on 'equanimity', but his pride in what he had done, and the horror and pain of what he suffered, was incongruous.

That stays with me.

That man would never use that arm again, and he was proud of what he'd done. It was strangely awe-inspiring and frightening at the same time.

I felt—small.

He was not a large man, but the force of his will was completely overwhelming. The men around him, glorifying his accomplishment, stared at me, keen to see how I might react to the show. All of them proud and reverent.

Despite my having nothing to do for him except send him North, they all thanked me, through Lucky's translation, before leaving—victorious—like champions of the world cup carrying a blackened trophy.

I was learning about the insurgency then, but didn't know it. In the same way Canada breeds camaraderie and tolerance with our heavy snow, Afghan men seem born to a seriousness of character, and an iron will, under their desert sun. They bear suffering in ways we, raised in sheltered comforts, cannot understand. They revere and subordinate themselves to suffering in ways that seem impossible. They don't all wear dead arms like badges of honour, but they seem to share an unfathomably unbreakable and unquestionable will.

I felt it in the kingpin that day, I saw it in that young man with the dead arm, and I saw it in the eyes of his comrades. I was beginning to see it all around me after that.

Tourniquets were everywhere out there. It was a new development in warfare that every soldier should carry one. We became quite proficient at putting them on, even if the taking off was left for surgeons higher up the med-evac chain.

Our medics saved a lot of lives with tourniquets.

There was one time that even a third tourniquet was not enough. That guy was an insurgent, trying to kill us, but we used three tourniquets on him to try to save him.

We had a balloon floating on a wire above the centre of the FOB with a high-definition camera keeping an eye on the village and surrounding roads. The insurgents clearly knew about it, because they shot at it every day. Sometimes the ricochets caught our guys in the butt or ankle, but mostly it was a bit of ineffectual whizzing. We could track the bullets though, and when the location of the firing positions were discovered an air strike was called. And it was something to behold.

I saw my first one the next day.

I was walking by the camera control centre in the headquarters building, on my way to the exchange library, when one of the infanteers called me in, "Hey Doc, check this out."

"What's up?" I asked as he ushered me in. Three infanteers were gathered around an array of screens. I'd been there before, and after the incident at the gate had heard they were keeping a close eye on that grape hut those three dudes had disappeared into. I could see the hut on one of the corner screens, one of the cameras permanently fixed on it, but on the middle screen they were watching a shepherd was doing unspeakable things with a goat in a field.

One by one he was taking his goats and pulling them backwards towards his crotch. Repetitively. And his pants were clearly down around his ankles. It was quite obvious what he was doing.

So that was burned on my retinas for all time.

I think they wanted to see the doc's reaction. They were laughing hysterically, and I was shocked, but again didn't show it.

I laughed along with them. Then some movement in the corner screen caught my eye. They were still watching the dude with his goats, but when I took a closer look back at that corner screen. I saw it again.

"Did you see that?"

The lead observer spun his chair and focused on the screen where I was pointing. And it happened again. A muzzle flash from the opening in the wall of that grape hut.

Someone was shooting at the FOB.

He scrambled to record and picked up comms equipment.

It got serious from there—all business. A form was filled in grease pencil—coordinates for an airstrike were relayed.

That bad guy was about to have a really bad day.

"You should come watch with us," one of them said as they rushed out. So naturally I followed them up the hill to their perch overlooking the gate. We had a clean view of that hut and it wasn't long before the shadow of an American A10 warthog arced out of the sky towards it.

It was silent and majestic and blocked out a small patch of stars as it glided. One of them handed me some binoculars, "I've seen this. You watch," he said.

A silent white trail cut across the darkening sky like an alien ship, impossibly strange and beautiful. It looked powerful, slicing the air like a hot knife through butter, too fast for the quiet. It seemed to warp the laws of physics. And we had a game seven, centre ice, on the glass kind of view, as it swooped toward its target.

Then from the silence a low-pitched explosion, focussed on one single moment in space and time, erupted over us, and a cacophony of lead; one tonne of munitions in less than a second. It sounded like the sky was barfing. Like nothing I'd ever heard before or since. And it obliterated that hut. Those muzzle flashes were cancelled. Done.

And the bringer of death was swooping away before a hole had yet to appear in the desert beneath.

It was frightening.

As quickly as it arrived it faded from the distant sky and it was immediately hard to imagine it had ever been there.

We stared in stunned silence. Not cheering. Not gasping. Simply drawn to the sense of absolute power.

Then a hole appeared and the surrounding sand was thick with red, and the air around was shining in the starlight filled with settling pink mist.

Some of these destructive events were used to support our counter-insurgency operations. I learned about that, and watched us struggle again with winning hearts and minds that day. The destruction we perpetrated, became an avenue for us to show support for the locals by paying locals for their flattened huts—with American cash.

The 'battle damage assessment' team stood-up within moments. Higgins went out with that team. They exited within an hour carrying a pile of US dollars, and body bags.

The cash said, we are here to help, but the implication seemed to me to be:

Those bullets fired from that hut we destroyed, could not possibly have been condoned by the owners of the destroyed hut. And please ignore this mess of flesh and blood that is scattered all over your yard. Here, have some cash. We are hoping it might help rebuild your precious hut. We are so very sorry the bad guys chose this place to shoot at us. It's all so very unfortunate. We know you had nothing to do with this... and we're here to help... because we care.

I clearly did not have the full picture.

It turns out there was more than one insurgent killed that day. Higgins told me later it was hard to tell how many. Wet, blood-soaked sand and bile covered the entire area and body parts were scattered everywhere.

But one of them was alive. He must have been on the edge of the blast zone. Higgins said he was staring and gasping for air, relatively intact, when he got there. But he was exsanguinating quickly from the burnt edges of a high leg amputation.

Higgins dropped in, applied a tourniquet, injected morphine, then placed another. He saved that boy's life, despite the voice in the back of his head screaming, "Leave him. He's already dead."

But he wasn't dead. Fluids were hung and they hauled him back to me at the medical station. I applied a third clean tourniquet, which was also ineffectual. It slowed the bleeding but the flesh still oozed blood over the stretcher and floor, so I explored the wound while that boy watched me, stoically, through an opioid-induced haze, and when I finally found the edge of his femoral artery, which had retracted deep into the meat of his pelvis, I clamped it off with a hemostat, and watched the bleeding finally slow.

I hoped it wasn't too late. I repacked the wound with a quick-clotting Israeli dressing and tied it hard around the bone that was left. I'd be damned if that bandage was coming loose. We got him on a bird within ten minutes.

We learned later, from the guard we'd sent with him, that the medic in the Blackhawk *needed* to change that bandage in flight, so that boy bled out on his way North.

It was hard not to cry again that day, for the life of a boy who, by virtue of circumstance alone, was earlier trying to kill me. Higgins and Lucky seemed the only humans on earth who saw the sadness at the heart of that. I was proud of the work Higgins did, and later wrote him up for a commendation. I should reach out to him and see if he ever got that someday.

The next day was another quiet one, so I decided to accompany Collins on his health and safety tour of the FOB. We watched our troops teach Afghan soldiers how to be an Army Defence force that day. The lessons were straight from our own basic training; how to use a map and compass; how to move together under fire; how to avoid IEDs; that sort of thing.

But their medics never seemed involved in those lessons. They seemed excluded for some reason. And I thought I might be able to help them learn a few medical things.

There were two Afghan boys, who seemed to be secret lovers the way they moved with one another, staying in a separate building from the rest. They called themselves the 'medics' and their quarters their *clinic*.

Lucky told me the platoon had made them their de facto medics because the others considered them the most effeminate. "That is their way," he said, although their 'doctor' was a gruff, masculine, denturist from Kabul. None of them had any formal medical training.

I did not presume to understand any of it.

They purchased medical supplies and pharmaceuticals at a nearby market and handed them out like candy. No prescriptions required. Antibiotics like Vancomycin and Gentamycin were sitting next to old vials of thalidomide or other chemicals we no longer use. None of them knew what any of it was for. But they handed them out. Thankfully it was mostly expired. I recommended they throw it out, and threw some of it out myself, but somehow, they would always have more by the following week.

It was the strangest clinic. A mud hut with tight knit rugs and blankets strewn about. A short table with a tea set and a small burner in the corner. And two medics lazing around on the floor together.

One day I brought a clipboard and made an effort at 'medicine 101' with Lucky translating. I showed them the basics of history-taking, and the physical exam, a few 'clinical pearls', and an approach to 'clinical reasoning'. But they spent most of the time laughing at inappropriate moments, and didn't seem to retain anything when I quizzed them. I gave up in futility within days.

But I tried to help in other ways. Troops would arrive in the morning, step into the middle of the room, say something in Farsi or Pashtun, chat back and forth with the medics, and leave with some vial of random medicine, or, more often, a handful of Werther's Original caramels. That was the extent of the medical work. Lucky wasn't hopeful I could change it. But I tried to pick out the more urgent clinical concerns and do my best to provide actual, evidence-based care.

On days I was helping, word got around quickly, and ANA soldiers would line up around the corner. Their denturist doctor tagged along those days as well. He would chat with Lucky between cases and try to discern what I was doing. They would laugh together, and I usually missed the humour, but laughed along with them. Fortunately, most of the complaints were not urgent. Some wanted to show me old scars, a few had questions about moles. Most wanted Werther's Originals.

Those days were surreal. Occasionally there was actual pathology: a sore throat, pus, swollen joints or skin infections, but for the most part the work felt completely futile. What it did afford was a chance to interact with Afghan soldiers. There was at least an entire company living on the FOB with us, and I was glad to smile with them, and laugh with them. I hoped they saw Canadians as kind, respectful, and useful.

The most memorable Interaction was a boy from Kabul who showed up asking for a 'sensitive' exam. I could tell he was sick by his waxy and gaunt appearance. He'd been keeping a terrible secret and hoped the "foreign doctor" could help. Three friends accompanied him.

Lucky relayed his story. He admitted to having jumped from a truck, some six months prior, and caught his testicle on the edge. He said it was not cut or scratched at the time, and didn't bleed, but it hurt a great deal. He figured it was that injury that was not healing.

But it wasn't that at all.

A lot of people do that, even in Canada where access to first world medical care is universal, they fool themselves. They delay and defer and tell themselves it's not there, or it's nothing, or it's "just taking a long time to heal".

Don't do that. Promise me you won't do that. Promise me if you're ever confused or disturbed or unsure about something changing in or on your body you will try not to fool yourself, and get it checked. This guy didn't have that option. He was born in the wrong corner of the world.

He stripped naked with none of the constrained modesty you see back home. His friends didn't react but you could tell they were watching me for my reaction. It was immediately obvious to me that he had an advanced form of testicular cancer. There was nothing else on the differential. What was once his right testicle was now a mass of fungating tumour that leaked pus and semen onto his scrotal surface. He had nodes of cancer stuck to his groin and belly and more in his axilla and even as far up as the supraclavicular spaces of his neck.

It was everywhere. His cancer was impressively advanced. Like nothing I'd ever seen. That he even had the strength to walk through the door was unbelievable. On further history it was clear his personality had changed and he was having headaches. He likely had metastatic disease to his brain. He didn't need a biopsy. He was too late for orchiectomy ('surgical removal of his testicle'). He was already dead. The universe just hadn't let him know yet.

I sent him North as well.

Poor kid. He had his reasons for hiding inside his story for six months, or a year, or maybe longer. But he knew deep down something was terribly wrong. They always know.

Lucky translated the word for him and he wasn't shocked. He was more resigned than shocked. It was a confirmation of his deepest fear, not a revelation.

He thanked me before leaving with his friends.

Chapter Twenty-One
FOB Dogs and Monkeys

Later that week Higgins shook me awake in the middle of the night, "Doc, you gotta come see this." I didn't sleep well most nights anyway, but this night a Navy SEAL had sidled into the UMS with a wound that needed my attention.

I didn't recognize him. He was a transient, passing through, as they did. One of the FOB dogs had found him in the night and ripped a chunk of flesh from his right hamstring. Higgins watched as I cleaned it up and patched it together as best I could (always keen to help, Higgins got some suturing practice that night.)

The SEAL spoke of his home in Kentucky as we sewed, but he didn't say much about what he was doing in Panjwai, and the very minute we finished he scurried off. I didn't see him leave. I was drawing up rabies prophylaxis in the back and hadn't had a chance to talk to him about that, or tetanus, and I came out to find an empty room. That man was on a mission to get somewhere quickly.

Higgins came back from chasing him, a little breathless, and said there was nothing he could do to stop him. We hadn't even noted his name or unit in the book. I was worried it was going to be hard to find him. He disappeared, like Clark had done at the range.

Higgins jotted down some info from their conversation, but that was all we had to go on. They had been chatting about the trident he wore on his uniform. Higgins was always keen to learn about SEALs. We didn't see many of them around. Word was sent back through the chain of command that, whoever he was, and wherever he went, he needed rabies immune globulin as soon as possible. All I could do was hope he would be okay, and document.

The dog, however, was not okay.

The next day people were talking about the dog with the bloody face. He was usually a docile, friendly dog, but he had changed. His routine was to lie around the barracks keeping fed and watered by the engineers, occasionally hopping the HESCO after some critter in the field, but generally hanging out with the hands that fed him. He was a good dog. A strong mid-sized runner. Maybe a cross between a Dane and a Mastiff. But when he attacked that soldier in the night it spooked everyone. He had definitely changed.

He was acting more aggressive and when he started foaming at the mouth, we didn't have a choice. Rabies is no joke.

If you don't know, rabies is universally fatal. If you don't get the immune globulin protection, or have the vaccine prior, you're basically dead if you catch it. It goes straight to your brain. You start prickling and itching and then the fever and headache starts, then hallucinations, and it's not a good death.

Unfortunately, despite all the signs, the only way to know for certain it is Rabies, is to kill the damn dog and search and culture the brain.

I did not want to do that.

But who else was there to do it?

One of the senior warrant officers from the infantry company offered to shoot the thing in the head, as it ran and played, thinking that might be most humane, and I was tempted to allow that, but it wouldn't help; we needed the brain.

My original plan, before the foaming and aggression, was to keep the thing in a cage under close supervision for ten days. If it didn't die or go obviously berserk, we might be in the clear. But it had already started acting strange. Brad and I discussed it the next morning.

"The dog has to go, Jack. It's the only way. There are obvious signs already. We need to culture the brain. Send me the head, on ice, today."

He always got straight to the point, and those were all good ones. I winced at the thought of it, but knew I had no choice. The SEALs don't mess around. They needed to weigh the balance of risks for their guy. From my perspective he needed the treatment anyway, but that's not how that went. Not for me to question. I got my orders and carried them out.

That was not my best day. We had sedatives to knock it out and a vial of volatile compound that sedates when inhaled. My plan was to wrap the animal tightly in a blanket and hold the soaked cloth over its snout, then, once it was docile, I would inject the drugs through a large vein near the groin. An American veterinarian at the airfield had shown me that before I left for the FOB. Intravenous Versed and Fentanyl for sedation, then intra-cardiac Pentobarbital through the chest wall directly into the heart, as the final act.

Dogs have surprisingly high metabolisms. I must have used four times the dose of drugs that would floor a human. Collins and Higgins got together and wrestled it into a blanket. Collins lay on top holding firm. Higgins and I wrapped the snout with a belt to keep it from biting. That was touchy. He was strong, and life does not go softly.

It's not easy to kill a thing.

That dog fought hard, sensing what was coming and I wondered if death was in the room. Or maybe possessing me. We were sweating and bumping and we knocked over a stretcher and a chair while I had to reload my syringe three times. Higgins tried to hold it tight but the thing got free more than once. Thankfully, we strategically avoided being scratched, or bit and finally got enough drug on board.

Finally, it began to wobble, then slump onto the blanket, and close its eyes.

I'd pushed syringes into chest cavities before. The usual approach is subxiphoid, below the ribs, angling up toward the apex of the heart. There is a life-threatening condition called cardiac tamponade, where the heart is being compressed by fluid around filling its surrounding sac, being strangled by the fluid. Every doctor knows how to treat that: Pericardiocentesis— placing a needle into the chest cavity and drawing the fluid *out*. Inserting a subxiphoid needle is not something you usually do, and never in the act of killing a thing. That was new.

That's how you kill a dog.

In case you want to know.

I did my duty that day. It had to be done. But it was hard, I like dogs, so there was no way I was severing the head. I contemplated it, briefly, because that's what Brad had said, and that was all they needed to test for rabies. But in the end, I couldn't do it. Instead, I sent the entire carcass back to Brad in a barracks box full of ice and dog.

I learned later they found the SEAL with the leg wound and had him treated. Probably before the rabies test came back. They probably didn't even need that dog's head. But I had killed it. I hoped it was a better death than dying of the disease, and told myself it was probably for the greater good. But the things I did for Queen and Country were getting harder to reconcile.

One can only bear so much.

I was starting to feel myself falling through the looking glass.

And that was only the beginning.

———

A mortar landed precisely on top of the headquarters building the next day. Right above the little room with screens where we'd watched that shepherd. Some of the shrapnel hit the gym where I was working out.

I'm not sure if it was a dud or if that air conditioner absorbed most of the blast, but you'd think a direct hit on the top of a schoolhouse would have gone through the roof and killed the command team below, but it didn't.

It was a perfect shot though, if that's where they were aiming.

Maybe they were getting better?

I had stepped off the treadmill heading for the shower moments before the shrapnel punched perfect circles through the double plywood wall, right above a low bar that I used for hooking my feet for sit ups. Metal tore clean through the blue mat and embedded in the sand below. My legs and chest would have been there if it were a half hour earlier.

I scrambled around looking for casualties but we got lucky that day. No one was hurt.

Not physically anyway.

Later, when I went back to replace the mat and do more sit ups, I could peer straight through clean holes that drew a perfect sight line through two sheets of plywood up to the shattered remains of the air conditioner on the roof next door. The very unit that supplied the cool air to our barracks.

It wouldn't be replaced for weeks.

———

We were getting ornery from the insidious, persistent, unavoidable heat when I learned about the monkey. One of the engineers had purchased it at the market thinking it might be fun to have around. This *after* the dog. I wondered if I was the only one who had ever seen the movie 'Outbreak'. Predictably it started biting soldiers.

For a while that cute little thing provided entertainment. But I never got to meet it that way. By the time it came to my attention it was an angry ball of hate. Acting erratic. There could be only one conclusion—Rabies.

"Shit," I thought, and said out loud.

And its owner capitulated.

Killing a dog was one thing.

Killing a tiny hominid is an entirely different experience. It's easier in some ways but much, much harder in others.

But we had experience. I wrapped the little thing in a blanket, held a cloth over it's cute little face, and injected sedative into his groin veins.

I probably should have covered his eyes.

He looked vulnerable, and sad, which I suppose he was. Mercifully his lids fell heavy within moments; much faster than the dog. A few more injections, and some parasternal Pentobarb later, and it too shuffled off this mortal coil.

By the very hands writing these words.

I think that broke me.

Later, when Brad sent pictures of the poor thing frozen and propped in the fridge with a cigar dangling from its mouth. I laughed, but I wasn't happy in the laughing.

Eid al-Fitr happened sometime later. September 10 that year. On a Friday. By that time, I had settled in and knew most of the players. When the ANA commander invited me to the celebration, I was grateful and felt seen. They sat me next to the denturist at the head table and I asked if they could make room for Lucky to translate, and they obliged.

"What were you discussing just now? Keep me up to date," I said as we sat down. They had been having a conversation and leaving me out.

"It was nothing. You would not be interested," he said.

"Try me?"

"We were talking about local politics. He is familiar with the Mullah here, and the tribal chief. He is from Kabul and heard the President is planning a visit this way. He wondered if I knew the chief he would be visiting. That is all."

"Do you?"

"Yes. I was speaking to him in the village last week."

"That's interesting."

"The local Mullah will be joining President Karzai's Peace Council... he knows Amalah's uncle."

"Oh, yeah? Is that how you met him?"

"No, no, everyone knows the Mullah. He is a popular community leader."

A man came around with a large pot and dropped a hunk of sheep spine on my plate. There was a bit of pomp and circumstance around that, and Lucky said they had saved a special piece for me. Apparently, that's a delicacy, which is nice, but it had some wool fragments on it.

I picked at it feeling queasy and thankful for Collin's advice to take pre-emptive Pepto-Bismol and ciprofloxacin before eating any local food. I don't know if that saved me from a terrible gastro, but the thought was there, and I never did get sick. So that was good.

We ate lamb and vegetables with naan. The naan was especially delicious, warm and fresh, despite my recollection of them stomping it to shape on the ground with their feet. The young soldier who brought it around was handsome and friendly.

Lucky translated for me, and I learned about the denturist's family in Kabul, and their hopes for a free and secure Afghanistan.

All in all, it was a pleasant celebration. By the end I had a sense they were proud of their progress as an Army, and thankful for our help.

Leaving that evening, walking back across the FOB with the moon high and bright, Lucky seemed happy.

"Thank you for inviting me," he said.

"I wouldn't have gone without you. Imagine how little I would have understood? You're a good friend, Luck. I'm glad when you're around."

"That is kind. Do you miss the girl?" he asked.

"A little, yes."

"She liked you very much. I could tell you were growing close."

"I hope she is okay," I said.

"Me too. I think she is. I saw her uncle near the village square yesterday. He seemed quite joyous."

"Well that's a start," I said, but wondered about the incident at the gate. "Was he not involved with that escaped prisoner last week?"

"I'm not sure what you mean?"

"I thought he was one of the men who helped that insurgent escape last week."

"I don't think so. He seems quite devout, but I don't think he's involved. At least I have seen no evidence."

"Okay, that's reassuring." I must have had Amalah on the brain that day. Maybe it wasn't him.

Chapter Twenty-Two

The Engineer

When I told Grace this next part, she said I was *sliming* her and asked me to stop. You may not want to hear it but the truth about war is bad things happen, and this was another one of those bad things. Not as bad as Amalah's baby brother but more accessible to me in all the wrong ways.

Collins and I and the Afghan soldiers in the back of that pickup were the only ones who saw this. Maybe the details are not important, but this is the stuff that comes back in the night, in bed, watching Netflix, reading books, or in church. It haunts me. I'm not sure it will ever go away.

It was a few days after the Eid celebration. I heard the explosion from inside the medical station. It was close and shook the walls and dust fell from the ceiling again. It was probably right outside the HESCO behind. At first, I thought it was another mortar. But it wasn't.

The Afghans had found an IED on the road. The kid who had brought my hunk of spine, careened that truck up the ridge toward us. I recognized others in the back from their laughing and cajoling at the celebration.

They were not laughing now.

I didn't recognize their dead friend. He might have been the one who served the naan but I couldn't be sure. There was not enough of him left to be sure.

They had picked him up and threw his parts in the back of that truck and when it careened up that hill, tilting from the speed, I don't know how they stayed in the back, sitting on the sides as they were, staring down at their dead friend.

The engine whirred as they backed in and the gravel crunched as they slid to a halt. The medics came out to see about the commotion but Collins and I stopped them. By the way those soldiers were staring, blank-faced, eyes to the floor, and by the grey matter and blood splattered on their faces, you knew. This was something to avoid seeing if you could. Not everyone needed to see what was in the bed of that truck.

He must have fancied himself a bomb-defusing engineer. They all must have stood around, probably in a perfect damn semi-circle, watching him brush away sand to expose the mechanism. He probably made some joke like "my countryman put this here, dopey doh, so I'm gonna defuse it."

They should have called our guys. Oh God, I wish they'd called our guys. That was their protocol. Our guys have turtle shell armour, and know-how. For God's sake I heard them teach that so many times: "Call us if you see anything suspicious on the road."

They knew that. *What the hell is the point of teaching them if they don't have any damn interest in learning.* He was probably gently brushing away sand. Probably saw the pressure plate. Probably crouched on his knees with his friends leaning in.

One of his forearms was missing so that must have been in front of his face when it tripped. I don't know how else to say this: his head was gone. The entire thing. Just gone.

Well, parts of it came back—embedded in his friends. Yes, I pulled pieces of his head from his buddies' wounds. That's the part you probably don't need to hear. That's the part Grace says I should keep to myself. I pulled a bone from his friend's eye that was probably part of the back of his head.

For a minute I thought it might be zygomatic arch from the protruding prominence but later I figured it was occiput. You could tell by looking closely at the ridges and contours and thickness.

Sergeant Collins and I nodded to one another. He held Joe and the others back and I approached alone and saw. There were four others with injuries but the part that really got me was the way they wanted me to fix him.

They thought I could help him.

I could see his trachea. White rings against the redness of the meat of the strap muscles of what used to be his neck. I actually had a morbid thought about how easy it would be to intubate.

That was the actual thought that went through my head.

What use is a thought like that?

What use was any of it? And they thought I could somehow piece him together so he could pop up and go defuse another bomb, or maybe distribute more naan.

That was not going to happen.

I shook my head and the boys in the truck seemed dejected by the shaking.

"Grab a body bag," I called back to Collins, and he came up beside me. When he looked into the bed he got stuck staring, and I put my hand on his shoulder and yelled back to Higgins, who went inside. Collins helped the other injured soldiers out of the truck and directed them into our trauma bays.

I got the driver and another to help me put the remains of their friend into a mortuary bag.

There's so much more I could say about that day. The sights and smells and sounds are immediately accessible. Like I never left. But it also seems too personal. I don't know his name. I will never know anything about that boy or his family. And I feel terrible about that. It seems wrong.

I'm sorry if you feel injured by reading this. I don't mean to hurt anyone. But I promised myself I would tell the truth about war and write "hard and clear about what hurts," to get it out.

So there it is. Like those D-Day heroes in the park always said, the truth about war is it's terrible. Don't let anyone ever tell you it's a good thing to go to war. No matter how important or necessary or justified it seems— it's terrible.

Chapter Twenty-Three

Keyser Söze and Alfred Tennyson

The next morning the air conditioning had finally been repaired and the medics were ecstatic. They gathered in the common room and turned on a flick: *The Usual Suspects.*

I'd seen it, so I got up and wandered about. I was pacing and thinking about Amalah again. I was hoping she was okay, trying to reconcile how that man who dove into that grape hut looked so much like her uncle. But Lucky had seen him since and didn't peg him for one of the bad guys. But something didn't sit well. I was hoping she was going to be okay.

Higgins was irritating Collins by repeating something over and over: "Keyser Söze, Keyser Söze." In a mocking tone and Collins was getting pissed off, "Would you shut that up. Just shut up," he said. "We're trying to watch the movie."

But Higgins couldn't help himself. They pressed pause and started wrestling on the couch and I stepped outside.

Keyser Söze is the antagonist in that film. I'd seen the movie long before. I didn't want to give away the surprise ending, but something made me stop and repeat the name. "Keyser Söze," something about that name triggered me.

And it made me think of Amalah.

What did Keyser Söze and Amalah have to do with one another?

Outside the sunshine hurt. I wandered to the kitchen for scrambled eggs. I had dust on my face, hands, and in my mouth, so I stopped at the ablution area to wash and rinse but that name kept ringing in my ears.

Keyser. Keyser.

I walked inside toward the meal line—then stopped suddenly in my tracks.

"Kayser-Fleischer Rings," I whispered.

Something obscure from medical school came flooding back.

Golden eyes. Amalah has golden eyes. Golden rings around the edges of the iris. Kayser-Fleischer rings... Copper deposits!?

"She might have Wilson's disease," I said out loud to no one.

The kitchen staff behind the sneeze guard slapped some bacon and scrambled eggs on my plate. I walked on trying to remember facts about Wilson's disease.

A copper handling disorder. Genetic. Leads to madness and early death from liver disease. One of those 'zebras' they talk about in med school. *When you hear hoof beats out your window, think horses, but sometimes it might be a zebra...*

"Does Amalah have Wilson's disease?" I sat alone and devoured my breakfast. Her stunning golden eyes were real, weren't they? All of that happened?

Amalah was real. Her parents. Her brother. Her eyes.

If she has Wilson's she will go psychotic and die an early death.

My heart beat a little faster.

Even if she makes it through this God forsaken war, she could die of something inborn and treatable. At that moment I was the only person on the planet who knew that. The only one having those types of thoughts about that little girl.

I felt an overwhelming urgency to do something about it.

To do otherwise was unbearable. How unfair would that be. Like the boy with testicular cancer. If he'd known sooner, he would have had a chance to survive. Wilson's is not inevitable. It is treatable. Psychosis and death could be prevented.

Amalah could be treated.

I stretched my mind. Penicillamine? Or something like that? Some oral copper binding agent. If she has it, and I was right, she could know early enough. I dropped my utensils and Melmac plate into the bin of sudsy water and rushed back to the UMS.

Joe was in the back sweeping. From the shelf above the comms, I lugged down a tattered copy of *Harrison's Principles of Internal Medicine, 15th edition.* I placed it on the desk with a thud and flipped to the back. Wilson's disease was chapter 384, page 2274. It's a large book, with gossamer pages, thankfully all there.

I read. *Yes.* "A genetic condition of impaired copper excretion... toxic accumulation... in the eyes and liver and brain... leads to mania and psychosis and early death... usually in one's late thirties or early fourties if not treated... every ethnic and geographic population at risk... ~1 in 30,000 affected... Treatable with Penicillamine—an inexpensive oral medication that binds copper preventing overload. Normal life expectancy with treatment...

"If she has it. She needs those pills," I said out loud.

"What was that?" Asked Joe from the back?

"NOT A DEATH SENTENCE," I yelled.

"Sorry?"

I read aloud, "The diagnosis is made using serum ceruloplasmin and copper levels... Hey, Joe. Do we have i-STAT cartridges that test for ceruloplasmin and copper levels?"

"Let me check." She rested her broom and grabbed the case marked i-STAT.

An i-STAT is a portable blood analyzer that we regularly used out there. It provides results in minutes. We had a rack of single use cartridges. Most ran standard common tests like basic chemistries, electrolytes, coag profiles, complete blood counts. But a few cartridges had biosensors for a variety of more obscure tests like blood gases, less common chemistries, cardiac markers, and endocrine studies—the zebras.

We had a few of those cartridges for just in case. And this seemed to me to be a really good just in case. If I was right.

"Yes," she said. "This one has copper studies on it. We've got, let's see, four of those. Why?"

"Awesome. All we need is her blood." I smiled so wide it hurt, feeling my purpose for being there wrapped up in those thoughts and that moment.

"What are you talking about boss? ...Is this about Amalah?"

"Yes! I think she might have Wilson's disease. Look here. Don't her eyes look like that?" There were pictures.

"Yes. They do," she said.

"Have you ever read A Prayer for Owen Meany?" I asked.

Joe looked at me sideways. Shook her head. And grabbed the mop.

"It's the story of a strange boy who believes God has a plan for him? And in the end, he might be right?... It's just... This feels like the reason I'm here."

I was certain that was true. Helping Amalah was an important thing. The only thing. I had to help that girl. I picked up the sat phone and dialled headquarters.

He picked up on the first ring. "Brad, it's Jack." I used his first name.

"Jack, how are ya? Your sector is being hit pretty hard. How are you holding up?"

"It's been rough," I said, "Listen, I called for a favour."

"Shoot. How can I help?"

"Remember that girl who was staying with us for those few days a while back?"

"Sure do. You did a great job finding her family."

"Yes. Well, that's the thing, boss. I'm worried about her. I just had a thought about her eyes. She might be sick, and need treatment."

"What do you mean?"

"Remember Kayser-Fleisher rings from med school?"

"Of course. Irises, copper thing, right? ...Wilson's disease? You think she might have Wilson's?"

"I'm not sure. It needs to be confirmed. But she has striking golden eyes. It's possible and I want to rule it out. I need your support for finding her and running a ceruloplasmin and copper level on her blood. We have what we need for the i-STAT here."

"I'm sure you do, Jack. You're a good man," he said after a moment's pause. "That's a very noble sentiment." He paused again and I could sense what was coming. "But you know we can't do that," he said.

"It's just one test. It could save her life," I said.

"Think about that. To what end? First of all, you don't know where she is. Second, if she had Wilson's disease she's dead anyway. I know that's harsh, but she would need specialist treatment that doesn't exist out here, and blood monitoring, and medications. This place is not conducive to a long life for those with chronic disease."

"She deserves a chance."

"It's just a hunch. You're probably wrong. Most patients with enough copper that you can see it in their eyes have already got it in their liver and brain, causing symptoms. Does she have jaundice? Was she ever psychotic?”

“No. But she could be one of the few. Harrison’s says quite clearly some kids get eye symptoms early. We could treat her and save her life. She would only need some cheap pills, which we could suppl—”

“But it’s probably not Wilson’s, Jack. She’s probably got pretty eyes. Stop stressing yourself. Stop worrying about some kid who is nowhere to be found and destined for a brief and tragic life anyway.”

“But—”

“Jack. Stop. I’m glad you called. And it is horrible to contemplate not helping, I know. But an Afghan girl out here doesn’t stand a chance. Her destiny was set long before she met you. Don’t concern yourself. Besides, there are a few ops planned for Panjwai this week, and we need you rested and ready. I need you to rest. Hopefully I’m wrong, but I suspect you’ll be getting even busier very soon. Don’t waste your time thinking about that girl. Whatever will be will be. Leave it alone.”

“But, Brad—”

“—That’s an order, Jack.”

I had been through too much. I flopped the book closed, leaned back in my chair, and pinched the bridge of my nose.

“...Okay boss,” I said.

“Listen, there’s a Commander’s Tour planned for next week. I’ll be heading your way to show the flag. Can’t wait to see what it's like out there. Looking forward to catching up."

"Okay. Sounds good." I set the phone down and slumped into that creaky chair.

"He said no?" Joe asked, placing the text book back on the shelf.

"Yes. He told me to put her out of my mind."

"We can't run a test? The i-STAT's right here," she said.

"I know. And that poor girl deserves to know. That's a terrible disease without treatment. It will end her."

"That feels wrong. But I suppose ours is not to reason why..."

Tennyson. Impressive.

"...Ours is but to do and die," I finished.

Chapter Twenty-Four
Lawful Commands

In a dream that night the monsters came.

All the horrors I'd seen. Killing the dog and monkey. The ANA *engineer*. Amalah. Mostly Amalah. Her golden eyes flashing past, closing in. All of it compressing. Her hand slipping away and the man holding her in that truck.

I jolted awake. Sweating in the dark and quiet. The dreams lingered.

All our resources for winning hearts and minds and what was it for? It meant nothing if we couldn't help one small girl live a normal life. Wasn't that the point of this entire thing? Our Army was going to let her die a miserable death in this desert. Without hope. *Why were we even here if not to protect someone as innocent as Amalah?*

Something shifted inside me.

Maybe it was the dark of night or the dream or my weariness but something snapped. I didn't care about the consequences. The consequences of doing nothing for Amalah seemed worse. Impossibly heavy. They weighed me down. I decided I was going to do something.

But the Army had said no. Major Ridgeway was clear on that. What could I do? I lay awake vibrating with frustration thinking about what to do. Time passed slowly as I tossed and turned. But when I finally decided what to do, a calm settled over me and I felt lighter.

Lucky. Lucky could help.

It was almost morning so I laced my boots. The dried blood still there—the splashes of blood all over those boots—I slipped on my combat shirt and pulled the Kevlar armour over my head and around my torso. I pulled the Velcro binding hugging it to my chest, strapped on my pistol, and grabbed my rifle.

Higgins, in the next cot, didn't stir. Someone in the back was snoring. I crept through the common area and out into the bright moonlight.

You'd think the moon would look different that far away from home. You'd think the angle of the craters would look different. They don't. The moon looks the same in Kingston as it does in Panjwai.

I hoped Grace was looking at the moon just then.

That night was as clear as a January evening. Not a cloud. About a trillion stars. Everything still. Joe was on night watch at the station.

Ours is but to do and die... I was thinking as I entered.

Lucky will be able to help.

"What are you doing awake, Doc?" she said.

"I couldn't sleep."

"Amalah?"

"Yes. But I was thinking maybe Lucky can find her, and bring her here. What do you think?"

"Maybe."

"And if she's here, then it's no big deal to run a simple test. That's not going to hurt anyone. And Brad doesn't even have to know. I'm going to ask Lucky to find her, and if he does, we're going to run that damn test."

"You sure about that? It sounded like he gave you a direct order."

"He did. But I don't give a shit about a direct order right now. It's wrong. It feels wrong. Like we're handing her a death sentence by doing nothing."

"I suppose…"

"She's a little girl, and she deserves our help, right?"

"I think so. But it's not my call."

"I'm going to find her. I'm going to see if Lucky knows where she is. And if she's here, then Brad will capitulate. I know he will."

"Okay. How can I help?"

"What time is it?"

"It's zero-dark-thirty, but the sun should be coming up soon."

"Hold the fort, will you? I won't be long."

"Okay. Boss."

I left the UMS and crossed the FOB climbing the ridge to where the interpreters live. There were two translators coming out on their way to the showers. I stepped inside and stood over Lucky's cot. He awoke in surprise when I touched his arm.

"We have a patient?" he asked, jumping up and began to throw his uniform on.

"No, Lucky, I'm sorry to wake you. It's about Amalah."

"Okay." He patted his hair and straightened his beard. "How can I be of service?"

"Do you remember the colour of her eyes?"

"Yes, they were golden. Quite beautiful."

"Yes, I'm worried that's a sign she's sick." I took a moment to explain about Wilson's, psychosis, and liver failure... "We can prevent her from dying."

"I understand. Yes. We should find her," he said. I was grateful he agreed.

"Do you know where?"

"I saw her uncle in the village. But I didn't see her."

"Can you find her for me and bring her to the clinic? Is that something you can do?" I asked.

"I think so, yes. I will put on my boots and go straight away."

"Thank you, Lucky!"

This felt exciting and purposeful and right. I was beaming as we parted ways. I considered going with him on his search but I knew I needed to be at the FOB if something happened. And Major Ridgeway would not be happy if I left. But Lucky was used to heading out there alone and I had hope he could be out and back with Amalah before anyone even knew he was gone. Maybe it was wishful thinking but I went back to the medical unit and asked Joe to get the blood draw kit and i-STAT ready.

She had already set it on the shelf inside the door.

Outside, the sun was rising. Lucky was already at the base of the hill making his way silently around the *ghar* to a place where the HESCO was low, close to the village. I'd seen the dog jumping in and out right there a hundred times. My heart felt light for the first time in a long while. He would bring Amalah back to us. I was certain.

Chapter Twenty-Five

Outreach

Finding Amalah was not as easy as I had hoped.

The next time I saw Lucky was at lunch the next day. He passed me with his tray as I entered the meal line.

"What happened?" I asked.

"I could not find her. I am sorry. I went back to the area where I last saw her uncle but they were not there. I asked around, but no one knew of her, so I came back for lunch."

"Well, that's disappointing."

"She may not be here any longer. I did not see her uncle either."

"Well, thanks for trying. I'm still hoping you can find her. I realize it might take some time."

"I will try, Jack. You are kind. She deserves your help."

"If we can't help one little girl what's the point, right?" He smiled at that.

"There is a village outreach tomorrow. Maybe she will come to that. You'll be there won't you?" I asked.

"I would not miss it," he said.

———

The next morning, we packed two ambs for the clinic outreach and headed out the main gate. We drove in convoy past ditches filled with dry vegetation that cut around a field of grape walls. The village was very close. We passed mud huts crumbling in the sun like dry concrete. Had we walked, we might have cut across a trail through the field, but we had been warned to stay on roads. Lucky liked to say the obvious trails were easily 'booby trapped' and he laughed at that phrase. He said, "That is an excellent and hilarious name for something so deadly."

Collins, Higgins, and Joe were in the amb behind us. It was a coordinated affair with other vehicles as well. We were led by a section of infantry and a pickup truck of Afghan national soldiers. They used our excursion ostensibly as an opportunity to teach about perimeter security, but mostly they helped set up our tents.

We didn't have far to go. Two turns and a few hundred meters. We could see our way back from where we stopped.

Nothing about that work felt dangerous. We'd heard stories about outreach clinics being hit with suicide attacks but that seemed unlikely. We set up in an open area near a well. We had line of sight around the entire perimeter, and the villagers seemed harmless and happy to have us. And with the infantry patrolling it felt safe.

Lucky spoke to anyone in the proximity and said he could tell by their demeanour if they meant us harm. I trusted his judgement and didn't worry.

I focused on care. There was a line of sore throats, rashes, and old injuries forming as we set up. I cleaned a few ears and pulled out a sliver. We'd been through a few of those clinics before. I wasn't expecting any complicated medicine. Joe and Higgins ran most of it on their own. They were reasonably independent and loved acting like doctors. They presented cases to me as if they were medical students. It was a good day.

Just before lunch I noticed Lucky had disappeared. There were other translators around, none of whom were half as proficient in English as Lucky, but they allowed us to struggle through.

We felt it when Lucky was gone.

I was finishing lunch when he finally returned, "Jack, I found her," he said immediately.

"Amalah? Really? That's wonderful. Where is she? Did you bring her?" I said quietly pulling him aside. Joe noticed but pretended not to hear.

"No. But she is not far. She went into a compound two blocks from here with some other girls and men."

"Oh Lucky. That's great. Can you bring her here?"

"I tried to call to her but she didn't hear."

"Well thank you for trying," I said. Disappointed.

"Jack, you should come with me."

"To the compound? You know I can't do that, Lucky. We have work to do here. And how would I be helpful?"

"If she sees you, she will come. And the men will listen if you are there."

"Why would they listen to me if they won't listen to you?"

"The Coalition brings American dollars. They might open the gate for you. It might be enough. They might listen."

"I'm sorry Lucky, but I can't. I've been told by my chain of command to forget her. And I've already over-stepped by asking you to search."

"You must come, Jack. She is not far. We could be back in moments. She deserves your help."

"I'm sorry, Lucky. It's not an option."

I was torn about that. Amalah's eyes and her cute embrace lingered. But Brad had been abundantly clear. I needed to put her out of my mind.

Lucky turned away in disappointment.

He didn't speak to me for the remainder of the afternoon. His frustration was warranted and I felt it, but I couldn't let Amalah's plight cloud my already cloudy judgment. It was true she deserved a chance to know her fate and avoid tragedy, but it was out of my hands. I'd done all I could.

I went back to work.

Then, as the clinic was ending and we were packing to go we saw in the distance the engineers deployed on the main road, blocking our return. There would be a delay.

The radio report said a suspicious object, an IED, had been found on the road. We had luckily missed it on our way in. Either that or it had been planted during the day, with our surveillance distracted by the outreach. Either way it needed attention. We could travel many miles around and through the back gate, or wait.

The command team decided to wait. So, we were stuck in the village until the engineers were done.

Our kit was packed and we were ready to return, but we were stuck. Another hurry up and wait scenario.

I sat back on a pile of folded tents and wondered how long it might be. The shadows were getting long.

Collins said, "The last time this happened we were stuck out here until well past nightfall. Better get comfortable." He pulled out a paperback and leaned back on the tire of the amb.

I looked at Lucky... Lucky looked back at me.

"How far away is she?" I whispered, and he smiled.

Then I spoke up, "Collins, listen, Lucky knows where Amalah is. She's not far. I'm going to take the blood draw kit and get a blood sample. It's a long story. Ask Joe. I won't be gone long."

"Wait. You're leaving?"

"No. I'm just going to get a blood sample from Amalah, she's two blocks away."

"Um. Ok... I'm coming with you."

"No, you can't. You're in charge while I'm gone. I won't be long. Wait here for us to return." I stood and grabbed the med kit. Lucky, smiling, jogged ahead.

————

Rounding the first hut we entered an alley and the walls closed in. We turned at the end and within moments the village had enveloped us. We turned twice and then out into a wider street and across into an alley. The clearing with the tents suddenly seemed far behind.

Lucky was jogging and I was trying to keep up. It was quiet. The townsfolk seemed to be indoors, or possibly at evening prayers, but I couldn't recall hearing the tower bell that chimed for those.

I followed Lucky, zigzagging through a couple wide streets and around a tight turn until we arrived on the edge of a broad square. He pointed up a short wall and hopped on a pile of stones leading to a rooftop. We crested the edge of the building. A cast iron table and two wooden folding chairs came into view: like a Paris street corner on a rooftop.

We stepped around a closed trap door that led down into the building below, and sidled over to the rail. Despite the fading light there was a good view of a stage at one end of a square. I pictured town festivals with dancers in vibrant, colourful costumes, people dancing and smiling.

The mud rail was low and over it, across the square, we had a view to a compound with a high stone wall and an iron gate.

"There," he said pointing to the gate.

Torches, lit from within, cast shadows in the day's fading light. We could make out a few buildings behind the wall. Only one with two storeys. The others were a storehouse, a stable and maybe a barn. Out front were two men smoking. Each held an AK-47 assault rifle, slung over their shoulders. Guards or just stopping to chat? I couldn't tell.

"Is she in there?" I asked.

"Yes. I saw her there with her uncle and other girls."

"Are those guards, Lucky? Are they protecting something?"

"Yes. I think so?"

"What? Why? Is this their home?"

"Yes. Archala Rahzani lives there. The Mullah we spoke of."

"Remind me."

"The one who served as Deputy Minister for Higher Education in the Taliban shadow government before its collapse. President Karzai trusts him."

"But why the compound and guards?"

"He has been asked to serve on the Afghan High Peace Council, representing the Taliban. We are hopeful he is key to peace in this region. He is a good man, Jack. I have spoken to him before."

"Well, Lucky, I thought we were going to a small home in the village not some compound with a minister and guards."

"It may look menacing, but he loves Afghanistan as I do, and desires peace. Amalah is safe in there. Her uncle seems to be in Archala's service. The guards there are also in his service. There are Taliban who do not want him to negotiate for peace."

A scene from *The Princess Bride* came to mind as I leaned back against the barrier. What have I gotten myself into? I thought, but said out loud, "If we only had a wheelbarrow..."

Lucky was confused. "Why a wheelbarrow?"

"Never mind... It's from a movie..."

If she's in there and we are this close. All I need is a small sample of her blood.

Drawing a deep breath, I closed my eyes and thought of Grace. She was smiling and her lips tightened and the skin of her chin bunched like it does, and I heard her say clearly, "If you're moving in the right direction, keep moving."

"Lucky, we mean no harm, right?"

"Right."

"We are here to help. Do you believe that?"

"Of course. Canada!" he said pointing to the maple leaf on the flag on my left arm. "Canada is good." He smiled.

"We're going to ask them about the girl," I said resolutely "We've come this far. We're going to speak to her uncle and tell him how the blood sample will help her."

The words resounded with more conviction than I was feeling. I rose and started down the way we had come.

"What do you think?"

Ignoring the trepidation in my voice he said, "How could we turn back now? We are this close. They will listen. Let's go!" He smiled and dropped down into the alley at the edge of the square.

I peered across at the men, some fifty feet away, smoking. Their silhouettes lit by the torchlight behind and the red tips of their cigarettes. Proud young men. We exchanged another smile. Then Lucky stepped out, striding boldly, and I followed.

As we moved across, one of the guards unslung his weapon and aimed toward us barking something in Pashtun, or Farsi, I could never tell.

We raised our arms.

Lucky responded, "Salaam Alaikum, deer wackht wosho na khary."—*Hello, long time no see*—and the weapon relaxed, dropping slightly.

They recognized Lucky and beckoned us over.

One stepped back but kept his weapon at the ready. Hand on the pistol grip, finger pointed down the trigger guard. The other slung his weapon and spoke to Lucky. A short exchange. Then Lucky turned to me.

"He wants to know why we are here and what we want." There was a look of hesitation on Lucky's face.

"What did you tell him? Tell him about the girl and the blood sample."

He nodded, "Yes, yes."

They spoke again and I watched the conversation go back and forth... and back and forth... and some time passed.

The two guards were young and fit with clean white clothing and grey-brown vests. Their weapons seemed brand new. I was trying to be patient, smiling back and forth, but I was starting to think this was a bad idea.

The exchange dragged on and emotions were getting heated. They were not opening the gate and made no movement to help us see Amalah.

I kept my hands in front, palms together, my C7 rifle dangled at my side, muzzle down from the ranger sling at my left shoulder.

Something in the fleeting looks between guards and Lucky, to me and back, was beginning to seem aggressive.

A tinge of fear was unmistakable.

But somehow anger and frustration pushed it down. We didn't have time for this, and Amalah needed us. These men were in our way. For no reason.

Finally, Lucky turned and said, "You cannot see her. And we should go."

"What?" I said, "That's it?"

"We should go, doctor," he said, stepping back.

They had discussed the subject for a good five minutes, and that was all? I was tired and my mouth was parched and I was done with this war.

"Why did we come all this way? ...It doesn't make sense."

Why had Lucky assumed my presence would help? He seemed to be trying, but ineffectual. I decided he was just not choosing the right words. "What did you tell them? ...Did you tell them it will *save her life*?"

Lucky placed his hand on my arm, "He wants us to go. He says to tell you—You may have watches, but we have time."

"I don't understand."

"He is saying you are not welcome here. That you will leave, now or soon… We are not welcome, Jack." He looked defeated, "This was a mistake," he added

I pictured Amalah. Alone. Orphaned. And these two boys, young and small, and not in charge of anything, were blocking us. We had come all this way. With everything that had happened. With all of the tragedy I'd seen. Being blocked now from a tiny act of kindness by these two boys seemed unpardonably wrong. If we could only speak to Amalah or her uncle this would be cleared up in an instant. I wasn't going to let it be for nothing. I was so completely fed up. It felt like a 'speak to the manager' moment.

"I'm not satisfied with that..." I turned toward the lead guard. Squared my shoulders and pointed at him. "Lucky, tell him I'm not taking no for an answer. Tell him, I'm not leaving here without a sample of her blood. The girl deserves our help. It's not fair they won't allow it. Tell him to go get Amalah."

I saw a flash of recognition in the guard when I said her name.

"Amalah. Go get Amalah," I repeated.

I'm certain he saw the conviction in my eyes.

Then he began to argue with Lucky again. Now more agitated than ever. The other guard began shuffling his feet and I saw his jaw clench. He pointed at me and then Lucky, commandingly. The muscles of his forearm writhed. And I realized it was futile. They were not going to help us. I could tell by their body language this was futile.

Suddenly the lead guard pushed Lucky hard and fast with two hands. And Lucky fell to the ground.

"Whoa. Okay. Okay," I said, reaching to help Lucky.

"We need to leave, Jack."

The lead guard was yelling. The other raised his weapon. Pointing it at Lucky. He cocked it. "What's happening, Lucky? -Lucky?" I said staring at the man with the gun who was yelling now.

"They are saying I am infidel being here with you—A traitor. They are saying I am not a Muslim. Not a man. They are saying I made my choice. We need to go... NOW..."

I was angry and confused. We were only there to help an innocent girl and I was blinded by my frustration and trauma and anger and not thinking straight.

I should have been running.

I raised my arms towards them and began to slowly back away. Then a scrabbling sound came from behind me, to my right, where Lucky was moving, and the man with the gun suddenly looked surprised, and scared and he pointed his gun. And before I could react—he pulled his trigger.

Clack, once. Clack, twice. Clack, clack, clack.

I stood in stunned silence and turned my head. I saw Lucky try to run. The first round missed. The second, and others, did not. He fell, sprawling into the square. A pistol he had drawn, I didn't know he had, was bouncing on the ground away from him.

He was dead before he hit the ground.

His body shifted as more rounds penetrated his torso. The men were yelling and it was like a dream.

The starlight and muzzle flashes lit the square.

Looking back—as I often do—I am surprised how little emotion I associate with the moment. The anger was gone. The fear was gone. I didn't flinch. I didn't move. There didn't seem to be a fight or flight response at all. The other guard lunged at me. But he was four steps away and before his body reached me, my anger was in charge of my movement.

I was *all anger.*

I raged.

He was a small person. Slight. Shorter than me. Thinner. But wiry. I'm not sure why he lunged and didn't shoot. Maybe he thought I could be taken hostage, and held for ransom. He must have known I was a doctor from speaking to Lucky. Doctors had value out there. Maybe he didn't want to kill me because of that. I don't know.

He should have killed me.

I surprised myself by my reaction. I spun out of his grasp. His momentum helped. I slew-footed him and he went down. I twisted and dropped on him and drove his head hard into the ground out of rage and anger. His face hit stone and blood splattered. He went limp.

I looked up, seeing surprise on the other man's face. His head was turning toward me. He was off balance as he brought his rifle around. And I brought mine up when I fell. Mine was already in line with where he stood.

I had twenty-nine rounds in a magazine and a thirtieth in the breach. I had never fired at a human being before that moment, but it was easy—too easy. Like shooting figure eleven targets, or critters in the attic. I clicked off the safety and squeezed the trigger. Gently. Like an orange. Once. Twice. Three times. Aiming for centre of mass.

The man, who moments before had killed my friend and was about to kill me, didn't get the chance. The third round hit him high as he collapsed. His legs were in the way. His body heaped then flopped sideways as he fell. He was pulling the trigger as he died and his AK-47 emptied its magazine in a curving arc, away from me. Then his weapon clattered to the ground.

In my memory he remains surprised, like the pattern of blood splatter on the gate behind him. I heard someone yell, "Noooo," from within the compound. Faces peered through the iron bars.

The other man was sitting up and coming for me, then scrabbling for his slung rifle as I pulled away. I ran across the square. Desperate. Hoping beyond hope that he would let me go, but his rifle cocked behind me and I heard him yell. Bullets whizzed high and to my right, and I had no choice.

I slid beside Lucky's corpse, and rolled back as I fell. He fired again and Lucky was hit again. The rounds smashed into his flesh saving my life. The proximity and violence of that was shocking. It's not like in the movies. Not a whiz and a 'pfffhtt'. More like the THUD of a sledge hammer. Desperate and exposed, I straightened my barrel again and fired three shots.

I've traced the paths of those rounds countless times. The man falls the same way, over and over, in my dreams. The bullets entered his chest and exited with flesh and blood painting the mud wall behind him.

Center of mass. Cardiac box. Exactly as I'd been taught.

In the brief silence I looked down at Lucky. He had a devastating wound to his skull and was unrecognizable. Dr. Chan's voice echoed in my ears, "Penetrating trauma to the cranium that crosses the midline is universally fatal."

I didn't check his pulse.

I stood and ran with a commotion erupting behind. There was more yelling as the gate clattering open. A searchlight cast my shadow up the building ahead.

I ran as fast and as far as I could.

First into the closest ally.

It was not until later I realized I had gone the wrong way.

Part Four:

Proximity and Violence

Chapter Twenty-Six

Heat and Injury

The village was not huge but it sprawled across the valley with no recognizable pattern to its streets. Ancient pathways followed geographic contours between mud structures placed in haphazard arrays. I ran blindly away from the yelling, stomping, and clacking behind me.

It might have been an army coming after me from all the noise. I wasn't thinking about the convoy, or the clinic outreach, or the road back. I juked around buildings as fast as my lungs would allow, and kept running as far and as fast as I could.

When I finished sprinting, I dug deep and found more energy. I jogged for my life until the noises began to recede.

In the distance, I could make out a mechanical buzz that sounded like motorcycles or trucks, so I continued jogging farther still. Then slowed to a trot, then a shuffle.

Eventually there was silence and I was alone in a sleeping village in the desert of Panjwai, far from home. The sun was down and I realized with a sudden pang of fear that I was lost. The convoy and FOB should have been my goal but Lucky had been my guide on the way in and I had been thinking of Amalah and surprised by how far we had to go and wasn't paying attention.

Now nothing looked familiar. Sand caked my nostrils and the image of those two men slumping to the ground in death was etching itself on my mind. The sadness that fills the holes was taking over.

"Why did I leave the team?" I said out loud and it echoed off the walls of an alley. I was not sobbing but my cheeks were wet and it was getting hard to see.

Another sand storm had rolled over the village. The moon and stars were dimmed by the sand. I was wandering in darkness. The hills were too far and shrouded to make out.

On the edge of town, I worried about IEDs and pressure plates. The obvious pathways, entries and exits, were frightening now. Locals would know which to avoid but I was completely lost.

I turned toward the next stout building behind a farm house with an open gate and a loose door and crept inside. Keeping to the shadows. Afraid to alert anyone to my presence. A farmer. A family. God only knows who might be nearby.

It was cool inside that hut. There were a few muddy vegetables on a centre table: radishes, apricots, pomegranates. There was a pile of wheat in bags in one corner. The apricots looked juicy but I had no appetite. I filled my pockets for later, moving aside the handful of Werther's originals from the morning clinic.

My canteen was empty. I was sucking on the last drops when I noticed my med kit was gone. I must have dropped it at the compound.

The burlap bags of grain were soft enough, and inviting, so I sat. Then lay down, and flashes of trauma flickered as my eyes closed. The two men first. Then fresh trauma from the FOB. Amalah's family. The killing of the dog and the monkey. Then images of the more controlled trauma back home. Car accidents and simple gunshot wounds. Wounds of the dying. Patients I'd born witness too. Fixed. Permanent. Like sculptures.

It was all meant to be in service to my fellow man.

All my work. All my choices, the striving and learning. Why had I done it? Why had I wanted any of it?

I was a killer. *We were only trying to help.* There in that sanctuary, alone, thirsty and tired, I tasted the poison of resentment and the bitter taste may never wash down.

Now my overwhelming hope was only to get back to the FOB—because the FOB was the way back to Grace— and to put this life behind. I wanted to leave it there in the dust. But home was far away and hope was fading.

Grace would say, "Soldier on, Jack... Keep moving." But I was tired and lost and needed to wait for first light.

I wrapped my arm around the sling of my rifle, buried myself between sacks of grain, and pulled some burlap over my body and head. Hugging my weapon I closed my eyes and the unavoidable sleep of exhaustion overtook me, despite the angle of Lucky's shattered mandible and the grey matter mixed with blood on the stones of that square. All of that, a meditation unto itself. A Rorschach blot beneath dancers in vibrant colours. I dreamed of the Joshua tree alone in the desert and of lambs to the slaughter, screaming and burning. I dreamed of a man crawling out onto a dry limb hundreds of feet above the ground. Like a sloth he crept toward the bone white tip as I tried to yell to warn him, but nothing came out.

———————

The sunshine pierced my eyes. I awoke sweating from the heat. With a jolt I remembered where I was, causing a surge of adrenaline and cortisol and a tightening in my chest. My heart jumped and I gasped. There were noises outside. People shuffling and yelling. I lay still and tried to sense if I was hidden.

I could feel the weight of burlap on my legs. But my face was open. Sunlight was cutting across my face, too bright to open my eyes. I was afraid to move. The pink of sunshine through my eyelids danced as it slowly dawned.

It sounded like children playing. My fear of soldiers searching floated away and I repositioned into shadow.

That's when I noticed the building had no roof. The morning sky was brave and blue between ancient wooden rafters. I was alone in that shed still unseen and hidden. I stretched and peaked through a hole in the wall. A soccer game was raging on the street outside. Children playing with a flat ball. One of the red and white ones that were stencilled with maple leaves trimmed in black and silver that we handed out at the role one. For winning hearts and minds. A reminder of our counter-insurgency war on terror.

Suddenly I thought of Ian, and Dylan, and Brad. Brad was not going to be happy. But he might be able to help. I hoped he would learn from Joe about my absence soon and maybe start to worry? Maybe send a search party? Standard protocol in the event of any missing soldier was to ramp up the entire task force pretty quickly. That should have been a consolation, but it wasn't.

The soccer game was quick. One of the boys was quite good. Taller. More agile. There were two girls playing, their dusty faces joyful.

It made me smile.

Across their pitch the terrain was more green than I remembered. Lush vegetation stretched over an open plain to a river—the Helmand River.

My heart sank.

In my confusion I had run downhill all night. Away from the FOB. There was now a village full of insurgents between me and my destination. I crouched against a sack and closed my eyes.

But it was also possible that running the wrong way may have saved my life. They would have chased me toward the FOB. Exactly to where I wasn't going. Maybe that was a good thing. *But what now?* From the confines of that shed, I wasn't going to get back. I'd have to figure something out. *Start by starting.*

I needed to find where I was and the direction back. The tragedy in the square would have alerted the village. My plan to save Amalah, seemingly so important the night before, now seemed patently stupid. Lucky was dead. I had killed two men, probably put a bounty on my head, and now I was lost, with a village of dangers to navigate if I was going to make it home. But dangers, real or imagined, that I wasn't prepared to face, would have to wait.

I was alive.

And the only way out is through.

————

I stacked the burlap back where I'd found it and stood to stretch. From inside that hut, I had no frame of reference for where I was or where I should be going. It seemed safe enough though. I could see through the cracks in the frame and high windows if anyone approached from the house or the road.

I needed a simple, useful, mindless task, to help me think.

My weapon was by my side.

It felt like both a burden and a saviour.

I could clean my rifle.

To this day I'm not certain how long a weapon can go without being cleaned before it stops working. In training we always cleaned after firing and my weapon had most definitely been fired. It had rested all night and I imagined carbon seizing the mechanism—and that scared me. It needed cleaning.

I opened the flap door in the butt and was pleased to find a fully stocked cleaning kit in its standard hiding place. "Thank the Lord," I said out loud. Half the time those compartments are empty. On exercise, back home, it was rare to find one full. But things are different in a war zone. I thanked the unknown storesmen for their diligence.

The dark green canvas sleeve wrapped a few brass fittings and brushes. It stuck at first but slid free with a yank. There was a small stack of white linen 'two by twos' for pulling through the barrel and a tiny squirt bottle of 'CLP' (Cleaner, Lubricant, Protectant).

I stripped my weapon *field expediently* by first removing the magazine and cocking the weapon, as silently as I could, and listened for noises outside.

A round popped out and bounced off the sack to my right landing in the dust. I picked it up, blew it off, and loaded it back in the magazine. I had about twenty-two rounds left and hoped I wouldn't need them.

How am I going to get back?

I depressed the take-down-pin and pulled it on the other side allowing the upper receiver to pivot forward. Then slid the cocking handle back allowing the bolt carrier out. My hands were blackened by the carbide residue.

I need to find high ground.

As far as I knew, that was the first time I'd cleaned a weapon that had been used to kill humans. I wiped my hands on burlap and finished field-stripping the bolt, placing the parts left to right in front of my crossed legs. The firing pin, retaining pin, the aluminum lining of the hand-guards, all caked with sand and dust. I wiped them clean.

From some place high up I can get a sense of distance. The FOB should be South East of the village. It should be easy to see from the roof of a building or high hill.

I dropped the pull-through into the barrel, as the bullet flies, attached the handle at the flash suppressor, and added a drop of CLP before pulling it through. It twists as it traverses, with the rifling in the barrel, just like bullets. Spinning the bullets to make them fly straighter. More accurate and true.

Like the ones that went through Lucky and those boys at the gate.

I was glad for the familiar task and smells but my mouth was parched. Cleaning my weapon might have been peaceful had I not been so thirsty, and I might have cried again as all that sadness percolated, but my plan was forming.

Stay in shadow. Make my way through the village. Find high ground. Set my direction. Keep to the shadows.

The weapon pieced together with familiar clicks. I worked methodically, happy for the work. I was stuffing the cleaning kit back into the hollow when I heard a noise at the door and looked up.

There were children standing there. The tall one front and centre, staring.

I froze.

They were jostling one another for a view of the lost soldier in the shed, but they did not speak, and made no move to come inside. They stayed in the doorway, appraising me. I clicked the compartment closed and continued. As a force of habit, I began my function test, which involves checking the safety and making sure the trigger mechanism works correctly. It ensures the hammer throws when the trigger is pulled. You check for a click and a clunk as the seer falls into place. It's a simple procedure that proves the weapon works as designed—and that you have reassembled it correctly—but the first step is to cock the weapon.

My magazine was on my right leg. There were no rounds chambered by that action, but the children noticed and flinched in fear, evidently aware that cocking a weapon is an aggressive act. They flinched but none of them dashed. The tall one stood still in the doorframe. I smiled at him. My weapon passed the test, and I pressed the magazine in place and cocked a round into the chamber. Still, they did not run. Then I placed it on safe and stood to sling it.

The tall boy in the middle smiled back.

Resolute, I pushed through them into the courtyard and they surrounded me as I moved. They were reaching for my pockets. Their tone was not aggressive, more pleading, and playful. They wanted something, and were smiling. I brushed them off and scurried out the gate but they chased, grabbing at my shirt and cargo pants.

"Hey," I said, "Leave me alone."

But they persisted. Then I recalled the children at the clinic outreach, and how they loved our Werther's caramels.

They hooted when they saw those. I stopped and handed one from my pocket to each of them. Then threw the rest into the air and jogged away uphill toward the village, as they fought over candies on the ground.

<hr>

I stayed to the periphery looking for high ground. Any sort of landmark would be helpful. The sun was bright and the sky was clear and the distant hills could be seen on the horizon, but I didn't recognize anything. I moved east toward the sun and up a hill. The children did not follow.

I was expecting more scrutiny from locals. A search party. Some violent action, but nothing seemed imminent. I was trying to stay in shadow, keeping a low profile, but it was hard to avoid being seen.

Luckily, for the most part, I was ignored.

A wandering soldier of little interest to most going about their daily routine. It felt as though I was passing in obscurity. Some villagers even nodded in my direction, but kept to themselves.

The sun was my guide initially. I moved toward it and kept it slightly to my left and came to a tall mud wall with an inset ladder with steps to a raised outlook. I climbed. From the top I had a view across the village to the hills in the distance and got a sense of where the skirmish and compound were. To my left and North.

Some of the distant hills were familiar: Massum Ghar the largest. Sperwan Ghar closer, probably five or six kilometres as the crow flies. I would have to make my way around but estimated a mid-afternoon arrival, if I kept moving.

Moving helped. The farther I went avoiding confrontation, the more my fear diminished. In time I began to feel insignificant. My presence seemed irrelevant to everyone. Then only children seemed to notice. They smiled and waved. Happy. Playing.

The townsfolk went about their business, as they seemingly had done for centuries. Toiling in that sand and heat—making their living in that relentless heat. One man was drawing a mule with a cart full of wares toward centre town. A woman stacking plants in a yard. Another chopping what looked like onions on an outdoor table with children running around her. All of them smiling.

Two men laughing as they stomped the ground beside a wood burning kiln, making naan. Another sharpened a scythe on a stone, pumping a peddle, which made the stone spin.

I was trying hard not to be seen, making quick movements to crouching positions. I couldn't be sure if I alluded them, or if they were simply focused on their work, determined and smiling, and made nothing of my presence.

A shepherd with his flock on a hill crystallized a sense I'd been written into a scene from the Bible. As if I had fallen through time. I began to feel oddly connected to the place. The strangest revelation. Like an ancestor might have walked up that same hill in the distant past. Possibly some pre-human ancestor had struggled up that very hill. And the joy around me was unmistakable and incongruent with my sense of foreboding and sadness. I tried to feel grateful for the sun on my face and for my life. I was alive and healthy despite horrors and the changes that come from killing. I focused on my breath and kept moving.

When you're moving in the right direction, keep moving.

My feet were blistered. My lips were cracked. My throat and canteen were dry. I kept to the shade when I could, but had to keep moving. My rifle weighed on my shoulder. Birds made quick shadows on the mud walls. I started daydreaming about swimming in cool water; of snow angels on a hill in Kingston; of catching snowflakes on my tongue, with Grace; of a crackling fire and the warmth of her arms; of cool bed-sheets, and wet kisses.

Keep the sun to my left. Keep moving.

I was thirsty and far too hot. Unbearably hot. And I was suddenly fearful. Heat exhaustion. Heat stroke. On the spectrum of heat injury, I was certainly close. I was so very parched. My throat was far too dry. I stumbled. Then fell to the ground.

If you've ever seen a juggler juggling tissue, or something cloth-like, soft and full of air. Like Kleenex. When they toss them in the air, they go only so high, and hover for a moment before falling. The juggler reaches up to grab them, pulling them to keep juggling. That's what seemed to happen to me.

A part of me was yanked from the centre of my chest and thrown in the air. Like tissue.

I hovered there for a moment looking down.

I could feel something beside me in my ears. Something familiar, and inviting, with hot, sweet breath. Inviting, hot, sweet breath, that scared me.

I wanted to turn toward it, but fought to turn away, and looked down to see myself lying in the sand. I watched a line of shadow cast from a nearby building move quickly across the ground. It was beginning to cover my body when I heard my sister's voice ring out, clear and true in my ears.

She had always been my connection to the spiritual.

She saved me that day.

I heard my sister's voice whispering an intimate homily in my ear. One I had a faint recollection of hearing before. One she had written many years ago about the remarkable, beautiful truth about suffering...

"When you accept your suffering, you transcend it."

She repeated it, saying it twice, and again, and it was close in my ears. Then I watched below as a man with a jug of water came around the building, and tipped my body onto his lap. He poured water into my mouth. And like a genie into the bottle, I was there, and felt the cold in my throat.

I sucked in breath and opened my eyes.

Dazed. But the man was gentle and tipped more water into my mouth. Cool and refreshing.

A profound sense of joy overtook me, and I felt my strength returning.

I stood and thanked the man in gestures, and pushed around the corner where I knew he had come, and he followed me with his jug toward the well.

My feet hurt a little less as my strength surged.

When you accept your suffering, you transcend it.

I had always missed the point of that homily, but it didn't matter. It didn't make sense at home, inside a cool stone church. But there in the desert sun, suffering and struggling to get home, accepting the suffering as part of the human condition somehow mattered more.

My stride picked up and I shook the man's hand and moved toward the well.

And when I turned back to smile, he was gone.

My shirt was wet though, so I knew he must have been, only moments before, there with his jug. But he feels more like a dream now.

I walked on thinking of the many millions of humans before me who had suffered more than this, and survived. Not only in that village or desert or country but everywhere throughout all of time. That one harrowing day, and a few life-changing months, were nothing in comparison.

I couldn't remember what my sister had said in that homily. Not exactly. Not word for word. But the feeling remained and it helped me survive that day.

I had to keep pushing my rock up my hill, maybe just for the joy of the pushing, but also to survive, and get home.

Whatever it is we're built for, it's not sloth. We're not built for sloth and not hedonism either. We long for instant gratification in our weakest moments, but we know, deep down, those are really the enemy. Hedonism and sloth are pathways to wallowing and despair and self-loathing. Naïve desires disconnected from truth. I never knew that more clearly than in that desert heat, filling my canteen from a wrought iron well. Pumping the wooden handle up and down, and up and down, wondering if water would come, but, seeing water having spilled around the nozzle, knowing it would.

On that day of struggle, alone, crossing an ancient village, stumbling, hot and tired, in my darkest hour, death as close as it had ever been, smelling its breath around me, sending it away with a force of will, I learned more about my human nature than a lifetime before or since. I survived that day with nothing but joy in my heart, a vision of my Grace, and a strange kind man with an ancient jug of water.

And then my fear was gone.

There was power in my legs and a beat in my heart and the love inside propelled me and wrapped me.

I don't know how else to explain that.

I kept repeating, *The FOB, then Kandahar, then Grace. I'll be home to you soon, my love.*

And somehow, turning away from that well with a full canteen toward the bustle of the noonday market in the distance, I knew I'd be okay.

I knew I would find my way back to Grace.

Chapter Twenty-Seven
The Demi-Team

I made my way through a few abandoned streets until I realized there seemed to be only one way through. I had to find my way around a market full of people but the village had walls and buildings that seemed to funnel me toward it.

I rested in the shade of a low wall for a moment and watched. There were stalls lining the perimeter bearing mostly fruit and vegetables, but also tools and wares. The monkey was probably purchased there. A man was selling animals in cages. Shop owners beckoned patrons, and the crowd was close.

I feared what they might know about the night before.

I was close to the compound here, and closer to the FOB. I tried harder to stay out of view, but it was difficult. Making my way toward the periphery, away from scrutiny, I passed behind the stall of a man selling knives, cloth, and wool, mesmerized for a moment by a colourful bird in a beautiful cage. It had a bulbous beak, and feathers of red, yellow, and blue. The sun shone off the brass dome of the cage. I had been distracted only for a moment when someone grabbed me.

I turned to defend but two strong men held my arms. I was weak from the day of wandering in the heat. They dragged me bodily into an alley, as I tried to stand. My feet sliding, kicking sand.

Then one of them spoke. "Relax, Jack, You're okay."
English. Canadian desert pattern fatigues.

I looked up into his smiling face. It was Jones. I'd never felt such relief. Those big shiny teeth, "Jones. Wow."

"What are you doing, Doc?" he asked.

I breathed, "You scared the shit out of me."

"We've been looking for you all morning. What the hell are you doing out here?" he repeated.

"I'm trying to get back to the FOB."

"Well, you're not an easy man to find. And you're not going that way." He pointing through the market. "Wait here."

He sat me down behind a wagon and said something to his team about signalling and bringing trucks around.

One lad disappeared into a doorway at a trot.

I looked at the sky and drank some water. Grateful for it, although it was already getting warm.

I emptied my canteen again.

The sun was completing its descent. Afternoon was fading into night. I lost a day crossing the village but never felt such peace as that, sitting against that wall in the shade of that alley.

These men were Canadian.

I was safe with them, and closer to home.

The smell of spices drifted in from the market.

Jones and another young soldier stood over me looking competent and strong. Scanning. Keeping watch.

Two birds circled overhead. Vultures, or hawks. Tracing long arcs that reminded me of that A10 Warthog. Silent, slowly swooping. I watched a single trout-shaped cloud on the horizon, drifting at the mouth of the alley.

They seemed satisfied with their defensive posture, so Jones crouched down by my side.

"Okay," he said, and I felt a sense of inevitability wash over me, "What the fuck are you doing, sir?"

"I'm sorry," I said. "It happened so fast."

"Try me."

"There was a moment. I thought I could save the girl. And Lucky said she was close, but she wasn't close."

"What girl?"

A profound sadness welled up inside, but I swallowed it down. "There was a family through the UMS a few weeks back, she was the only survivor. She's an orphan. And I think she has a medical condition that needs treatment."

"And you ran off to find her? To get her treatment?"

"Well, sort of, yes. It seemed the right thing."

He sighed.

A pair of scorpions were locked in a fight, or possibly copulating, beneath us by the wall. We watched them dance in silence for a moment.

It's hard to look away from those sorts of things.

It was getting dark.

Jones seemed to be swallowing down an ebbing rage for a moment. "I know it's hard to see this suffering but, you can't save them all, Doc." He was staring at the scorpions as he said it.

"I know."

"You're lucky to be alive you know."

"I know. But the girl is..."

"There are a lot of orphans out here, sir."

"Yes, but she wouldn't even be here if I didn't hand her over to her uncle. And I'm not even sure it's her uncle... And, Wilson's disease is deadly... if we confirm it, and catch it early, she could have a chance. She might live a normal, happy life."

"What's a normal happy life?"

"I don't know."

"Can I speak freely, sir?"

"Of course. Always."

"I don't know if it's my place to tell you about your business, but she's *not* your priority, man. It's a fucking sad story, yes. I get that. I get how you wanna help. She's an orphan, and I'm sure she's super cute, or whatever. But she's not your problem! You are here to take care of us, Doc. Why are you wasting time on some piece of shit little girl who is going to die out here anyway?"

He was in no position to see my side of it. "I don't know... It doesn't feel right to leave her to die that way... I just... feel... compelled to help her."

But I was starting to see his point.

"It's not your problem, Doc," he said with an unmistakable violence. "Not your circus. Not your elephants. She was born into this shit. You can't change that. I'd be pissed if you got hurt out here and we were down a doc because of this bullshit. And now my team is exposed, because we're out here searching for you. It's so fuckin' irresponsible. You have to own that."

"You're right, Jones." He was right. "I'm sorry... I thought… if I could only help one girl. It might make all this shit worth it... It doesn't seem fair…"

"It's not about fair, Doc. None of this is fair. Her whole miserable life isn't fair. This whole situation isn't fair..." Then he trailed off.

The scorpions broke free and scurried under a rock. We heard the rumble of engines through the building and the lad he'd sent away popped back, "We're good, Sarge."

"Are you ready to put that shit out of your head, and get back to work now?"

"Yes," I said, stretching my legs, feeling defeated.

He grabbed my shoulders, "If she dies or gets killed out here, that's not on you. It's her fate. It's hubris to think it has anything to do with you. None of us have control over where and when we die and she's no exception."

"You're right."

Jones seemed certain. In his mind, his path was righteous and just, and his unmistakable capacity for violence, coloured all of that. But for me, right and wrong, just and unjust, were blurry.

Amalah might be seeing her last few sunsets, and it felt like my fault. My inability to fix that weighed on me. Too many fragile frames snuffed out by this godforsaken war.

Jones reached out to take my hand. "Don't let it get you down. You're a good man. But just one man. And you can't save them all."

I held his hand a moment as he pulled me to my feet. "Wouldn't it be great if we could though?"

"If it were only possible... Let's get you home."

———

Passing through the building into the far street we found his demi-team. Two GMV's (General Military Vehicles that looked a lot like American Humvee's) were idling there.

I recognized a couple of the troops from the ranges.

And then I saw Clark. He nodded and smiled. The look of relief on his face reminded me why they were all here.

For me. I was their mission. Americans call it a 'DUSTWUN', "Duty Status, Whereabouts Unknown." That was me. The entire Coalition must have been ramped up looking for me.

I was missing in action. But found.

I climbed in the back of the rear truck, with Clark, Jones, and their driver, feeling dejected. The soft seat was too inviting.

"You look like shit, Jack. Are you okay?" Clark asked.

"I'm okay."

"We've been looking for you."

"Yes. I'm sorry about that."

"That's fine. It's what we do. You left your clinic outreach and ran off into the village though. What the hell were you thinking?"

"I got lost."

"Clearly. But why?"

"He was looking for an orphan girl," said Jones from the front.

"You were what? Wandering the village looking for... You realize you're in Panjwai, right?"

"Yes. It's a long story... I just... It's complicated."

"You're a physician. That FOB is as far forward as you're ever supposed to be."

"It won't happen again, sir."

"Damn right it won't."

The trucks ambled down the winding streets.

"But I'm glad we found you." He smiled over to me like an older brother might and this lightened my spirits a bit. "But what were you thinking?"

I rested my head on the window and seat back. I was groggy and thinking about the men I'd killed and about Lucky and how everything I'd done had led to that slaughter.

I wanted Clark to know the truth. I was clearing my head about the truth. But also wanted to be back at the FOB, which felt so imminent then, because that was where my journey home to Grace would begin.

Oh Grace. What would Grace do if she were here?

Grace would tell them the truth. The whole truth. All of it. Without hesitation. And she would tell me to take responsibility for everything I'd done. And she would be right. There was nothing to be ashamed of. I had done it all with good intentions.

But Brad had told me to forget about that girl. He said it out loud, "That's an order." And that made me hesitate.

Why did I leave the outreach?

I started to try to explain to Clark, but my mouth was dry. I reached for my canteen. But it was empty. Clark fumbled behind for his, and handed it to me.

After a long draught I finally found some words, "I was looking for an Afghan child who lost her parents."

"You ran off looking for an Afghan child. Alone. Do I have that right?"

"Umm. Well. Not alone. But, yes."

"What do you mean?"

"My translator was with me... But, he's dead"

"Dead?"

"Yeah. Shot last night. That's how I got lost. I was running for my life."

"Ok. Well. That's something. Dead translator. Where?"

"He was trying to help me into a compound where he saw her."

"And they shot him?"

"Yes."

"Okay. And... this kid. What is she? Some kinda sob story?"

"Something like that. I think she has a medical condition. If I can catch it early. It could save her."

"I see. I figured there'd be some kind of noble explanation for all this, Jack, but I can't find my way around the stupid. You're needed at the FOB, man. Whatever compelled you to find that girl was patently misguided. And now your translator is dead? You need to forget about that girl."

"Yes, sir," I managed.

"We will get you back to the UMS. We have another mission that is time sensitive. And, I was coming to find you about it before all this went down. You might be able to help us with it."

"Whatever you need, sir."

The trucks rumbled on toward the FOB. Clark booted up his Toughbook on the centre console between us, and passed it forward to Jones, "Can you bring up those images from last night? I have a theory."

Jones clicked the keyboard and I could see him open a folder full of image and video files. He pulled one up, "I think this is the one."

Clark manipulated the video, "Right, yes."

It was an overhead view of a group of buildings. Possibly shot by drone, maybe satellite. Three men with AK-47's in a compound. A group of children loitering. The front wall hid the buildings from a town square. Grape fields stretched into the distance behind. In the square out front, a form in a heap. A body. Dark sand pooled around a shattered skull...

"Lucky," I gasped.

My hand moved to my mouth.

Clark noticed my hand, but it wasn't clear that he heard me over the din of the vehicle. He was distracted and didn't seem to noticed that I had recognized the compound, and my dead friend in the dirt out front. He continued scanning the video.

It was hard to believe all of that had happened only yesterday.

Why are they even looking at that? Did they know that was Lucky? Did they know I was there last night? Am I in a world of hurt?

He found an image and zoomed in, "You did a medical exam on a prisoner at the FOB last week."

"Yes, sir."

"I have your report right here." He pulled out a duotang and slapped it into my hand. A page with my handwriting. The form I'd completed on the fat man in the vest who got away.

"How did you get this?" I asked, feebly.

"Doesn't matter. Does that look like the same man?" he pointed to the screen.

The picture was grainy. What I noticed first were the two men lying in caskets in the centre of the courtyard. Women were cleaning the bodies with buckets and soap of the two men I'd killed.

I had to steal myself from feinting. I wanted to disappear, but focussed instead on the pot belly and colourful vest of the man striding through the compound.

"It could be him, yes," I said. "The belly. The beard. And the vest, look familiar. But I can't be sure. Do you have a close up?"

"No. Look closely. If you had to bet?"

"Yes. I would say that's the same vest. It looks like the same man. You don't see many like him."

"That helps, Jack. Thank you." Then to Jones, "We have him." And Jones smiled.

They immediately started a planning cycle.

"I'm getting excited, sir," said Jones.

"Well, hold your horses. We've got to get the team on this first."

But Jones was anxious, "See here. This front wall is a façade. Open to the fields behind. Here. And here. You would assume they've mined this area... Back up the tape... There... troop movement... here and here... If we were to assault... I'd recommend this way, and this way, at first light..." I watched them bounce ideas for an assault on the compound as the truck rolled on.

I was staring at the screen. The fat man. The three others with rifles. Two women. Seven children. Then down in the corner, a colour caught my eye. A tackle box with a blue lid.

"That's my med kit," I whispered to no one. They hadn't heard. Sitting alone in the picture, beside the med kit was a child, who appeared to be reading.

Amalah!

She *was* in that compound.

I pulled the screen closer. She was sitting beside my med kit reading. Maybe the book I'd given her, "Colonel," I said. "That girl. I think that's the child I'm looking for... "

"What?" he said, and looked at the screen, then back at me. A puzzled look on his face. "What are you talking about?"

"Her uncle claimed her from our FOB after her parents were killed in a blast."

"How? Was that the compound? Is that... There is no way... That girl is a suicide bomber, Jack."

"A what? ...No."

"Yes. There's nothing more true than that. We have twenty-four hours of video on that compound. Footage of those kids trying on suicide vests.

"But. That's Amalah. Her name is Amalah."

"Well, she's involved in his schemes, and they are planning something big."

"I can't imagine... Her family was just killed... I watched them die."

"Kids without parents are Mustaq's modis operandi. He grooms them."

"But she's only there because of me."

"How can you be sure? Maybe she's been groomed since birth."

"I don't know. But I think it's true. And if I'm right, she's only caught up in this because of me."

"That's neither here nor there. She looks like all the other kids."

I wondered how much I could trust about what I felt from those few days with her. My conviction was waning.

"Jack, it's best you consider that girl wants us dead. I'm sure of it. Like the others. The man you examined last week is Mustaq Akbarzada. He's a very bad man. We're going to capture him tomorrow. And he will be killed, or locked down for good. Guantanamo. Immediately. And anyone who gets in our way will not be pleased. If that girl ends up collateral damage I won't shed a tear."

Then Jones added, "The last time we underestimated him, three of our guys died in the crossfire. Any resistance will be met with overwhelming force and superior fire power." And he smiled.

"That girl though, she's innocent."

"They're all innocent. Right up to the moment they strap on the explosives and start chanting. And they believe they're innocent even then." Clark pointed to the screen. "That man is the mastermind behind fifteen suicide bombings, this year alone. All of them, children who seemed to go willingly to their cause. He arranges it all. He is a monster. And those fifteen are just the ones we know about. I won't let him get away with it."

None of what I felt for Amalah factored in to Clark's calculus. In his mind she was close to the epicentre of an enemy combatant until removed. The futility was overwhelming.

I was so tired and sore and his conviction was compelling. I began to worry about telling him more about the night before.

It was bad enough being lost outside the FOB, but the killing was something else. Lucky was dead and I'd killed two young men. Clark would not be wrong to hold me accountable for those things. Maybe even for Lucky's death.

He could have me arrested.

Clark seemed in that moment to be one of the wolves.

I wasn't sure about anything.

I was spinning.

I wanted to trust him. It sounded like Mustaq was a terrible human, and needed to be stopped. I had to hang my hat on the idea they would protect an innocent girl if given the choice.

I wanted to believe the Army could be her saviour. Even without me breaking rules to help her. That's why I was there after all. I believed in the Army. And outsourcing Canada. And Clark was the personification of all of that.

But they'd lost men trying to take down Mustaq. And revenge is a different kind of motivator; even for these professionals. If she got in the way she didn't stand a chance.

"I believe she's innocent," I said again, meekly.

But they weren't listening.

————

The trucks were moving quite slowly through the narrow streets and the two wolves were still talking.

"Think it through with me, Jones," Clark was saying, "It makes a lot of sense. They were trying to throw us off the trail. But we know the suicide bombings triangulate to this village. We have solid reasons to believe they are operating out of this compound. And now Jack confirms. He's there."

Jones zoomed in on the image of Lucky's shattered remains and the trails of blood in the dust where two others had been dragged into the compound. "When we caught this image of dead men in that market square last night..."

Sweat dripped down the back of my neck, and beaded on my brow.

I should clear it up and tell them.

"That skirmish is consistent with intel about infighting between Mustaq's group and the other Taliban militias."

That's not right. That's not why there was a skirmish there.

But I was confused and tired and remained scared of consequences.

I need to tell them. Interrupt and explain how all of that was me. And how Lucky got there. Tell them how he died. How I was the one who lured him to his death, with my stupid ideas about the girl...

I swallowed hard, choking back bile.

Clark continued, pointing to a mound of fabric straps in the back of the compound, "That material is the same webbing found on suicide vests."

He flipped through another series of photos of captured suicide bombers, and the fabric of their vests. "See, here." He was making a good case. Some were laid clean on tables, others bloody lying across mutilated corpses.

Then, back to the compound, "That stack of crates appears U.S. in origin. Possibly the stolen C4 raided from that convoy in West Helmand three months ago." He pointed to a corner of one of the roofless buildings.

Next, he pulled up a heat map of the compound, "This is live. Seventeen souls inside now. Numbers have fluctuated from twelve and twenty-eight over the past eight hours."

"And Mustaq is one of them," Jones said, through gritted teeth.

"Yes. Which means our source is compromised. We had him on an aircraft to Pakistan two nights ago, but that appears wrong. Jack here confirms." He smiled over to me as the image zoomed on the portly man in the vest again, and their silence compelled me to speak. But I only nodded. My dry mouth creaked open, but nothing came out.

"Sounds convincing to me," said Clark with a chuckle, "It confirms our intelligence has been suspect for months."

"We've got him now though," said Jones.

"I think so."

They were both excited about that.

"Their main weapons cache is probably here. Sleeping quarters here, and here. Soldiers and these children may all be threats. We'll need to get the team together quickly. Standard rules of engagement. Protect the children if we can..."

The assault would be planned from bottom up. The door kickers started time appreciation from the pointy end, and worked back through stages of command ending with the present moment. I would have liked to witness that, but they were fixed on getting me back to the FOB and UMS as soon as possible.

And my head was still spinning.

I leaned against the window and closed my eyes.

I had broken rules. Three men were dead, and no one even knew I was involved. But this ordeal would be over soon, and they would be off to focus on their own mission.

Maybe I'm right to keep the killing to myself?

I didn't want to struggle with that question. But I was glad for their help, and infinitely safer in their presence. They were confident, and competent, and dangerous.

The truck continued rumbling through the streets toward the FOB. The sky was pink as far as I could see now.

Sunsets can be breathtaking in the desert.

We passed an alley on the edge of town and entered a familiar street where, in the distance, I saw the building where Lucky and I climbed. The first stars were appearing beyond the patio set on that rooftop, and I thought of Lucky. He was lying there still, one block over, rotting in the street.

He deserved better. I thought of Amalah. She deserved better too.

I was drawn to her by some supernatural pull. A need to fix it. Helping her felt more important than ever. I could only hope they would keep her safe. I had to trust they would. But Jones was right. I was needed at the FOB. I never should have left the team. I'd done enough damage.

My head rested on the window and soft headrest, and suddenly I was floating above Lucky in the square, like a drone over ground zero. "Clark, Clark," I was pleading and watching the team approach. Their night vision goggles perched over eyes, weapons at the ready. "It was self-defence," I was yelling, but the sound absorbed in the din, like in the back of that Herc.

"They killed Lucky in cold blood," I tried to scream, but no one stopped moving to listen, relentlessly marching forward on their deadly mission.

Then Amalah was staring at me from a bed inside the compound. Her golden eyes came close to mine, and she was angry at first, then sad. Sorry for me. As if I'd done something terribly wrong. She reached up and pulled me down. She was pulling on my arm and shaking my head and I was trying to reach for her but she was too far away and slipping into the depths...

And I awoke suddenly, as the world went silent with a bang and a pop, and I was blinded by a flash of light.

———————

Silence. Then tinnitus and vibration. The blast had been loud and fierce. The Humvee to our front was in the air, rolling to its side in slow motion, and time seemed to stretch. I saw every detail. Metal twisting, fire spreading. Our windshield shattering.

Our driver slammed on the brakes and we shuddered to a halt.

"IED, IED, Get Down!" Jones yelled.

The mangled truck ahead, on its side, was leaning against a building, burning, and blocking our path.

Dust filled the air. Thick and choking.

"Niner Charlie, niner Charlie, do you copy? Over." Clark's voice was steady, but there was no answer. Just static.

Then bullets were hitting our truck.

Through the dust and commotion holes appeared in our cracked windshield and I ducked. The sound of the clink-clinking of metal being frayed was frighteningly close.

The rest of the occupants were already exiting with their weapons at the ready and I lost site of the team.

I opened my door and fell to my left onto the ground. There was a melee beginning around me. Jones and the driver were engaging to the front. The air was thick with the smell of burning fuel and rubber.

I reached back into the truck and grabbed my C7 and crouched by the tire, trying to get my bearings.

It was all dust and motion.

Past the front of the vehicle, I saw a group of Afghan men streaming out of a building to my right.

Insurgents.

Jones killed two of them efficiently, then jumped between the buildings to our left. I crouched as the insurgents engaged the rolled vehicle. No one would be getting out of there alive.

I turned back in time to see Jones running across the road with his weapon up, away from someone in the alley. He was shooting backwards. I trained my weapon on the alley, and when an insurgent emerged, I pulled my trigger and dropped him.

Jones looked over to me with a nod, then took up a firing position near the wall.

Then a muzzle flash from a second storey across the street aimed toward him. I saw dust fall from near his head.

It's hard to explain what happened next.

They say you don't know how you're going to react.

I recall thinking about home. My cot at the FOB, and the futility of everything I'd done. All the horrors I'd seen, and how my skills as a physician had saved so few. My feet were blistered and so very sore.

But when I saw Jones shot, and watched him fall...

It made me angry. I raged. And something inside took over.

"Jones can't die," I yelled.

I stood with my weapon at my shoulder and began firing, first at the window on the second floor, and watched as a bearded rifleman in tan linens fell out onto the hard packed gravel.

Then at the insurgents around the rolled vehicle. Three of them fell in succession before they noticed me.

They seemed confused as they fell.

I mustered all the speed I could and ran to Jones. Within seconds I was with him. The drops of blood were still falling to the ground from where my rounds had penetrated the nearby men. The rest of the insurgents seemed to have dispersed into darkness.

The shooting stopped. All that was left was the noise of one engine. And crackling fire.

The current threat seemed to have disappeared as suddenly as it arrived. Clark and the others must have been nearby but I couldn't see or hear them either. I rolled Jones over and took a look.

His wounds were severe. The worst penetrated his thigh exiting above his popliteal fossa at the back. The round had torn a gaping exit wound that I'm certain contained parts of his femoral artery which was pumping blood onto the road.

He was exsanguinating quickly.

"Where's your tourniquet?"

"Left pocket." He looked scared. Pale.

I opened and emptied its contents: a notepad, pens, a protein bar, and two empty wrappers.

No tourniquet.

I tried the other side. Nothing. Checked his other pockets, losing precious seconds.

"Shit. I used it on Mac," he said.

"And I don't have one," I said.

I quickly removed my belt and wrapped it around his upper leg. Pulled tight but couldn't find anything to secure it. A tourniquet has a metal windlass that helps cinch it. My belt was leather and I had nothing to secure it to, there's no holes in the leather at that spot... but I pulled with all my might and tried to pierce it with the point of metal at the buckle and wrap it tight...

"We need to get some cover. Can you move?"

"I can try."

With more strength than I remember ever having I lifted Jones to his feet. With one of his legs dragging, his head drooped, I wrapped his arm around my shoulders and pulled him along. I could see inside one of the nearby buildings, it was empty. I pulled him to a corner there and set him down. I placed his rifle in his hands then turned to survey the scene. The dust was settling and I could see bodies everywhere.

Then one of the Canadians on the far side of the mangled Humvee seemed to be moving. I didn't think. I ran to him. It was no more than fifty feet and I scanned my environment with my weapon at the ready as I ran. I dropped down at his side and quickly triaged.

Two obvious bullet wounds. Left calf. Right shoulder.

His pulse was thready. His eyes glazed over.

I had nothing clean to pack those wounds but did my best to apply pressure to the shoulder. Then found his tourniquet and cinched his leg.

"Let's go." I said, and picked him up and dragged him over to the building with Jones. I set him on the opposite wall with a better view of the entrance. And gave him his rifle.

Then ran out again.

I had to see if anyone was alive in the wreckage. And if there was a working radio.

I was on my knees reaching up into the back of the mangled Humvee, I could see the occupants. Not moving. Blackened from the still burning fires. I was reaching for the pretzel switch of the radio in the back when something struck me on the back of my head and everything went black.

Chapter Twenty-Eight

Damage Control

There were no dreams. No epiphanies. No white lights.

I don't know how long I was out, but when I came to, I was in the dirt on my back with two insurgents standing over me. One had his gun pointed at my chest. The other was bent, slapping my face.

He saw my eyes open and squatted lower.

"Dakter -You Dakter?" He undid my helmet and threw it to his friend. My head bounced on the road. He grabbed my hair and pulled.

"You Dakter?" he asked again.

He was close and spit into my face as he said it.

He looked vaguely familiar. Maybe from the village outreach, or from the gate the night before. I don't know, but he seemed to know I was a doctor.

I nodded. "Yes, I'm a doctor." My head was pounding. They dragged me to my feet but my legs were weak. I couldn't stand. I was fading. They seemed angry, and began to argue as I slumped back to the ground.

Above them the constellations were shining.

In Panjwai there are more stars than I have ever seen. More than over the big prairie skies. Out there, the milky way is an elliptical slash from horizon to horizon almost completely full of light. It's beautiful.

I thought again of Lucky lying beneath those stars as I lied there. All because I had hope for a little girl. That she might live a little longer.

Doing nothing, even then, felt like letting her die. How could any of this be okay? Clark's words, *collateral damage,* rang in my ears. The girl with copper eyes who loved stories: collateral damage. An orphan with no hope, and no one to look out for her. Her family already slaughtered by this stupid war.

Orion's belt pointed at the man with the gun.

I was drifting. Fading. I held on to the beauty of the moment for as long as I could. But there was nothing I could do. Darkness overcame me.

———

The next thing I remember was the movement of the ground. My hands had fallen forward and were dragging. I flinched against the sudden pain as my fingers racked against the spinning spokes of a motorized cart I was draped over. Blood splattered and I winced. I gasped in fear and cried out, almost falling.

The engine noise to my right was an old army-green motorcycle with a sidecar. Two insurgents were taking me somewhere. Fast. We were careening through the streets.

The one in the sidecar saw me flinch, and smiled back. He pulled his friend's shirt and thumbed toward me.

I rolled into a more balanced position in the trailer. My hands were abraded across the back. Not deep, but bleeding. My head was throbbing. The cart was otherwise empty. My weapons, and body armour, and helmet were gone. My pockets were empty. Even my boot laces were gone.

When we entered the village square, I recognized the compound immediately. Lucky's corpse was covered in flies and dirt. That horror contrasted the care taken with the other two beyond the gate. Those dead men had been washed with care and draped with cloth. They were surrounded by colour. Flowers and frames on a dais between them. A funeral parlour in torchlight. We circled them. Despite my pain and predicament, I felt profoundly sad. They were still and serene and far too young. And I had killed them. They were someone's son, someone's lover, maybe someone's father.

No matter how just or necessary don't ever let anyone tell you war is not a crime.

My medical kit was in the corner on the ground. It's blue top stark against the pale wall. Three men came out to greet us. They clasped arms with their friends and gathered around my cart. I was pushed against the wall as they lowered the tail. They grabbed my legs and pulled and I fell onto the ground landing hard on my left hip. They held my ankles firm, laughing as I twisted trying to pull free.

They dragged me struggling across the stones through the compound to a back building.

I was unceremoniously dumped into a small room.

The door slammed, and the latch clicked.

There was a low straw mattress in one corner. I crawled over and collapsed onto my back, my head pounding, my hands bleeding, my hip now throbbing and sore, and my feet blistered and swollen.

But I was alive.

The voices in the hall sounded joyous. They were laughing as they faded away. In the silence I closed my eyes, but heavy footsteps returned, and there were voices again in the hall.

The night sky was dark through the slits in the ceiling. Exhausted and in pain I looked at my hands.

Filthy, but the blood had clotted.

The door opened and the man with the vest and portly belly stepped through the door. He was balancing a metal wash basin and had a towel over his arm. In his hand, a bar of soap.

Mustaq.

"Hello Doctor," he said.

"You speak English?"

"Yes. Some. I am glad you could join us."

I said nothing.

"You need wounds cleaned," he said in a deep, fatherly tone as he placed the basin and towel on the floor and dropped a bar of soap in the tepid water. I squatted and immersed my sore hands. It was soothing. I washed and examined.

One step at a time.

Sore but manageable. Nothing terribly deep. Nothing over joints. My fingers were not broken.

Neurovascularly intact.

Abrasions. No lacerations. I cleaned and blotted and held pressure with the cloth. My hands would be ok. He stood watching as I focused on my task.

"Two of my men need you, Doctor."

And there it was. I was alive because they needed a doctor.

A glimmer of hope.

"Why should I help you?" I asked quietly, focusing on my breathing, as he stepped closer.

He radiated heat. Like he'd been lounging by a fire or lying in the sun but the sun was down. It was unnatural. He was crunching something in his teeth and smelled of cloves. His smell filled the room. He was menacing. But peaceful. Reminiscent of a deacon in my sister's church. An aura of religious authority. The same peaceful smile behind his beard.

"Are you not a doctor? Have you not taken an oath?" And I knew I would help him. "There was a box left outside last night. Dropped by the man who killed my nephews."

I dried my hands on the towel and said nothing. "Not me!", "That's interesting?", "Tell me more about that." Were the first few options that ran through my head, but I said nothing.

My thoughts were racing...

I tried to calm my breathing.

I was thinking of the killings. Those men falling. The blood splattering behind them. The surprise on their faces.

I didn't know it at the time but killing had marked a dividing moment in my life. There was before and there was after.

Like Grace.

"They tell me the man at my gate was a doctor. Were you here last night, Doctor? Were you at my gate?"

I was confused and afraid. I was also sad. And peaceful. And from within that complicated mix of emotion came a searing, blistering anger again.

It welled up quickly from within and was overwhelming in a moment. My scrabbling for calm through boxed-breathing was futile. It threatened to harm me, to break me in two. It threatened to end everything. I knew I should stay silent. All the conduct after capture protocols said so. Say nothing at first... "I can't answer that question." The safest, most intelligent response. I knew I should leave it at that; 'I cat Q'... but, I knew this fatherly, holy man was the perpetrator of unspeakable horrors... And my anger was overwhelming.

"Mustaq," I said with aggression, and saw the surprise in his eyes. He stepped back a half step as I turned. His brow furrowed and he looked more closely into my face and eyes.

"Yes. I was there. I killed your nephews. I killed them, and I'm happy that I did." My teeth were gritted. "They killed my friend and tried to kill me." My fists clenched. I was taller and looked down into his eyes.

His eyes burned with anger and I hesitated.

He stepped forward and placed an iron hand on the centre of my chest. I reached for it, but couldn't budge it from its perch. He pushed me back with shocking force. It frightened me. My back was suddenly three feet back against the wall. My feet were on the edge of the mat. I had almost fallen but he held me up, off balance for a moment.

"You will pay for that," he said.

"It was self-defence," I tried, struggling against him, but his strength of *will* was insurmountable.

I couldn't move.

"They were my nephews," he sneered and his words sunk through me like sand. He held me still. His eyes drilling into my soul and I knew he would have me suffer, that I would pay for those deaths with my blood.

I had killed his family. Their souls haunted me, staring back through his angry eyes.

When I realized we were alone, and he seemed unarmed, that frightened me even more.

He saw my surrender and relaxed his grip, "You will help my friends. Then we will speak of justice."

He turned, briskly, and disappeared out the door. It latched behind him.

Alone I collapsed onto the bed.

Defeated. And scared.

———

I must have passed out. In a moment there were two men grabbing my arms. It was dark and I was exhausted. They took me down the hall into another room which looked like a hospital ward but more like the one the Afghan medics had set up at the FOB.

Two sick men were convalescing under blankets on raised tables against the wall with beads of sweat dripping down their faces. Their eyes were closed and both were panting and still. There was medical equipment, but none of it seemed utilized.

Two IV stanchions, surgical tools in a tray on a table, a wash basin with soapy water, bandages and rags, and a white metal cabinet with a glass door, full of vials.

The room smelled like a morgue. Like death.

Mustaq was there, "These men were shot five days ago. You will help them. You will fix them," he said.

Another man pointed a rifle at me.

I hesitantly crossed the room to look at the first man. He was awake but his eyes were glazed and his pupils were pinpoint. Poppy husks and vials of brown liquid were on the side table beside him.

They are using pure opium for his pain.

The skin of his face was hot.

Fever. Radial pulse too fast. 115 bpm.

I pulled the blanket down. No flinch as I pressed his soft belly. Non-tender. A wet and bloody bandage was draped across his left arm. The wound beneath was dripping pus.

I removed the bandage revealing a festering bullet hole through bone, heaped with swelling, erythema, and leaking pus.

Infected.

It had spread up his arm and onto his chest. The bullet had shattered his humerus and lacerated the flesh of his back. It didn't seem to have penetrated his chest.

The wounds were filthy and probably would have benefitted from suturing days ago. Too late for that now. There was an old wooden maternity stethoscope in the cabinet. I grabbed it and listened over his chest. Intimate, but effective. Breath sounds bilaterally. No pneumothorax. His lungs were intact. I finished my secondary survey, checked his legs, pelvis, and head.

"His biggest concern is that infection. He needs antibiotics. Yesterday. I may have some in my kit," I said.

I turned to the second man. He was less fortunate. Three bullet wounds. One shattered his left heel.

Not properly packed.

"He is probably going to lose this foot," I said, lifting it slightly.

Mustaq appeared to wince.

The foot was infected and what was left of his calcaneus bone was mush. There was fibrin deposition, and some clot forming around the bone fragments, all the way up to the level of his talar dome.

He won't walk again.

That was an unfortunate outcome, but not as life-threatening as his other two wounds. Bullets had penetrated his abdomen and I could only find one exit wound.

An odd number of bullet holes in a torso is a bad thing. It means one round was still inside. Possibly lodged in his pelvis or spine. Possibly close to a major artery or nerve. He had survived five days, so massive internal hemorrhage was less likely, but his bowels were probably penetrated and festering.

"This man is almost certainly seeping feces, shit, into his peritoneum, his belly... He is septic... He needed damage control surgery five days ago. A wash out and a bowel run now might help," I said.

Mustaq was listening. He stayed near the door.

"You will do this," he said.

I ignored that. I couldn't find a blood pressure cuff. There was definitely no sat monitor. Nothing useful. The best I could do was clean and pack the wounds, and hope. A pulse at his femoral artery was reassuring that there was some blood pressure there.

The basin had dirty water. I dumped it on the ground and wiped it clean with a dirty cloth, "I need clean water. Preferably warm. Lots of it. Bring me more bandages if you have them, and the medical kit with the blue lid in the courtyard."

He barked and his henchmen ran out. In short order one of them returned with my med kit. Another brought water. Initially the basin I had used to clean my own blood in the other room. It was still awash with my own blood.

I rolled my eyes, "CLEAN water please," I said and dumped it on the ground. He left again.

I found a vial of Ceftriaxone at the bottom of my med kit. That was something useful. An antibiotic. Although it was not enough. I drew two grams in a small syringe and affixed a twenty-two-gauge needle. I cleaned an injection site on the first man's leg with an ethanol wipe and injected the medicine into the meat of his thigh. I did the same for the other man, but that was not particularly hopeful.

"This man needs surgery," I said. "They both need medication daily and I don't have enough. They need to be in hospital. Otherwise, they will die."

The other man returned with clean water and placed it reverently at my side. Mustaq began pacing as I cleaned wounds. His hands behind his back.

"You are a surgeon, no?" he said at last.

"No. I'm not."

"Yes," he said. Louder. His eyebrows joined together and he frowned. "You are. You are his surgeon."

"No. I really am not. He needs an operating room and imaging. And intensive care. There is a bullet somewhere in his belly and his bowels are leaking into his gut. Nothing can be done here."

"You will operate," he said.

I jumped when he slammed a fist on the table with the tray. The surgical tools bounced and clanged.

He barked more orders and another man left.

The arm wound needed a pressure dressing.

"I need more bandages," I said. One of the men opened a drawer under the table and pulled some out. They were clean. I used them on the arm and the man's back.

Their hope that I would save this man with belly wounds was laughable. What he was asking was ludicrous.

I thought about the month I'd spent at Sunnybrook. About the handful of abdominal surgeries I'd watched in med school. A handful of appendectomies, c-sections, and a few bowel resections. The most I'd done was hold a retractor. I had always cheekily asked successive preceptors, "Would you like your sutures cut too-long or too-short, sir?" Which endeared me to them. And they would show me more things in the body cavity where we had our hands. But I was not studying surgery. I was observing. An emergency room physician and a family doctor does not perform major abdominal surgery without an extensive amount of directed training, and even then, it is rare. Some things are best left to surgeons.

I could handle the odd minor surgery but an exploratory abdominal laparotomy was not even a remote possibility. There was no way I was going rooting around in that man's belly, in the middle of the desert, with no anesthesia, no lighting, and no help. I didn't even know what proper tools to use, but they were certainly not in that room, and even a surgeon wouldn't do it without imaging first.

At gun point or otherwise it would be murder.

And I'd killed enough people for one lifetime.

Those men needed a hospital.

"You might as well shoot them," I said.

"Doctor, I need you to try," he said, and stepped toward me.

"It would be asinine for me to attempt an exploratory laparotomy here. Even if I could do it. I can't."

I stepped away from the two men toward the door, but he stepped in front of me.

"They need imaging and an operating room and anesthesia. If you don't get them to hospital, you are killing them."

"The hospital is in Kabul. We cannot get them to Kabul."

"Well, you ought to try."

"YOU WILL HELP THEM," he yelled. And he seemed vulnerable. There were tears forming in his eyes.

"I have given them antibiotics. I have one dose left for tomorrow. They will need more after that and the next day. I have more at the FOB. We can bring them there. We might be able to help them there."

"You will help them, here," he said.

Exasperated, I turned back to the patients, and continued to clean their wounds.

Chapter Twenty-Nine

The NICU

At that moment I heard a shuffle in the hall and when I looked up, I was shocked to see Amalah standing at the door. She stepped into view in the wake of Mustaq's yelling. She was rubbing her eyes and clutching something in her hands. A pillow. She was wearing a sleeping gown. Her eyes lit up when she saw me, and she ran past Mustaq across the floor at top speed, her hair flowing behind her in the air. I smiled and crouched and wrapped her in my arms. Her forehead tucked under my chin.

In that shitty, makeshift hospital ward we had a moment of eternal happiness. I felt like her champion and suddenly I knew I had been dreaming of that moment, and believing it would happen. I had been asking the universe for it. And then she was there. And there was hope.

"You know this girl," said Mustaq.

"Yes. Her family died with us."

"She knows you. She likes you."

"I read her stories."

Then he spoke to Amalah in harsh tones and she stepped behind me and peered around me as I stood.

"She should not be out of bed," he said.

"This is the girl I was looking for when I came here last night. Look at her eyes." I said, then added, "It's okay, Amalah," and, "Look at her eyes. She might have a sickness. A sample of her blood would tell me..."

He looked at me differently.

It might have been esteem.

The angle of his jaw tilted.

"Doctor, you were here last night for this reason?"

"Yes, this is why I came. For her. This is why my friend was killed. And your men attacked me. She needs a blood test."

"Her eyes. What does this mean?"

"I think it's copper. Too much copper in her body accumulates in her eyes and eventually her liver and brain. No one can survive without treatment."

"How long?"

"That depends. Very few live past forty years and most go crazy long before."

Then he began to laugh. A deep hearty laugh that confused me for a moment, "Doctor, you are an enigma. She will live for a month, yes?"

"Of course... But if I could just draw her blood to see, she might live a normal happy life."

Then he laughed again. A natural laugh. Not forced but joyful. Finally, he settled and said plainly, "No. There is no need for your blood test."

"Why?"

"This girl will not live to see forty years." Then he squatted and reached out his hand to Amalah. He spoke gently in his own tongue and she moved toward him.

I grabbed her arm and pulled her close. "What do you mean?"

"Let go Doctor. She is not yours."

Just then the man returned with her uncle and when she saw him, she came back to me and pushed her face into my arm again. Hiding.

"Your ideas do not concern us, Doctor. She is prepared to serve our cause. Our glorious future depends on her faith. There is a plan for her."

"No... You can't."

"She is a beautiful child. No? Her eyes are a blessing to our jihad. She will get close to President Karsai next month. Afghanistan will be in the hands of the true believers once more. You cannot stop this from happening, Doctor."

Her uncle came forward and grabbed her by the arm. I tried to stop him by pushing his arm away, and didn't see it coming...

He struck me. A short blunt punch to the face. His sharp ring lacerated my nose and cheek. I was not expecting it and it hurt. Blood splattered as I fell to the ground. And a memory from my time in medical school flashed before my eyes...

I was working as a clinical clerk in the neonatal intensive care unit. Neonates occasionally need tiny transfusions of blood. I had ten cc's in a syringe, more than enough for an infant that size. We checked the stickers, confirmed the match, and I began my first ever neonatal transfusion.

A senior resident and the baby's parents were looking on. The neonate was in one of those clear plastic incubators with openings on the side for hands. An IV cannula was in place infusing a trickle of saline TKVO (to keep the vein open) through an umbilical vein. My syringe with the blood had a male adapter that slid into the female opening on the IV line. No sharps. Nothing too complicated for a learner. Easy, peezy. I pushed the syringe onto the opening and tried to depress the plunger—but nothing happened. I pushed a little harder.

The resident was speaking to the parents and didn't notice my struggling with the syringe. Confused, I pushed harder still. The plunger was stuck. Blood can be sticky. I took my hand off the line and drew the plunger back and felt it release with a click. Great. With a better grip, I pushed again. And all at once the tip slipped off and— PFFFFFffffttttttt—ten cc's of bright red blood splattered all over the baby and the inside of that incubator.

It looked like a blood bath.

I was mortified.

The mother was stunned.

The father fainted.

All that to say ten cc's is a tiny volume, but looks like a lot of blood. It painted the inside of that incubator and covered the baby. The splatter of blood on that stone floor in Panjwai was reminiscent... After that uncle punched me in the face.

And that is why I laughed out loud.

I was certain the blood looked worse than it was, and I laughed remembering that father fainting. They looked confused by my laughter, and stared. Amalah looked scared. She was between the two men. I wiped my hands on my pants and stood, grabbed a clean cloth, and applied pressure to my minor facial wound.

"You're a funny man, Doctor. You will care for these men. And we will talk about what might be done tomorrow."

"How do you know I won't harm them? Like you've done to me?" I asked quietly.

He put his arm around Amalah, "Because I have something you want."

"You are already planning her death."

"Well, if that is not enough, then come with me Doctor," he said and turned toward the door.

I followed him into the hall. In the room next door there were eight tiny bunk beds filled with sleeping children.

Mustaq gently guided Amalah to hers and she climbed in.

Scanning the room quickly I noticed a stack of crates to the right of the door marked with US Army stencils, C4, placed here maybe for storage, or maybe for some more nefarious purpose. Clark and his team would not have seen these on the drone footage. There were more under the beds, and more stacked along the back wall. But he wasn't showing me those crates. He was showing me the children.

"All of these children are orphans, Doctor. And I promise you they will suffer if you allow more of my family to come to harm. I trust you will do your duty, as one who has taken the Hippocratic oath. You will heal them. Let this room inspire you."

He tucked Amalah into her bed. She was staring wide-eyed as he pulled the grey blanket to her chin. They pushed me back down the hall into the room with the injured men on stretchers.

———

Mustaq departed and another man came in with a straw pillow and a rough wool blanket and threw them at me in the corner.

"You. Sleep," he said, sitting in a chair beside the door. He rested his rifle across his lap and took out a pack of cigarettes. He offered me one. I declined.

The laceration on my face was clotting and I was weary. My hip was sore. My hands were sore. My feet too. The only glimmer of hope was Clark's team. My only hope was they were regrouped and ready for an assault. They knew about this compound. I'd seen their photos. They wouldn't wait. They couldn't wait. And if they were close, that was both reassuring and frightening. I was on the inside, and they'd breach with weapons free. I couldn't be sure if they didn't know I was there, or about all that C4 in the room with the children.

Maybe they were watching. I moved to the window and looked up to the sky. Searching for a drone. Hoping beyond hope someone might catch a glimpse of my face. But it was dark and I was bandaged and their pictures were taken long ago... I doubted they'd be keeping an eye on that window.

I set my med kit beside the pillow and went to the injured men again. I looked them over as if what I did would make a difference. Their living or dying had been predetermined long before I arrived on the scene. Nothing had changed. I took a clean towel, folded it, and placed it against my own wound. Then sat on the blanket and went through the kit searching for something useful: IV setup, rubber tourniquets, vials for blood, syringes, various individually wrapped needles, a pack of alcohol swabs, some individually wrapped 4x4 sterile gauze. I used some of those on my face. Below were vials of antibiotics, a dark bottle with a black metallic cap.

I pulled that out and read the label. It was the volatile compound I had used to knock out the monkey and the dog. There was half a bottle left.

I closed the kit.

The man lit another smoke.

He was young, thin, and wiry, like the rest. He wore a striped lungee turban draped across his shoulder. An AK-47 pointing in my direction across his lap. Cigarette smoke filled the room. It smelled of acid in my throat.

"Do you speak English?"

Some guttural sounds. Then another gesture to my cot.

"You. Sleep."

I lay in the dirt against the wall and pulled the blanket over my shoulders. My adrenaline pumping, mind racing. What could I do?

The compound was quiet. They had seen my wounds and my limp, the sores on my hands and face, and had left this one man to guard me.

I could run. But where? There were traps on the perimeter. I wouldn't get far, and Amalah and the children were in danger next door. *I need to be patient.*

Clark and his team were coming. They had to be coming.

First light. They said something about first light.

But I wasn't sure if these walls could stop stray bullets.

I needed a plan and I needed to stay awake and be prepared.

The boy guard was a chain-smoker. He lit back-to-back cigarettes from the cinders of the last. Probably trying to stay awake. I'd done my best to lie still, keeping one eye open staring through my lashes. He picked his nose and flicked it. To him I was asleep.

Staying awake was not difficult despite my fatigue and pronation. The ground was hard and my adrenaline laced with fear helped. My heart was racing.

On his third cigarette the man began drifting to sleep. He propped his head against the wall and crossed his arms. I stared at his weapon trying to trace the sling. Was it wrapped around his leg or arm or just lying flat across his lap? I couldn't tell.

Eventually sleep overtook him and his cigarette dropped to the floor. It smouldered in the sand and I waited, watching.

His breathing steadied as the trail of smoke slowed and stopped. I imagined myself sitting up. If I moved slowly, he might not stir. I could brace into a crouch. He looked comfortable. Asleep. Breathing deeply. I could move to the lid of the med kit. It was not latched. I could open it silently and remove the brown vial of volatile anesthetic. I had left it on top.

He remained still.

I imagined twisting the metallic lid of the vial. It would sound like fingernails on a chalkboard. But maybe not. Maybe the crystals in the glass grooves were wet. But how difficult had it been to sedate that dog? The monkey was easier but it was small and weak.

This soldier did not look weak.

Still, he slept.

I imagined folding the cloth, covered in my blood, and pouring the liquid from the vial then placing it in my right hand and winding up like a spring. He was three strides away. Four tops. I could get there. I'd have him. He'd breath in deep from the shock. It could work. And I could go to Amalah's room and get outside with the children into the moonlight.

But the skin on his face in the light of the moon from the window was soft, smooth and pristine above his short beard, like a young man's skin.

And my hip and hands and face were sore. I would
need to find strength that I did not think I had.

Then he snorted. And repositioned.

Then a noise from the compound woke him.

A bell was clanging down the hall and through the open
window. Someone was sounding an alarm. The boy with
the gun stood suddenly. His rifle clattered to the ground
and he turned toward the door. In his waking stupor he left
his gun and ignored me. I was struck by the suddenness of
the sounds and his standing abruptly. He stepped into the
opening of the door. A light from down the hall cast his
shadow into the room.

I was bigger than him.

But he was much quicker. And probably stronger. If
I jumped him, maybe I could wrestle him to the ground?
Or maybe I could get to his gun before he turned his head.

Then the noises from the compound recurred. And I
knew it was them. The assault. It was starting. There was an
explosion and gun fire.

I had no choice but to move. I jumped up and sprang
toward the gun. He turned when he heard my movement
but I had already closed the gap. We both dove for it. My
arm slid beneath his chin and I flexed and pulled hard. He
had the gun but I rolled on top of him. He kicked back at
my legs and shins and rolled me over. One arm came back
and gouged at my leg. He kicked my shins but his soft
shoes only bruised.

Amped and frightened I shifted and jostled to avoid
his kicks, and failing, and holding on, despite the pain in

my hands and shins and hip. My arm wedged against his throat.

I was more scared than I have ever been. Clark and his team were coming and I was locked in a struggle with a boy. And the children and the explosives were so close.

I consciously tried to crush his trachea.

I'm not proud of that.

But I was scared. It seemed my only hope. He was trying to yell. I had to overcome.

There was a gun battle raging nearby. Inside the compound. The assault had begun. OBUA. I pictured them stacking in. I twisted and strained against him. My eyes squeezed tight and all the horrors returned. The engineer's exposed trachea in the back of that truck... Amalah's baby brother... Those men falling with blood splattering behind them on the gate... The Canadians burning in the back of the mangled Humvee. Humans and animals. Death and destruction... It was too much to bear.

And this boy was another.

I couldn't kill another.

I relaxed my grip.

My Grace was there spinning in a white dress, snow falling, Wolf Island in the distance. A little girl beside her. Two white dresses spinning together on the hill. That beautiful picture was pressing down on my chest, and it hurt and I ran up the hill toward them, but the harder I ran the farther they seemed.

The boy stopped struggling.

I gasped. Fearful.

The human brain can survive without oxygen for about eight minutes. Could it have been that long?

No.

I could hear the gun battle raging in the compound and my eyes were blurry and wet. When I let go of the boy my arm wouldn't straighten. It seemed permanently flexed across his neck in the way, as children, we would push against door frames and feel our arms float away from our sides, up, in defiance of gravity, and hover.

He smelled of cigarettes and sweat and his dark hair had come loose in the struggle and was in my mouth.

I rolled him off and strained onto all fours and felt for his carotid pulse.

My tears tasted like salt and iron.

There were gun shots in the distance.

Thwaak. Thwaak. Thud. Thud.

They were distracting me from checking the pulse.

But I found it.

For a moment it was mine or his on my fingertips. But it was his. Mine was faster.

"Thank you Lord," I said out loud.

I scrambled to his weapon. Thinking about the children. They needed to be far away from those crates.

Bullets were filling the air that very moment. Any one might stray and hit a crate and I wasn't sure if they would explode, but I knew that heat and pressure was required and it was hot and bullets create a pressure wave. I'm not an expert, but maybe shooting plastique explosives in the heat would be enough to cause an explosion. I was worried about that C4. And the fact they stashed it with the children.

I ran to the door and checked the hall. The fighting was distant. The hallway was empty.

I bolted next door.

Chapter Thirty

Left Behind

The sky was lighter through the window of the children's room. The air was hot and still. The children were sitting on their beds. Amalah looked up and ran over to me. I gestured to the others and with Amalah's help gathered them in the hall.

They were listening as Amalah spoke, directing. I tried to move one of the crates of C4 to place it on the floor out of the line of flying bullets, but it was too heavy, and my hands were too sore. I left it, chest high, in the children's room.

I moved down the hall with the children following. A door at the side of the building opened to a field that sprawled across the back of the compound, and to the grape fields behind.

The battle was raging on the far side toward the front of the compound. There was no one around but I was afraid, holding a weapon, that I might be mistaken for an insurgent, so I dropped it, suddenly, by the back door as we exited.

We made our way to a distant clearing beyond the corner. I sat low and the children sat around me. We could see men scurrying around the sides of the buildings.

Flashbangs blasting inside and all around. JTF2 troops were moving through in their standard way. Methodically. *Slow is smooth and smooth is fast.*

You could hear the faint din of the odd "clear" every few moments. Thwaaks and thuds echoed toward the clearing where we sat.

Dark silhouettes glided around a corner. Like death stalking. Tightly wrapped in night black gear, their movements fluid, night-vision goggles perched on their helmets. Smooth and fast. Deliberate and quick. One of them turned toward us and I was afraid.

"Canadian. CANADIAN," I yelled and crouched. It was the only thing I could think to yell, as loud as I could, raising my hands. The children slumped low behind me.

He left us and turned back to the fight. Two others passed gliding smoothly into the far building, ignoring us now. Their short C8 rifles, with elongated flash suppressors flashing, as they moved. Men fell at their will.

Then I saw a child standing in the doorway of the building. She was tiny. Smaller than Amalah. I couldn't believe we had left her behind. I thought they had all stayed with the group but I wasn't counting. We had moved into the distance quickly and must have left her behind. She was there poking her head out of the open door. I watched as she stooped and picked up the weapon I had dropped and fell back inside.

I had to stop her. She could be seen as a threat with the weapon. But I couldn't imagine she knew how to use it. I stood up and ran toward her.

And that is when the building exploded.

The pressure wave and shrapnel hit me like a wall of flame. I flew backward in a rush. There was a ringing and a bright light.

Then Grace was smiling on a hill overlooking the lake in Kingston. Her white dress flowing as she danced and spun.

And I lost time.

———

The next thing I remember was a searing pain in my side and arm. I was clenching my teeth as I opened my eyes, and Amalah was there. She had a hand on my head, and a JTF2 soldier was crouched above her, in a kneeling position, with his weapon pointed back toward the compound.

"Doctor Henry, are you okay?"

I gathered myself and strained to sit.

"My arm," I winced.

"What are you doing here?" he asked.

"I was taken... at the ambush."

"Don't move," he said. That was not hard. My right arm was not working. The children were gathered around, still and quiet, and low. The building was gone. There was a hole in the ground where it had been and the next building had collapsed as well.

The soldier spoke into a microphone at his jaw and exchanged hand signals with a man in the distance.

The noises were beginning to slow, like popcorn in a microwave. I strained into a seated position to take a look around.

When they finally stopped, the team gathered in the compound. The soldier at my side stood from his crouch, then taller and straighter, and pushed on his ear bud. When his muzzle lowered, he looked relaxed. Then he removed his head gear and I recognized him as one of the troops from the range.

"All clear," he said in a gravelly voice that reminded me of Saturday morning cartoons.

The first morning rays were spilling over the wall and buildings. A broken line of sunshine cut across the dirt, folding in the crumbling parts and highlighting the imperfections. The compound was filling with light and it seemed smaller, and for a moment the sadness, horror, and pain were gone.

"Is it over?" I asked.

"It's over," he said.

I looked at Amalah and she smiled. Her golden eyes sparkled in the morning sun and I lay back and closed my eyes as she tucked her head under my arm.

We were together in the dust for a long time as the sun rose.

———

The man who called himself her uncle had not survived. He was there in the rows of bodies near the wall. I shrouded Amalah's eyes as we passed. The soldiers responsible were proud of their work and congratulatory, as they dealt with the business on hand. They were not joyous, but no one seemed unhappy.

I never saw Mustaq though I heard they had him in custody.

Other young men were sitting in rows, legs crossed, hands cuffed with zap straps behind their backs. A few looked like men, but mostly they were boys. Most of the youngest had survived.

I held Amalah's hand and made my way across the compound. A Blackhawk helicopter was landing in the square. We passed the gate where Lucky's corpse had been. Sand had covered the stains and washed the blood away.

A SOF medic near the landing zone was working over a patient on a stretcher.

Colonel Clark was there beside them and beckoned me over.

"You look pretty banged up," he said. "Let the medic here sling your arm then this bird will take you back to the FOB. They've got some work to do on you."

Some of Clark's men needed mending too. One, already sitting in the Blackhawk, was holding a bloody bandage against his shoulder.

"I'm taking this girl with me," I said.

He looked at me. And at the girl. And back to me.

"Jack, you're nuts," he said.

I said nothing.

But he saw the conviction in my eyes.

We embraced briefly, one arm only, as I winced in pain. He didn't ask questions but helped Amalah up into the chopper. Then moved away directing and planning.

The most severely injured would be back at the role three in Kandahar that day and, quite possibly, I'd be joining them. A medic threw a sling on my arm. Any movement caused searing pain and I was certain it was broken and worried I might pass out.

Two Blackhawk helicopters were circling above us. Protecting. Amalah was beside me, to the inside, my good arm wrapped around her. The door remained open and I braced myself against the frame. I looked out and down at the village as we lifted off. We rose quickly and the FOB came into view. Not far. Locals were toiling in the space between. Like a scene from the Bible. Shepherds in their fields. They didn't look up as we passed.

We touched down at the FOB and the jolt hurt. The medics grappled on to us and ushered us to the medical station.

Amalah ran ahead when she saw Joe and they embraced. I followed up the hill, leaning on Collins.

In the UMS I was a patient.

One of the medics leaned in as I sat on a gurney, "Let me take a look at that arm, and that face, and those hands..."

I tried to smile.

"Your humerus is broken, and this will need stitches. Normally I would ask you to do those, boss, but Warrant Baker came out this morning. He'll be right over."

Warrant Baker, the Physician's Assistant whom I'd replaced, my roommate in KAF who I never met, was doing triage. I was one of his injured patients and this was a 'mass casualty' event for him. He was directing a medic packing a gunshot wound. He seemed competent and that was reassuring.

FOB medical stations are usually staffed with PA's. It was rare to find an emerg doc out this far, but the fact he was there, suddenly made my heart sink. They must have sent him out as soon as they learned of my absence. Which meant Brad had been involved.

It shouldn't have been a surprise, but the realization that Brad was involved meant he knew I had run off. There was no telling what his reaction to that might be.

I was not only missing, but possibly a deserter, and possibly disobeyed his direct orders.

He wouldn't be happy.

Warrant Baker moved quickly to each patient, and finally over to me, "Let me check your wounds, Doc," he said as he approached. I was lying flat staring at the ceiling.

He lifted my shirt to see my side.

"These lacerations need stitches."

I looked at the wound as he prodded. It was a painful gash but it hadn't penetrated the cavity. No urgent need for surgery. And my fracture wasn't compound, the bone hadn't pierced any skin. I couldn't see the slash on my face but that required stitches too.

All in all, though, I was lucky. I would be ok.

"I'm not going to ask where you've been," he said. "It's none of my business. But I'll clean you up if that's alright?"

Another medic was starting an IV on my arm.

"We're going to need to sedate you to set that arm?"

"Sure. Thank you." I winced at the sharpness as he examined, trying my best to lay still with my thoughts as they worked. When they finally got around to pushing the drugs, the sleep was welcome.

———

I awoke, with my arm in a cast, and clean bandages on my head and face and hands. A soothing ointment was seeping through the otherwise clean white cloth.

Joe noticed me stir and came over.

"You're awake. How are you feeling?"

"Tired."

"Jack, you were right!" she said and showed me the lines on an i-STAT cartridge. She had run the test on Amalah's blood.

Then I saw Amalah sitting beside me, reading. A tiny piece of cotton taped at the bend of her arm. She smiled at me and waved. Then reached up to hold my hand.

"She's very positive for ceruloplasmin and copper. Too much of a good thing," said Joe.

And I was happy. Relieved.

And then concerned.

"Joe, you have to hide that test."

"—Why? This proves you were right. She has Wilson's disease. We can get her help. They'll trust you. You were right. You were doing the right thing."

"Throw it out. Burn it. Get rid of it," I said.

"I don't understand. We can help her... Are you worried about Major Ridgeway?"

"No. no."

"Well, you don't have to worry because Warrant Baker ordered the test. I told him about her and he registered his own order in the log. You are off the hook. You didn't disobey the order."

That was kind.

"Please thank him for me. But I think we should get rid of the test."

"Why?"

"I'm not sure how immigration works."

Joe looked puzzled at that, and I continued.

"If they know she's sick. I'm not sure if Canada will let her in. I'm worried it might be hard to take her home. They might not let me take her home if they know she's sick."

I was stammering.

She was stunned.

Then she processed, and smiled, and hugged me.

Chapter Thirty-One

The Journey Home

My TAV ended earlier than anticipated. No longer any use to the task force with a broken arm and bandaged hands, I needed time to heal. Warrant Baker had taken over at the FOB, so the only thing that remained was to get me home.

When I passed through Kandahar, Major Ridgeway wanted to talk, "Get in here, soldier," he barked.

I was in the hallway outside his office and he didn't sound like he was kidding. As best I could, with my arm in a sling and painful sores, I marched in and stood to attention at the head of his desk.

We were alone in the room.

He came around toward me.

"Tell me one thing, Captain Henry. Did you disobey my lawful command?"

I stammered, "—I don't know, sir... I suppose I intended to." He let me speak. Giving me the rope. "I was going to find the girl. You told me to forget about her. But we had a quiet moment and it felt like it would be simple. She was close... and I... I wasn't thinking..."

"Damn right you weren't. You abandoned your team and got—" he shuffled papers on the desk, "—Achmed Yazdani—You got one of our best translators killed in the process."

"Lucky," I said, quietly.

"What?"

"...his name is Lucky," I repeated softly feeling something break inside of me. Not because of Major Ridgeway's anger, I didn't care so much about that, the emotion was for Lucky, and it caught in my throat. I hadn't cried for Lucky. And when I came to that realization the tears welled in my eyes and my lip began to quiver.

Brad stopped.

He looked at me then back at the papers, "I don't know what to do with you, Jack," he said finally, "They are telling me you saved some Afghani children. Is that true? Is it true you saved some kids out there?"

"I don't know. I wasn't supposed to be there."

"No. You shouldn't have been."

I began to sob and couldn't stop it.

My thoughts began with Lucky, but moved quickly to the dead men, and the child in the doorway, and the building exploding. My eyes still ached from the flames. *What might have happened if they were all inside?*

"Are you okay, Jack?"

"I'm fine," I said, standing and taking a breath. I wiped my tears and stood for judgment.

"I don't know exactly what happened and I don't care. If they want to give you some damn award for what you did, so be it."

I looked up. Confused.

"The JTF Commander, some guy named Clark, wrote you up for a commendation. I'm still processing this. I'm pissed at you running off. But it appears you did some good out there."

I flushed. I wanted Lucky to be alive, and all the terrible things to have never happened.

And, most of all, in that moment…

I wanted to be home, with Grace.

I certainly didn't want any damn award.

I found myself stepping back against the wall and sliding down to a crouch and hiding my face in my cast and crossing arms and crying uncontrollably for far too long.

I don't know how long I cried.

But Brad let me cry.

———

Rolly was not there when I passed through Mirage on my way home. Then "third location decompression" came next. That's a requirement prior to repatriation. A standard protocol for soldiers leaving a war zone. Lessons learned from previous wars.

Three days of quiet contemplation. Examining your experiences. Processing. Sitting through structured programming. Thoughtful lectures meant to minimize the mental anguish, prevent 'shell shock', 'War Neurosis', or 'PTSD'.

There's lots of good evidence it works.

I'm not sure it worked for me.

Mine was at a resort on the gulf of Yemen at a ridiculously opulent (someone said "seven-star") resort. There were marble floors for days. Even a sprawling spa with multiple experiences including ice, cedar, mist, forest, sauna, all meant to relax and give the client time to process.

The lectures and videos about "Returning Home a Hero", and "Adjusting to Life Back Home," were vaguely familiar in an otherworldly sense from something learned in med school, but I wasn't paying much attention. Being off-cycle, and a doctor, no one scrutinized my attendance. I was given a bit of a pass.

I snorkelled in the gulf of Yemen and played horseshoes on the beach with a lonely padre who spent most of his time listening to house-music wearing nothing but a banana hammock. Poor guy had been there for the duration. Not a bad gig I suppose, but the entire experience for me was more frustrating than relaxing. All I wanted was to be home.

I wanted to see Grace. Even now it seems like a story I was told or a dream that happened to someone else. The entire time, I was only interested in that one thing: Getting home to Grace.

———

She met me at arrivals in Toronto and captured all the light in the concourse. Every sunbeam passed through her eyes and smile directly into my heart.

Her beauty was painful. And that embrace was for the ages.

She was more fit and healthy than I remembered. Wearing a stunning dress and new purple coat, she smelled like heaven. We held each other firm and fast and, despite my casted arm, I spun her around as time stood still.

Grace had rented a limo.

Of course she did.

We climbed in the back and embraced behind that dark screen holding hands and smiling. And immediately poured over all the pressing things. That two hours, down highway 401 to Kingston, passed in a blur, we panted and breathed and fell into one another time and again... Then, over the hum of tires, we sat still in each other's arms and spoke of too many tragic things.

Our letters and phone calls hinted at some of those emotions. But we had time now, so she asked me to start from the beginning.

I tried to tell her all the things, but soon I noticed tears. Around the time of the engineer she asked me to stop, so I stopped.

I never got to the part about the killing.

It was too much for me to say out loud anyway. As if that would make it real. I was glad Grace asked me to stop. But those parts remained inside... too easily.

"Tell me more about the girl who stole your heart," she said.

The girl with the golden eyes had been a large part of my letters. She mostly wanted to hear about Amalah.

I told her all about her. How she tried to read, her infectious smile, the precocious way she flips her hair, and how unfathomably strong she had been through it all. Through all the darkness, and into the light.

And then I showed her a picture.

And Grace lit up when she saw her eyes.

"She's beautiful," she gasped.

"She really is, isn't she?"

"I'm so very sad for her."

"It's tragic, about her family."

"I can't imagine."

"I know... They are all gone. It's too much."

"Do you think there's a way, Jack? Do you think they would allow us...?" She fell silent then, and moved her fingers across the photo, holding it close and staring.

I knew what she was thinking. -

And my heart filled with joy for her.

For both of them.

When she looked up, she blushed to find tears in my eyes.

"I know it's crazy, but maybe there's a way we could adopt her?" she said, "I know you're not thinking about fatherhood right now, but—"

"—Grace," I stopped her with a touch, "I was trying to find a way to ask you the very same thing." And a look of profound love and happiness flooded her face, "I was trying to find the courage... I was hoping you might consider..."

"Oh, Jack. Do you think it's possible?"

"I don't know. But we can try. I've asked the social workers to look into it."

She turned and snuggled into the crook of my neck and whispered, "I love you, Jack. My hero."

By the time we pulled into our home in Kingston, a life we hadn't even begun to imagine was beginning anew.

———

The adoption process was not straightforward. Much more difficult than we anticipated. The paperwork was overwhelming. Brad and Joe helped from their end. Amalah was placed in regular contact with our Canadian authorities and they did their best to grease the wheels and keep in touch.

We could only hope the system would work its magic for us.

We were informed Amalah wanted to come to Canada and reunite with the friendly doctor she had met that fateful day in the market.

The Afghanistan administration confirmed she had no surviving relatives and was eligible for adoption. She was an orphan who needed a family and we were as good as any. I could only hope that being a doctor and a 'returning hero' would help.

So, she entered the system, and our waiting game began.

We were good at delayed gratification. All our years in school proved that, but this would be some of the most difficult.

So, we went back to work. Grace first.

I had "post-deployment leave" to burn.

————

Despite the trip to the resort in Yemen, and all the lectures, the military also conferred three weeks of post-deployment leave. Naturally, a blessing.

Those were strange weeks though. I felt like a stranger in a strange land. Going directly back to work would have been difficult. Canada was the same, but things were inexplicably different. Psychiatrists might call it depersonalization, or derealization. You have this pervasive feeling of detachment from self and surroundings, as if awake but dreaming.

The world looked and smelled the same, but it was different.

And I felt guilty all of the time.

About nothing. Sometimes about everything.

About owning a car.

About having fresh sheets.

About eating old cheddar.

About the damn fresh air.

I spent the time occupying my mind by finishing our basement. Sixteen hours a day of pure focus—carpentry, insulating, wiring, completed ductwork, drywalling, mudding, painting, sanding, and painting again. I even built a bookcase door in the wall on a pivot hinge, just to keep my mind from wandering back.

But the demons always came.

It took a long time before the nightmares began to recede. I don't remember how many times, in those early days, I awoke crouched at the headboard, white with fear, with a vague lingering sense I had been yelling at something. Grace would be there holding me. Hushing and holding. Until it dawned that I was safe and home. We got through it together one day at a time.

In the end I was ready to try to go back to clinical work. All the studies say returning to normalcy, re-entering the real world, as soon as possible, is helpful. And so, eventually, I got back on my bike and pedalled back to the base hospital.

In my little office, I put my green uniform back on, having left the tan one tucked away, and slid back into 'sick-parade,' on the way nodding to all the 'welcome backs' and 'how was its'—politely getting back to business. I needed to keep on keeping on. The Royal Canadian Medical Corps never sleeps.

In those first few days I saw some twisted ankles, managed a few chronic diseases, examined some belly pains and headaches, treated some rashes, and provided some supportive counselling.

It was all the same as it had been before. But it was all so very different. And inevitably, each night, the demons returned. I felt numb. Sometimes, as though I wasn't even there, as if it wasn't me but someone else practicing medicine, and I was watching myself from the corner of the room.

And then one morning it all came to a head.

At the end of a long clinic, near the end of my first month back, I picked up a chart: "twenty-two year-old male with a rash". It looked like an easy chief complaint to end the morning.

Probably acne, or poison ivy, or some other contact dermatitis. These young soldiers rarely show up with zebras.

I was on cruise control. From the doorway I saw the boy was skinny. His uniform was dishevelled. His hair was too long for an officer cadet, and he was sweaty. He was writhing a bit too, nervous about something. As I entered, he stood from his chair abruptly and moved toward me mumbling under his breath.

Then he reached into his pocket and my senses converged.

I dropped my clip board and lunged in a fit of protective rage slamming him against the wall. I dropped on top of him clinging to his arm. He was yelling for support as I managed to prevent him from removing whatever he had in his cargo pocket.

I wrestled to get a grip on his arm and neck. To protect myself and stop the inevitable pain that would follow. He was strong and deadly.

But so was I.

When someone grabbed me from behind, I was certain there were two of them assaulting me. I refused to let them kill me after all I'd been through. I struck a blow and drew blood. But they were strong and subdued me against the floor.

It was cold on my face. The asbestos tiles were ugly and scratched. Clean enough but cold against my cheek. And I wondered where the tiles came from. The ground was sand only moments before. Now someone was holding my face against cold tiles.

Why are there tiles.

The drops of blood, in my line of sight, was the splatter in the compound. But *that* blood was from my face, and that cut had healed. And this boy with the rash hadn't cut me.

My face was cold, but not in pain.

The blood could be from my nose.

But my nose felt fine. And the tiles didn't make sense.

I could smell cigarettes and cloves.

Then the voices were English and I heard my name. A familiar voice: Sergeant Jimmy Sheffield was holding me down and speaking softly, and kindly. He was helping me to my feet. The boy with the rash was not Taliban. I brushed off. The boy was apologizing for scaring me, and showing pictures of his rash on his phone, from his pocket. I was confused. He still looked jumpy. Then it dawned that he was probably half asleep, or hungover, or still drunk. He certainly didn't seem threatening.

Jimmy guided him away and had him seen by another provider then returned to find me sitting at my desk. He handed me a glass of water, "Doc, you're really jumpy. You almost killed that kid."

"I thought he had a gun."

"There are no guns here, Jack... Are you okay?"

"I don't know... I think so..."

"Jack... Please... Get some help... You need to take some time."

I wasn't processing that like I should have.

I sat there staring at the wall.

"Go home. Get some sleep. We'll cover for you."

Then I sat alone at my desk for what seemed like an eternity.

———

After another week of waking in the night Grace finally dragged me to the doctor. Without her, I would not have had the courage to go. Knowing what you need to do is not enough.

It is hard to admit that.

Even though the signs were there, and I was trained to see them, I could not find my way through. Not without Grace.

She dragged me to the doctor, and spoke on my behalf. Eventually I accepted help. I might have turned to the bottle if not for Grace. She found a way to help me as she always does. She sees me, and loves me. I am so very grateful for my Grace.

And for all you struggling veterans out there, please hear this. Never let anyone tell you our military mental health systems are lacking. They are stellar. World class. If you need help, please ask. It did not take long for the wheels of recovery to set in motion. I met a counsellor that same day and a psychiatrist shortly thereafter. They were smart and gentle and kind and knowledgeable, with a firm and compassionate approach.

They worked magic with 'eye movement desensitization' and finally, after months of hard work, meditation, and focus, the symptoms began to subside.

Along the way, someone suggested I write this book, as a form of 'exposure therapy'. So, that's what I did.

And my first reader was Grace.

I still scan a room when I enter and never sit with my back to a door but the nightmares are fewer and farther between.

The memories will always remain, under the surface, and sometimes they intrude, but they don't control my life any longer.

I am living proof that you can 'have had' PTSD. It is not something you need to lug around like a ruck sack or wear like a badge of honour. It fades with time and effort.

But as with most things worth doing, you have to put in the time and effort. Having help is not enough. You need to accept it too. But there is hope. I promise.

By the time Brad came home, early in the new year, my cast was off and my scars were fading. I was through the bulk of my therapy and feeling as close to my old self as I may ever be. He asked me to join him at the mess on a Friday and I was happy to go.

We sat at the 'medical branch table' in the corner near the window with a view across the snow to the frozen lake below. We drank a glass of dark draft beer and fumbled over awkward small talk before our conversation turned more serious.

"I want to give you something," he said as he unzipped a brass zipper and pulled a piece of paper from a leather folder.

He slid it across to me.

It was a charge report.

I'd seen similar, the last under canvas near the Byward Market, but this one had my name emblazoned across the top.

He was smiling.

I was silent.

"I wrote that up the morning you went missing. I waited to speak to you before making it official and I'm glad I did. I almost had you thrown in jail, Jack."

I was reading it in stunned silence.

The implications were immense.

He was my direct superior and had ordered me to let it go, but I ignored him. Disregarded orders. It was well within his right to have me charged.

"That's yours to keep," he said, "Or destroy. Those were difficult days for all of us."

I stared in disbelief at the form in my hands.

"My emotion almost got the best of me," he continued. "I thought it was important for you to see that. I want you to have it. It's the only copy."

"A soldier is charged the moment the offence is reduced to writing," I said, recalling the phrase I'd used a thousand times in training. "This paper means I was charged, quite literally charged, for disobeying a lawful command." My head was spinning as I read in black and white.

The essential elements of the charge...
the evidence received...
the credibility of witnesses heard...
the representations submitted.
Maximum sentence: Two-years-less-a-day.

My mind was full of that as I stared at the crisp white foolscap. "That's no small thing," I said, "That's jail time."

"I know. That's why I wanted you to have it. If I submitted that while you were out there... I can't even—It was a stressful time."

He paused as we let it sink in.

"I want to apologize for almost having done that to you, Jack. It would have been wrong. It would have been a mistake. The way these things work, it would have swept you up, you probably would have…" He paused and looked outside.

"It was your duty. Your right. I would not have blamed you."

"It would have been wrong. We both know how the system works. The Army has its truths."

"You would have been correct. Rules are rules. And you told me to forget about that girl."

He smiled, "I did. But that was maybe too much to ask."

"Maybe." I sipped my beer. "Maybe we try too hard to do the right thing."

"Our ideals might be the end of our humanity."

"I hope not. I've been thinking about my humanity lately. Trying to reconcile some of the things that happened over there. I did some things…" I trailed off.

"War is hell," he said without an ounce of irony in his tone.

"It is, isn't it? The darkest parts are probably as close to hell as you can get on earth."

"The old timers warned us, didn't they?"

"They always did," we smiled.

"Where do we get fitted for our blue coats and grey slacks now that we're war vets?"

"Ha. Yes. Right. The legion, I suppose…"

There was a moment of silence again as we sat watching the sun on the snow outside. It wasn't awkward. It wasn't rushed. We were comfortable there. Sitting with our thoughts about the war. Sipping.

"I see now why they had so much trouble telling stories though."

"Yes... right! Some things are impossible to talk about."

"Right! And some things are right there blazing in your memory but when you try to find the words to talk about them the words never quite fit."

"Words don't capture the expanse of the thing that barely fits inside your head," he said.

"Exactly. I always thought it was the opposite. Like maybe they had nothing interesting to say. Or they wouldn't tell stories because they couldn't remember the most interesting parts to tell. Like they could only remember the boring parts and all the monotony. But it's not that at all. It's just hard to talk about it."

"Well, there certainly was some monotony. But that's not what I'll remember most. Maybe they just weren't story tellers."

"Aren't we all story tellers though, to some extent?"

"I guess."

"I tried to write poetry about it for Grace."

"Did you?"

"I did. But when she read them out loud I was more embarrassed to hear them than anything."

"I can see that." He muttered through a mouthful of beer.

"I mean... there were some horrific things and it's hard to talk about those things, but there's also this fear that some of the things were shameful. Like a crime was committed. And out of context some of it could be considered criminal, couldn't it? It's only justifiable in context. But telling it outside the context, feels wrong because of some arbitrary set of boundaries and feelings that you can't replace. Some arbitrary set of ideals that only exist in that place. That's hard to reconcile."

"But maybe that's the point. Maybe all we can do is live up to our own ideals and hope we're on the side of good on balance."

"Maybe... I hope we are the good guys."

"It sure feels like we are," he said, and our glasses clinked.

"I'll drink to that." I took another sip. We watched a flock of geese in the sky, and a squirrel bound across the snow and up a tree.

"That day in my office at the role one. I'm sorry for putting you through that."

"It wasn't you, Brad… I was in a dark place."

"How are you now?" he asked.

"It's been a struggle."

"Nightmares?"

"Yeah."

"Have you spoken to someone?"

"Yes. I'm functional... Different, but functional"

"You certainly are different."

"Ha. Thanks, man."

"That reminds me, Clark certainly thought you were different."

"Oh yeah?"

"Yes. He spoke very highly of you, and eloquently too. He said your actions saved some lives at that ambush out there."

"I'm not so sure about that," I said as he reached into his folder again.

This time he pulled out a dark file protector and a small box, "You left this in theatre," he said.

I had missed the medal ceremony at Kandahar Air Field. He handed me a brown box that snapped open to reveal a gold star-shaped medal on a burgundy and black ribbon, "Your campaign star. For service in the presence of an armed enemy."

It was beautiful. "Thank you, sir." I stared at it. I'd wear it proudly on my chest.

"And," he continued, "As you know, that charge report might suggest some things about your actions in theatre, but Clark had a different narrative. Did you know he submitted you for a commendation."

"Really?"

"Yes. And it was successful."

He set aside the case and opened another foam lined folder and turned it toward me. A small bronze oak leaf adorned a cardboard placard that was affixed to the corner of a frame. The frame displayed an embossed certificate adorned with the Queen's crest, signed by the Prime Minister of Canada and Minister of National Defence:

"Mention in Dispatches—This national honour is awarded for valiant conduct, devotion to duty, and distinguished service

"I didn't think you'd want a big fuss."

I didn't know what to say. It was a high honour. One I was never expecting. "Thank you," I said.

"It's been published in dispatches. The task force heard the story and your name at the final parade. I'm sorry you missed that."

"This is exactly how I would have hoped to receive it. Thank you… I've never been one for pomp and circumstance." I ran my fingers along the embossed Dominion Crest contemplating all that had come to pass.

"And I have something for you," I said at last.

I had been working on it for months, written it and rewritten it a thousand times trying to make it right. Trying to encapsulate all the Army had meant to me, from those early years in Petawawa, to medical training, and my time in war. It began as three pages of philosophizing about highlights of my career, filled with reasons and choices and justifications.

But in the end, I boiled it down to a single sentence:

I, Jack Henry, having reached the end of my obligatory service, formally request a release from her majesty's service.

For weeks that memo had been folded in the right breast pocket of my combat shirt. I took it out then and handed it to Brad. Not much more needed to be said after that.

He read it out loud and smiled.

"I gotta say, Jack. I didn't see that coming. Thank you for your service."

"You too, Boss, you too."

———

The Army life is behind me now and I miss it sometimes, but things are going well for Grace and I. She was promoted quickly in the halls of academia and encouraged me to teach. So I do. It's hard to believe this disaffected, fatherless son of the seventies, is a professor of medicine, but I am. I teach at one of the most prestigious medical schools in this country, and I love it.

Emergency medicine lost its lustre after Afghanistan. The adrenaline rush hits a little different. I still do the odd shift to keep my skills up at the peripheral hospitals, but my true joy is teaching Family Medicine.

The day after my release I pulled out that old leather doctor bag and went looking for a place to set up shop. I did not have far to look. Grace had space at her clinic downtown.

Of course, she did.

She has always loved her work from the very beginning and her patient's love her implicitly. We discussed how working together might have its picadillo's, but came to the decision quickly. I placed my shingle on the bricks below hers and got to work.

It seemed the proper thing.

And in the coming weeks and months Grace showed me the ropes of full-service family practice. It has renewed my love of medicine. She even mentored me in obstetrics, and we delivered babies together for a while. Now that's a bloody business! I love it.

Starting over, in a sense, has not been easy, but the struggle, and constant vigilance to ever-changing guidelines, is right up my ally. And our work makes a difference.

Last month a young man came in with a lump on his testicle. Within days he had an ultrasound and blood work that confirmed our suspicion—testicular cancer. When I told him the news he was scared. I held his hand through the process of surgery and chemo in rapid succession. And he is already, for all intents and purposes, cured.

I can't tell you how satisfying that is. Family doctors don't run around the hospital pulling clots from arteries, or performing life-saving surgeries, and we don't wear capes, but when the system needs a hero, your friendly neighbourhood family doctor fills that role, now and then.

————

A year or so had passed and we were settled into our new life. My release from the military was becoming a distant memory. Grace and I enjoyed our morning coffee and commute together... but we were beginning to wonder if it might never happen.

Although, we never lost hope.

And then, she arrived.

It was snowing. I was waiting by the window as she stepped from the back of a dark sedan and stood at the end of our walk holding hands with a kind Canadian official.

"Grace! Grace! She's here!" I yelled as I ran out to greet them in my socks.

Amalah was catching snowflakes on her tongue. I nearly bowled them over.

The first thing she said was as clear as a bell, and many times more joyful, "Hello, Doctor Henry. I missed you."

I knelt down to hug her. She was taller than I remembered, and her English had improved. We embraced for a moment in the snow. And then Grace was speaking behind me.

"Hello young lady," she said smiling. She had taken a moment to put on shoes.

They locked eyes with tenderness as something beautiful and unspoken passed between them. Grace reached out to hold her delicate hand. And when they touched I felt our world shift as the final piece of our family puzzle clicked into place. I held them both there in the street as joy rushed in to fill the spaces war had tried to steal from the man I was before I left.

We saw a specialist friend within days and had Amalah started on treatment for Wilson's disease—a few simple daily pills. And soon it was as if she had been there all along.

She is expected to live a long and happy life.

And we're told her eyes will keep their golden sparkle.

Acknowledgements

For Kelly, my Grace. Thanks for putting up with me, for being my champion, for building this life, and raising these beautiful children with me (and for being my very first reader—I'm sorry you had to go through that) ...You never cease to amaze me.

To my children, You are the light of my life and my reason for being. Thanks for giving dad some space to write. I love you all mostest, mostest, mostest.

For my mother and sister, thank you for being supportive early readers and for your amazing story and copy editing skills (honestly, if I had a nickel for every comma removed).

To my other early readers (Jason, Romney, Aileen, Ruth, Alastair, Richelle, Katie, Randy, Loretta), thank you all for your encouragement and advice—even if I didn't always take it.

Ben, You have no idea how much your enthusiasm for this story made it possible to complete. I never would have written another draft without your reaction to that early (crappy) version... You were the first person to really engage and tell me (I assume with veracity) that you loved it... So thank you.

To Phil Halton, James Leslie, and the team at Double Dagger, thank you for your patience and encouragement and advice. A debut novel is hard. You made it easy.

And to every soldier who sees some part of themselves here and understands...

Thank you, from the bottom of my heart, for everything you do.

Author's Note

This is my first attempt at crafting a complete novel. Over the years I have written short stories and multiple outlines for novels but never tried to finish one. I was inspired by a book about the 'writer and his craft' that I found on a dusty shelf at Sperwan Ghar. It contained a lot of wisdom: "Writing anything more than the truth would be too much", "Always write hard and clear about what hurts", "Never think that war no matter how necessary nor how justified is not a crime".

A few years later I picked up a copy of "A farewell to Arms" with the original introduction (written in 1948). The foreword of the most recent version was written by his son Patrick, who had been (spoiler alert) unceremoniously written into the story as a 'miscarriage'. That was a revelation to me… I could write about my TAV to Afghanistan and not worrying about making it a 'memoire', or about self-indulgently needing to emphasizing the coolest parts, or gloss over the boredom… I could wrap the scenes I'd written in Afghanistan into an overarching story and with a fictional narrative around them.

So this story is a "hero's journey" set in the Afghanistan war in 2010. I happen to have served as a physician in the Canadian Army on a short TAV in 2010 (like Jack) but Jack's time was much more interesting than mine—my war diary would bore you. The clinical work was routine and the occasional trauma was manageable because I was surrounded and supported by a phenomenally trained and skilled team. The scenes depict terrible things have been embellished for dramatic effect and only tinged with truth. Any resemblance, to real persons, living or dead, is purely coincidental (except for a few amalgams of people who know who they are).

Also, I consider Mustaq a little cliché. He is a fabrication and meant to be evil, so hopefully easy to hate. I had trepidations about personifying evil in such a figure, so if he is offensive to anyone, I regret that, but the story needed him. (Isn't it tragically Canadian to feel compelled to apologize for that?)

And finally, it is hard enough to talk about a wartime experience, let alone write about it, for many reasons. Partly because the people who were there will be critical. They will look at this and see holes and incongruences. It's hard to put this out knowing it is so terribly imperfect.

Also, because human misery alone does not make for a good story, a fiction about war needs a hero with a compelling character arc. And my attempts to structure this, and embellish things, might come across as disingenuous, but it is true that my writing has helped me process my own trauma from that time. So no apologies for that.

When I told my wife about the wounds and amputations and other things, she asked me to stop 'sliming' her (which is reflected in Grace's reaction to Jack). I considered removing some of it... because vicarious trauma is real and complicated... but it weakened the narrative. My personal memories of gunshot wounds and bomb blast injuries were purely clinical, and relatively easy for me to digest. I suspect being a doctor helped with that. But I needed to invent a story around those experiences for other more selfish reasons.

The stark contrast between the opulence of our lives back home and the austerity of life over there was the beginning. That was hard to reconcile. Experiencing the third world in war left me with a feeling of guilt that took a while to shake. We 'won the cosmic lottery' being born in Canada. It is a privilege that we take for granted. That feeling was hard to shake. I was metaphorically pacing on the beach, like that soldier in the opening of "Saving Private Ryan" with his arm dangling in his hand, but it wasn't my arm it was another heavy thing. Intrusive thoughts, not about blood or wounds or explosions, but about people. Locals who were part of our routine. What might have become of them. For example, the best translator at Massum Ghar really was a young man named Lucky (Achmed, I think?). He asked for my email address, and phone number, but he never wrote or called, and I often wonder what became of him.

Another boy I met, on a hillside in Panjwai, was smiling as he walked away into the desert holding hands with a stranger. There was nothing particularly traumatic or life threatening about that moment, I had sown a flap of skin on his head earlier in the day, and didn't think much of his walking away. But he also lingered. That child became the orphan of this story. He haunted me until I fictionalized an ending for him. I gave her a chronic disease that only Jack might diagnose, and a happily ever after. I'm glad to have finished. Hope you enjoy reading as much as I enjoyed, and needed, to write.

Matt Simpson
July 2024, Kingston

About The Author

Dr. Matt Simpson, Major (Retired), is a married father of four, family physician, and Honorary Colonel. He joined the Canadian Armed Forces at 16 and rose through the ranks from a young reservist to a young Sergeant, before entering medical school at the University of Ottawa and joining the Regular Force. He retired in 2015 after completing nearly 25 years of combined service.

Although highly fictionalized, his debut novel, *Before I Left*, draws inspiration from his experience as a General Duties Medical Officer deployed with the Role One Medical Contingent on a short Technical Assistance Visit (TAV) to Panjwai, Afghanistan, in 2010. It's a story about healing and resilience, the weight of duty, the cost of war, and the quiet moments of redemption in between.

He and his wife, both family physicians, now teach in the Department of Family Medicine at Queen's University. When not writing or seeing patients, he can be found coaching hockey or relaxing at the lake with his family.

DOUBLE‡DAGGER
— www.doubledagger.ca —

Double Dagger Books is Canada's only military-focused publisher. Conflict and warfare have shaped human history since before we began to record it. The earliest stories that we know of, passed on as oral tradition, speak of war, and more importantly, the essential elements of the human condition that are revealed under its pressure.

We are dedicated to publishing material that, while rooted in conflict, transcend the idea of "war" as merely a genre. Fiction, non-fiction, and stuff that defies categorization, we want to read it all.

Because if you want peace, study war.